PENGUIN CRIME FICTION

TURNAROUND JACK

Richard Abshire was with the Dallas Police Department for twelve years and a private investigator for two. His first novel was *Dallas Drop*. Abshire is currently a writer and producer for Law Enforcement Television Network and is working on his third Jack Kyle mystery. He lives in Dallas.

TURNAROUND JACK

A Jack Kyle Mystery

Richard Abshire

PENGUIN BOOKS

PENGUIN BOOKS
Published by the Penguin Group
Viking Penguin, a division of Penguin Books USA Inc.,
375 Hudson Street, New York, New York 10014, U.S.A.
Penguin Books Ltd, 27 Wrights Lane,
London W8 5TZ, England
Penguin Books Australia Ltd, Ringwood,
Victoria, Australia
Penguin Books Canada Ltd, 10 Alcorn Avenue, Suite 300,
Toronto, Ontario, Canada M4V 3B2
Penguin Books (N.Z.) Ltd, 182–190 Wairau Road,
Auckland 10, New Zealand

Penguin Books Ltd, Registered Offices:
Harmondsworth, Middlesex, England

First published in the United States of America by
William Morrow and Company, Inc., 1990
Reprinted by arrangement with William Morrow and Company, Inc.
Published in Penguin Books 1992

1   3   5   7   9   10   8   6   4   2

PUBLISHER'S NOTE
This is a work of fiction. Names, characters, places, and incidents
either are the product of the author's imagination or are used
fictitiously, and any resemblance to actual persons, living or
dead, events, or locales is entirely coincidental.

THE LIBRARY OF CONGRESS HAS CATALOGUED THE HARDCOVER AS FOLLOWS:
Abshire, Richard.
Turnaround Jack: a Jack Kyle mystery / Richard Abshire.
p.   cm.
ISBN 0-688-05268-1 (hc.)
ISBN 0 14 01.5836 7 (pbk.)
I. Title.
PS3551.B84T87   1990
813'.54—dc20   90–35613

Printed in the United States of America

To Carol and all our kids,
and to my colleagues at
the Law Enforcement Television Network

TURNAROUND
JACK

CHAPTER ONE

I REMINDED MYSELF of Philip Marlowe in *The Big Sleep*, all decked out in his best blue suit and his shoes are shined and everything. He is wearing the dark blue socks with the clocks on them and he says he is sober and doesn't care who knows it, because he is calling on a million dollars, or something like that. That is the part where he is going up to this mansion to meet Colonel Whatsit on this big case. I was cleaned up pretty good myself when I climbed out of my car in the big round driveway at the Borodin place in far North Dallas.

The place may not have been as tall or fancy as the one where Marlowe had his meet with the colonel, but then a million dollars does not go as far nowadays. It was big enough, about the size of your average small-town Holiday Inn. I had written the guy's name on the back of one of my business cards and I took the card out of my shirt pocket to check it one more time. G. BORODIN. I had the right address, and as I pushed the doorbell I wondered again what the G stood for. My secretary, Della, had taken the message and said there had not been any extra conversation involved, just the day, time, and address.

I did not have to ring twice. Half of the big door swung open and a dark-complexioned man stood looking out at me. He was a head shorter than me, but stood very straight in his white jacket.

"Yes?"

"Jack Kyle to see Mister Borodin."

He looked me over and was not impressed.

"I have an appoint——"

"Follow me, please," he said, and stepped out onto the porch, tugging the big door closed behind him.

The very straight little man marched off across the front of the house toward the corner to my right and I fell in behind him. It was a bit of a hike to the corner, then around and down the side of the place toward the sounds of water splashing. It was a hellishly hot August day, and I thought I heard the clinking of ice cubes in a drink.

My guide led me to the back of the house into the shade of a bright orange awning the size of a circus tent and in its cool darkness I saw a man standing at a well-stocked bar cart, making himself a drink.

"Mister Kyle," the little man announced.

I would have sworn he snapped off a curt little bow from the waist, and I thought he might click his heels together, but he did not.

"Good morning," said the man making the drink. "Or should I say good afternoon."

I checked my watch. A quarter to one in the afternoon, the hottest part of the day. I was a few minutes early.

"How do you do," I said, offering him my hand.

"Guy Borodin, Mister Kyle. Welcome to my humble home."

He took my hand and shook it as if he might have meant it. He did not try to impress me with his grip or anything. He pronounced his first name like "ghee," and I was not sure how he spelled it until I saw it on the contract later.

"Yeah, humble," I said. "That's the word I was looking for."

He laughed and so did I. What the hell, the guy spends a million more or less, he deserves to have a fuss made.

"I know it's early in the day, but . . ."

"Scotch on the rocks, Pinch if you have it."

He laughed again, and looked through his stock of booze. No Pinch, but he held up a bottle of Chivas Regal and raised his eyebrows to ask if that would do.

"That's fine," I assured him.

Borodin dismissed my little friend with a thank-you and I watched the white jacket disappear around the corner of the house the way we had come.

"Here you are."

He was not selfish with his liquor and that meant a lot to me. G. Borodin and I were hitting it off so far, as far as I was concerned. He put the hefty drink in my hand, and only about half of the weight of it was the cut crystal tumbler.

"Thanks."

"Never trust a man who doesn't drink," he said with a wink.

"My sentiments exactly."

"Make yourself comfortable, Mister Kyle," he added, motioning toward a white wrought iron chair with a comfortable-looking orange cushion which matched the awning overhead. I started toward the chair, but the sound of more water splashing caught my attention. Looking past Mister Borodin, I saw the swimming pool that stretched from just beyond the edge of the awning's shade not much more than fifty yards out into the blinding sunlight. The surface of the water was a dancing glare, but the splashing had a rhythm to it. My host glanced over his shoulder toward the pool and smiled a little broader. Again with his hand he waved me toward the chair.

"You make a nice drink," I told him after I had settled into the chair and tossed off the top third of the Chivas.

"It's just scotch and ice," he said.

"That's what I mean," I assured him.

"Do you carry a gun?" he asked.

"What?" I answered.

That was a very bad sign. It was a question that came up from time to time, but this was much too early in the game for it. As a matter of fact, I did not carry a gun. The state of Texas does not allow private investigators to go armed. That was one of the things that made the job what you might call challenging, because I often found myself in places where I was the only one who did not have a gun on.

"A gun, do you go armed?"

"That's none of your business."

I liked his drink and he looked as if he could more than afford my services. And I sure as hell could use the business, but you have to keep a certain tone to these things.

"I beg your pardon?" He looked confused. "I thought—"

"It doesn't matter what you thought, Mister Borodin. If you want to talk about guns . . ."

As much as it went against my nature, I put the drink down on a table that was handy and stood up.

"Please, don't misunderstand. Sit down."

"I don't want to waste your time or mine, Mister Borodin. If you're interested in guns—"

"But I'm not, I assure you. I only asked because . . ."

He looked from me to his drink and his brows knotted up as if he were deep in thought. He did not look out into the sunlight where the splashing was, but I did, and I saw something dark and graceful shimmering.

"Because what?" I prompted him.

"Because I very specifically do not want anyone with a gun involved. I do not want a . . . gunman, if that is the right word, working for me."

"I hope not. Because I'm not a gunman. I'm a private investigator."

"Exactly. Please sit down."

I sat back down and retrieved my drink. It was a hell of a hot day, and it was a very good drink. I had nothing better to do. I told myself the man deserved the benefit of the doubt.

"I am new here," he said. "In Texas, in Dallas, I mean. I've only been here, what is it now, a couple of months."

"Yeah? Where are you from?"

"Back East," he said, then he smiled again. "Way back East, originally."

12

Like somewhere around the Mediterranean, I told myself. His English was awfully good, if I am anyone to judge, with my Texas accent. But it had something foreign around the edges of it, and he was foreign-looking, in a way I had trouble putting my finger on. He was a handsome man, sixtyish, with thick dark hair showing a touch of gray at the temples. His eyes were light-colored like a cat's, maybe gray. He lived well, and it showed in his paunch. But he was broad in the shoulders and thick-chested. His manicured fingernails twinkled when the light touched them, but his fingers were thick and his hands looked strong.

"Anyway, I'm afraid maybe I've heard too many stories about you Texans. When I first came here I expected to see men walking around on the street with guns on their hips, you know."

"Yeah."

"Listen, I'm sorry I brought up the gun business. That was clumsy of me, and I apologize."

"Okay."

"I don't mean to offend you, Mister Kyle. This is . . . I'm pretty new at this."

"New at what?" I asked.

"Hiring a . . . hiring someone to do this kind of thing."

"That's a pretty good place to start," I offered. "What kind of thing is it you want to hire me for?"

"A very sensitive job."

"It usually is."

"A personal matter," he confided, lowering his voice.

I could not help noticing that the thing that was making the splashes in the pool had come to rest at the end of the pool nearest us, only a few dozen feet away. There was a quick, slithering whisper on the surface of the water as whatever it was sounded and disappeared beneath the opaque light of the sun-sparkling pool. I waited as Mister Borodin sat silent, considering the personal matter he wanted to hire me for, and a long moment passed before the water blathered again and then I thought I knew what kind of creature was there.

"It is my wife, Mister Kyle."

"It often is," I said a little too smugly, and I regretted having said it because he looked up at me with pain in his eyes. "Sorry, go ahead."

"I suppose you are accustomed . . ."

"It's my turn to apologize," I said. "I don't mean to be flippant, it's just I am experienced in these things. You can tell me anything."

He accepted that and went on with his story. It was not anything I had not heard before, but I tried to look him in the eye as if I gave a shit.

It was the usual thing. He was a businessman and he admitted that it was as much his fault as his wife's. He spent most of his time making money and she was a young woman after all, a woman with normal appetites. Not that it was a purely sexual thing, you understand. If he were crippled, God forbid, in an accident of some kind, he knew she would be faithful to him. I thought that a bit odd, but I did not interrupt him to offer an opinion. He was getting his story out, and I wanted to hear it all. I also wondered about the thing in the pool, the thing that by now had snuggled up to the near end so that I could only see part of it, two parts, bobbing languorously out from the poolside just beneath the glistening surface.

Time. That was the problem, Borodin assured me. I nodded. He did not spend enough time with his wife. Quality time, he said, and I wondered where he had picked up that expression. Maybe even moneymakers from way back east took time out to watch a little daytime TV. Who knew? Or maybe his wife had taught him about quality time. The thing was, he did not blame her, not really. He had neglected her shamelessly, but then again, that was only because he was working so hard to keep himself rich so he could support her in the manner she deserved. It sounded like a soap opera to me, or one of those made-for-TV movies. But that was me, I knew. Life seems like that to me. It was a character flaw I had had pointed out to me on occasion.

What it all came down to, naturally, was that she was

14

cheating on him. I happened to feel that this was what they call a value-loaded term. It was only cheating if she was giving somebody else something he wanted. From the way he had described their situation, I figured she was just exploring alternative markets, more or less. Making an arrangement. But then I remembered being in love with a woman and how it had felt to know that she was with someone else, and I warmed up to Mister Borodin a little.

"So," I said, but he did not offer anything more. "What do you want me to do?"

"To confirm my suspicions," he said.

"I can do that from here," I told him. When he put a puzzled look on his face, I went on, "Look, I don't exactly get paid to give advice, but I've had some experience in these things . . ."

"Yes?" he said, leaning forward as if he thought I were going to tell him something that mattered.

I could not help thinking that my experience had been as much personal as professional, but I did not tell him that.

"You know your own wife better than anybody. If you think she's . . . seeing someone else, probably she is. What good will it do you to know the who, what, and where, the gory details?"

"You don't understand, Mister Kyle—"

"Just go ahead and do what you need to do," I interjected. Like hell I did not understand. "Make up with her, take some time off from your work and take her on a romantic cruise. Or throw her out, if that's what you want to do. What difference does it make who the guy is? You'll only make trouble for yourself."

"I see. Yes, you're probably right. But it's a bit more complicated than that."

I thought so. Her daddy's money. Somebody's daddy's money. I liked that. To me, all the real motives had dollar signs in front of them. I was comfortable with that.

"No matter if it does make things . . . more complicated, messy. I have to know absolutely everything. I don't expect you to understand."

He kept underestimating me. But he was rich, or somebody was, and that colored my judgment of him.

"It's up to you, of course," I said.

"Yes. Have you photographic capabilities?"

"Yeah."

"Videotape?"

"That too."

"With sound?"

"I'm not in the business of making porn flicks, Mister Borodin, but I can do whatever you need done, I imagine."

Actually, I could just about shoot a recognizable still, if the lighting was not tricky and you did not rush me, but I had a friend by the name of Speed who could capture anything that happened on film, or videotape either, for that matter. The thing was, I did not mind making promises.

"Good."

He smiled at me and I thought he looked satisfied. If there had been some kind of entrance exam or audition going on, I figured I had gotten by it. He was wearing swimming trunks with a matching short-sleeved shirt which had two pockets. He reached into one of the pockets and pulled something out and handed it to me. It was a lined page out of a cheap spiral notebook, a small one. There were two addresses on it and some car tag numbers.

"You'll need these," he said.

The addresses interested me. One was on Industrial Boulevard, a really colorful strip laid in between downtown and the Trinity River, a place where some of the seediest honky-tonks and strip joints in town would be crushed if the high-tech signature Reunion Tower with the lighted ball on top ever happened to fall over toward the river. The other one was in Oak Lawn, which is the name both of a street and of a section of town that would be Greenwich Village if it could. I liked Oak Lawn, it had pretensions.

"The license numbers?" I asked.

"The first one is hers. The others I am not sure. You can research them?"

16

"No problem." I nodded smugly. By researching them, I guessed he meant run registration on them, which anybody could do who had time to run down to the county courthouse. It was public information, but most people did not know that. No big deal.

"What kind of car is this on?" I asked, showing him that I meant his wife's license number.

"A Mercedes," he replied, with a look that said he took me for a rube not to know that.

"Right, but what kind?" I rejoined.

"I can't remember the numbers," he admitted. "A little two-seater, robin's-egg blue."

"M-m-m," I answered, as if I understood exactly the one he meant. If he had asked me point-blank, I would have said he meant the 450-SL, although of course I knew even less about Mercedeses than he did. I suspected I knew a hell of a lot less.

"I want you to follow her wherever she goes," Borodin said, leaning toward me as if it were a matter of life or death. "No matter what. I *must* know where she goes and whom she sees."

I was impressed. Almost nobody I knew ever got the "who" and "whom" right.

"I see," I said reassuringly.

"Time is running out," he added, and then stopped to suck down a healthy percentage of his drink.

"How do you mean?" I asked.

"It's not important. Only that you understand that time is of the essence, that's all."

"The hell it is."

"I beg your pardon?" he asked, his eyes big with the question, making me think people were too careful how they talked to him.

"Everything about this deal is important to me. The more I know, the better job I'll do for you. If you can't trust me with everything, you can't trust me with anything. That's the way it works."

"You're right, of course." Borodin shook his head in agreement and hid his face in his drink for a moment. I finished mine. "I think she means to leave me," he added.

There was no point in my saying that if she felt that way it was probably best for him if she did, because I knew how he would feel about that. I understood that logic had no place in all of this.

"When?" I asked.

"Soon. I'm afraid I can't be more specific than that."

"Okay. I hope you don't expect me to stop her, if—"

"Nothing like that."

"Good. Because it's important that we understand each other. My job is to collect information for you. I tell you what I find out, what you do with it is—"

"Up to me. Understood."

"Okay."

"That is why I asked about the gun business earlier, Mister Kyle, and I apologize again . . ."

"No need," I assured him, wondering at the same time whether he would offer me another drink.

". . . but I am adamant that I do not want you to . . . interfere in any way. Not to do anything to her, or try to stop her, or . . ."

"I understand. I really do," I promised him, rattling what was left of the ice cubes in my empty tumbler.

"Good. Good, I see that you understand me."

"Of course, it's just . . ." I did not finish what I was going to say, and then forgot what that might have been altogether, because the thing at the edge of the swimming pool had emerged.

She drew herself up the side of the pool in a single supple motion, arising like some mythical creature out of the sparkling water to stand on the cool marble at the edge of the awning's shade. She was dark from head to toe, with no tan line to suggest that she had ever heard of a swimsuit. Her hair ran slick and wet between her fingers as she pushed it back and it coiled like snakes around her throat and over her shoulders. She stood naked and carefully poised with one leg bent as if she did not trust her weight to the solidity of the deck. I could not help noticing the heavy and piquant perfection of her breasts, the tapering indentation of her belly, the wet dark invitation between her lean and tensing thighs.

"This evening, no later than eight, Mister Kyle, you must be at this address," Borodin instructed, pointing at the Oak Lawn address on the paper I held in my hand. "You should find her car parked in the place reserved for that apartment. She may stay there all evening or go out. If she stays in, she almost certainly will have company. If anyone comes to see her there, I want photos, I want to know everything about him. Do you understand, everything!"

"Mister Borodin," I said.

"Yes?"

"Aren't you afraid she'll hear you?"

"What?" He turned the way I was looking and took in the naked woman beside the pool. "Don't be silly, Mister Kyle. That's not my wife." He laughed. "Would you like another drink?"

I said I would.

CHAPTER
TWO

OKAY. SHE WAS not his wife, she was not anybody's wife. I knew that, or I would have figured it out, if I had not been so busy marveling at the way she looked. The sunlight sparkled over her wet skin as if she had diamonds in her pores. She was lean and hard where she should have been, but her breasts beckoned like a mother's arms. I was so taken with her, the way all that mystery and flesh hovered in shimmering curves and angles like smoke up from the point on the poolside marble where her feet almost did not seem to touch the ground at all, that I was not exactly thinking clearly.

Borodin laughed at me good-naturedly.

"Mister Kyle, this is Sasha." He turned toward her and motioned with his arm at me. "Sasha, Mister Kyle."

I rose from my seat and smiled with a polite nod of my head. She nodded too, but did not bother to smile. She did not have to, and she knew it. I did not mind. She pivoted like a dancer, turning her back to us as she walked away from the shade of the awning toward a lounge chair in the sun on one side of the pool. I did not mind that either. When I had stopped looking at her I sat down again. Borodin had the bottle of Chivas in his hand and I held out my glass for him to refill it. He did not bother replacing the melted ice.

"I can imagine what you are thinking," he said, still smiling.

"Can you?" I asked. I might have been leering.

"It's not what it may seem, I assure you. Sasha is my niece, my brother's daughter. She has come to live with us."

"Okay."

"My brother wants her to live in America, learn the business. He doesn't think there is much future for her in the old country."

"Which country is that?"

"Cyprus."

"I see."

What did I know about Cyprus? I ran it through the cluttered file cabinet in my mind and did not find much. Newspaper stories, pictures on TV, Arabs killing Jews on a boat, somebody, probably the Israelis, blowing up Arabs in a hotel. It occurred to me that I had read somewhere about Cyprus being a crossroads, some kind of smuggler's haven, like Istanbul and Lisbon in World War II movies.

"And I must admit there was a little more to it than that."

I did not ask what it was because I knew by looking at him that he was going to tell me anyway.

"She had a lover," Borodin confided in me, leaning closer so Sasha would not overhear him. "A young boy my brother did not approve of. He didn't want her running off with the boy, so for that reason also he sent her to me."

"Makes sense. And she works for you?" I asked. It did not seem altogether fair that someone who looked like she did had to work too.

"After a fashion. I am not a very good slave driver, I am afraid."

"Yeah, family, huh?" I sympathized.

"Exactly," he said, spreading his hands beyond his shoulders and grimacing good-naturedly. "What is one to do?"

I did not offer any suggestions, but my face might have

shown what I was thinking as I sat looking at the girl lounging in the sun. She was rubbing oil on herself in most of the places I was interested in. It was a sight, more than enough to take my mind off of business. What is one to do, indeed.

"Here, here, Mister Kyle," my host chided me. "One might think you'd never seen a girl sunbathe before."

"It's been a while," I admitted.

"If you like, I can have her get dressed or go inside."

"You wouldn't dare. I mean, no, that's not necessary. Really."

"If I have your attention, then," Borodin said a little pointedly, making me think I might have offended him, ogling his niece or whatever she really was. "I think these will be of interest."

He handed me a manila envelope which I opened to find half a dozen photographs. They were all of the same woman, naturally, and Borodin said it was his wife, Sylvia. There was just the slightest hum inside my head as I looked them over. Not even a buzz really, much less an alarm. Just a hum, the kind of little thing you might get from somebody's hot breath tickling the fine hairs on the nape of your neck. It was a faint, intuitive kind of thing you would ignore if it stood between you and some money.

"Something's wrong here," I said.

"Oh?"

"For one thing, a couple of these shots look like surveillance photos, so you've had somebody tailing her already. And these two here."

I showed him the two I meant, a couple of party pix of Sylvia with a man who was not Mister Borodin, although he had the same look about him, like he might be from Cyprus too, or wherever Mister Borodin was really from. The man was a lot younger than Borodin, nearer his wife's age, and he was not bad-looking. He had kind of a military bearing, straight-backed and barrel-chested, and a row of perfect white teeth set off by black hair that was brushed straight back, with a little gray showing stylishly at the temples. Maybe, like the luscious Sasha at poolside, he was family.

"Who's he?" I asked.

"An acquaintance," Borodin said, like he was letting out some pretty valuable information.

"What's the connection?"

"He and I used to do business."

"Uh-huh. When were these pictures taken?"

"Recently."

"Is that a problem?" I asked. "Recently your wife got her picture taken snuggling up to some guy you don't do business with anymore for reasons you don't seem eager to explain. Don't make me drag it out of you, Borodin. Like I said, if you can't trust me all the way, you can't trust me at all."

"You're right." He poured himself a new drink and freshened mine. I made a deal with myself that this would be my last one of the day. When he had taken care of his bartending, he took a deep breath and started talking. "There is more to it than infidelity. It's business, too."

"I see," I encouraged him, nodding.

"That doesn't sound very good, does it, Mister Kyle?"

"Don't worry about it."

"The man in the photograph with Sylvia is . . . let's just say he's not to be trusted. That's why I dissolved our partnership. If Sylvia is involved with him she may be getting herself into serious trouble."

"What kind of business are we talking about, and what kind of trouble?"

"Investments, a little import-export."

"Okay."

The money angle again. He had not gotten around to telling me about her money or her daddy's money if there was any, but the money thing was there. I like that, it was the kind of motive you can keep a handle on when things get mixed up the way these cases do sometimes.

"I'm sure I don't have to tell you there are plenty of shady operators in the investment business these days," Borodin said.

"Hardly. I heard on the car radio on my way over here that there was another bank closed today. How many does that make in Texas this year, about a hundred?"

"Eighty-three, I believe."

"You could be right," I said. He was right, according to the radio news.

"My friend there may have had something to do with bank number eighty-three. If not, then almost certainly with several of the others," Borodin said, jabbing the photo of Sylvia and the smiling wheeler-dealer with a stubby index finger.

"Fraudulent loans?" I asked.

"Anything. A banker who so much as has lunch with that one is like a swimmer in a shark tank."

"What's his name?"

"Galipolus. Stefan Galipolus."

"Maybe you ought to write that down for me," I suggested.

"If you like."

"Please. Where were these pictures taken and how did you get them?"

"There was a party. I did not attend, but word got back to me that Sylvia was there. There are usually photographers at these things, society page and all that. I had my man look into it, hoping to find whom she was with. Imagine my surprise when it turned out to be my old friend Stefan."

"You didn't think he'd be there?"

"I didn't think he was in this part of the country anymore. The last I knew he had gone back East."

"Cyprus?" I asked.

"Not that far, only to Washington, D.C."

"You say you sent your man to look into this. Who would that be?"

"Anton. You met him."

"The white jacket who answered the door?"

"My butler, yes."

"And did he take these?" I asked, holding up the photos taken of Sylvia in what looked like a parking lot somewhere, walking. They were the ones I thought looked like surveillance work.

"Yes."

"Then what do you need me for? Let Anton keep tabs on her."

"He was lucky that time, not so lucky other times. He's not a professional. Besides, he has his own job to do."

"Okay," I said, slipping all the photographs back inside the envelope. He was lying about the party pix, I could tell by the lighting and the pose, and what little I could see of the table to one side of the smiling couple. I was pretty damned sure those shots had been taken some place less gala than a society bash. But lying a little was par for the course in this kind of a case. The rest of it felt pretty solid, and the slight little hum I had heard earlier had died away. I folded the piece of paper with the addresses and car tag numbers into a square and put it in my shirt pocket. Then I tugged my contract out of an inside jacket pocket and handed it to him. "You need to look this over, sign it at the bottom there, both copies."

Della had typed the contract for me after taking Borodin's call. It was a standard Board-issue form, with specifics to be typed into the appropriate blanks. Basically, it said I got two hundred dollars a day and expenses plus twenty-five dollars an hour for anything over eight hours in a day, that I would make timely reports to the client of any information that developed, and some stuff a lawyer had said he thought might discourage clients from suing me. Borodin read the one-page form quickly, tracing from side to side with a finger as he went. I thought he looked as if he knew his way around a contract.

"It seems in order," he said, and he signed both copies with an expensive-looking pen he pulled out of his shirt pocket.

I gave him his copy and tucked mine back inside my jacket. He went to his bar cart and produced a checkbook. He scribbled on it and then handed me a check for two thousand dollars. It was on a local bank and the check number was pretty high, four thousand and something.

"That's ten days," he said. "Less if you work more than eight hours a day, which I imagine you will. You understand I want to know everything she does."

"I understand."

"I don't know how your office is set up, Mister Kyle, whether you have a staff or if you subcontract, and I don't particularly care. That's up to you if you want to split the money with someone else or not. I am only interested in results."

"Fair enough," I answered, smiling. There was no staff. Kyle and Associates was just me, and Della part-time. If this thing ran on for very long, I would have to sub some of it out. I had been thinking about that already.

"That's it, then?" Borodin announced in a way that I knew meant he thought he was dismissing me. Nicely, of course.

"Not quite. There's one thing I always make a point of getting clear up front on these surveillance jobs."

"What?"

"I need to know which is more important to you, that I don't lose her or that I don't let her know that she's being followed."

"Both, of course. I don't want you to lose her, and I certainly . . ."

"I understand that, Mister Borodin, and I'll do my best. But the thing is, there almost always comes a time when I have to go one way or the other. Like if she catches a light on me or something. Then I can either play it cool and take a chance on losing her for a while, knowing I can pick her up again, or else I can do something noticeable, like run a red light or something, which means she may spot me, to make sure I don't lose her even for a few minutes. I know both things are important, but I need you to tell me which is most important. If we understand each other now, it makes for fewer hard feelings later."

"I see," he said, looking thoughtful.

I let him think it over, because this really is one of the most important things to get ironed out in a case like this. Client education is a very important part of the business. You cannot afford to have a client expecting too much of you, while at the same time you naturally cannot afford to talk yourself out of a job before you start either. One problem is that clients watch too much television, they are used to seeing one guy driving the same car day after day tail somebody all over town for weeks on end and never lose the guy or get burned. In my experience, both with the Dallas Police Department and on the private side, I had found that in every tail job one or the other thing happens at least once, sometimes several times. So you need to know which way the customer wants it played. I always like it when the client says he does not mind if you lose the target temporarily, because I know it is probably going to happen anyway before it is all over.

"For the time being, Mister Kyle, it is most important that Sylvia does not suspect she is being followed. I believe you will find a pattern in her activities, so that if you lose her you shouldn't have too much trouble finding her again."

"Good," I said, nodding to show him he had made a good call.

"However," Borodin went on, "there may come a time in the next few days when that will change. Then, I must insist that you do not lose her, no matter whether in doing so you reveal yourself to her. Do you understand?"

"I think so. I'll keep in close touch with you, you let me know when the ground rules change."

"Yes," he said. Noticing something about the look on my face, he added, "It's nothing so mysterious, Mister Kyle. Only that I believe she may have plans to travel in a few days. If so, then I want very much to know where she goes. Probably, she will fly. I must know what flight she takes, and I really don't care at that point if she suspects that I am on to her. All right?"

"Makes sense."

"So that is everything, then," he said, dismissing me again. Only I did not get up to go.

"Another thing or two I'd like to clear up," I said.

"Very well," he said, and I got the impression he was tiring of me. Maybe I was keeping him from his niece, Sasha.

"First, why do you think your wife may be traveling soon?"

"She is supposed to be out of state now, visiting relatives, due back in a few days. I happen to know she is in town, but—"

"I see," I cut in so he would not have to go into it anymore.

"And the other thing?" he asked.

"Her daddy's money," I said.

"How did you know about that?" he asked. He looked surprised when he said it, and I flattered myself that he may have been impressed.

"It's my business to know," says I, laughing inside. What the hell, all my hunches can't be wrong. That did it for me, made me put the little hum out of my mind and feel pretty good about the case all the way around. Borodin was not a lovesick old fool I would have to worry about doing something stupid if things got tacky. He was a businessman. Maybe he loved Sylvia, maybe not. She was younger than he was by a couple of decades and a good-looking woman, if you could go by her photographs. But I like that her daddy's money was part of it too. I thought Borodin was looking after his capital at least as much as his feelings. More, probably. I did not think he would make the kind of trouble for me that some husbands do when it's all passion and smoke. Okay, I told myself, you're in business.

Borodin was actually explaining to me about Sylvia's family's money. He was a rich man in his own right, he assured me more than once, and Sylvia's family fortune did not matter to him. I stifled a laugh. But, being her devoted husband, he was naturally worried that someone less honorable than he, like specifically his ex-partner Galipolus, might be after her for her money, leading her on and like that.

I held up a hand to let him know he had explained the whole thing to my satisfaction, and he seemed the least bit flustered as he stopped talking and shot a look over his shoulder in Sasha's direction before polishing off his drink.

I finished my scotch and remembered that I did not want another. Looking at Sasha stretched out like a seal at poolside was the kind of thing you could do for just so long before you had to try to do something about it. I did not think there was much future in that, so it was time for me to be on my way.

28

CHAPTER THREE

THE AIR CONDITIONER did not work in my car and since I always left it with the windows up and the doors locked, it was about the temperature of a sauna inside when I climbed in and drove away from the big house down the circular drive. But I did not roll the windows down or take off my jacket until I was out of sight. I had only recently scraped together enough extra cash to have the dented right front fender fixed, and the money probably would have been better spent on a tune-up anyway. The air conditioner was on my list, but not right away. The two grand from Borodin, assuming that his check would clear, and I knew it would, was welcome news. It would catch me up with my office rent and take care of the next month's child support. There was always something. My kid was a preschooler. I would only be able to pay for his college if I died accidentally so my policy would pay double. I figured he had a pretty good chance of collecting, the way things had gone for me lately.

I was just about well after catching a slug on my last case, but it had taken longer than I would have liked. Your body does that when you get close to forty, it takes its time healing as if it was trying to tell you something.

Two hundred a day and expenses plus twenty-five an hour for everything over eight hours a day. A twenty-four-hour tail meant six hundred bucks a day. For that I could hire some help, and I would need some. I would also need some kind of a van. Sitting in my car in front of a yardman's truck in the shade of some trees that stood near the curb between a couple of estates down the road from Borodin's house, I rolled down my windows and peeled off my jacket. I waited to see if my new client might send his butler out to tail me. There was no reason for Borodin to do anything like that, but I try to be careful. I had not waited more than ten minutes when I did see old Anton drive by. He was at the wheel of a well-polished two-door black BMW I had not seen at the Borodin place. He was not wearing his white jacket anymore. He had not been sent to follow me, and I was pretty sure he had not noticed me as he passed. I had no reason to tail him either, but I did. It does not hurt to find out what you can about the people you work for. And I had the time. But I did not learn much for my trouble. Anton led me north on Preston Road almost forever, across LBJ, past Valley View Shopping Center and still north, across the line into Collin County where Preston Road changed its name to Highway 289, past the ranch where 544 crossed, with its pasture full of buffalo, for Christ's sake. Only a couple of minutes before I would have blown it off and turned back toward LBJ and then west to my office, Anton turned east onto a two-lane road. So I stayed with him, hanging well back. Lucky for me, there was enough traffic even that far out that I did not have to be obvious. Besides, Anton appeared to have this on his mind. I thought he might have been up to something, because nobody drives as scrupulously legally as he was doing. But the bottom line was I watched him drive out to a smallish frame house behind a big chain link fence and feed a brace of evil-looking Doberman dogs what looked like raw meat he tugged out of the trunk of his shiny "beemer." Okay, so maybe I had wasted half an hour. Anton stood with his hands on his hips admiring the beasts, and I went back to town.

Della was in, and I was glad. When I stepped off the elevator, she looked up from whatever she was doing and flashed me a big grin.

"How did it go?" she asked.

"Fine," I assured her, trying to act like I got a new client every day. "Why shouldn't it?"

"Let me see the contract!"

"Take it easy, kid. You've seen them before."

"I've seen one before," she reminded me, without a thought of malice.

"Okay, okay. Here, you can file it if it'll make you happy."

It made me happy. Della was a leggy kid, a bouncy blonde with a dazzling smile and blue eyes. She should have been in show business. I watched her bounce up from her desk and swing into my office, and I poured myself a cup of coffee from the community urn in the waiting room that I shared with my fellow tenants. We all shared Della too. That is, she did typing and was a receptionist for all of us. There were several other offices, accountants, a couple of lawyers, some guys whose jobs I had never bothered to find out. Della liked me best, but that was only because she read a lot of private eye novels. Mike Hammer was her favorite, and I did my best to live up to him for her sake.

"What kind of case is it?" she asked when she came back.

"Too big to talk about," I told her.

"You always say that."

"What you don't know can't hurt you," I assured her.

"Ah, you don't—"

"Harrumph!" That would be Mrs. Farragut from the corner office. She was the only person I ever knew who actually made that sound. She didn't just clear her throat or cough or anything, she really made that sound.

"Yes?" Della turned a perky smile at the old woman.

"Have you finished my typing?"

"Just a sec."

"Yeah, you'd better get back to work," I whispered at her as I passed on my way into my office.

Della giggled and by the time I reached my desk her Selectric was clattering away.

I dug through my stuff and found the number my friend Joe had given me, but when I called it a suspicious-sounding lady said either that Joe was not in or that nobody named Joe lived there. She had a Spanish accent that was pretty thick, and I could not be sure which she had said, so I asked for him in Spanish, which was pretty presumptuous of me. I could talk it well enough to find a place to eat or a taxi, I guess what you would call tourist Spanish. Most of the vocabulary I knew had something to do with sportfishing, because that was why I went south, to fish and spend time on boats away from people. I did better in the tropics, where it was hot and humid, because my back felt better there. That was why I didn't mind the dog days of our Dallas Augusts like most people did. The lady at Joe's phone number warmed to me a little when I at least made the effort, and said that he was out. After a little more conversation, I guess she decided I was all right, and she gave me his pager number. I punched it on my phone and got the little stuttering beep that tells you it is a digital, so I punched in my number and hoped I would hear from him.

Speed is almost always hard to find. I must have had half a dozen numbers for him, his apartment, a couple of places where he was supposed to work—I did not know for sure what the others were. He was a free-lancer. I was not sure what his line was, but I did know he was a whiz with a camera. Not just that he could get a picture you could recognize, he knew all about oddball gadgets that came in handy from time to time. He had what he called a right-angle lens that let him take your picture over here while he was pointing the camera over there. He had used that for me on my last case, and it had worked fine. He was generally taken by the people who knew him as some kind of writer or reporter, maybe a free-lance photographer. All the newspaper guys knew him and would let him sit with them at Joe Miller's, but I could not remember ever seeing anything in print with his name on it.

The closest I could get to finding Speed by phone was one

guy who said he would try to get a message to him. I told him I would appreciate it.

I had to get my hands on a van. It's the only way to go on a surveillance like the one Borodin had in mind, unless you could wangle a room. You could not sit for more than about half an hour in a car in most neighborhoods without somebody calling the police on you. The officers were usually okay, and all you had to do was show them some ID and tell them you were on a deal, but it was not the low-profile way to go. I knew a couple of people who had vans, and I gave them a call.

One was a private investigator in town on a pretty big scale. I did not know for sure where he came from, he was not a local ex-cop like most of us. I had heard he had been FBI, but I did not hold that against him so much that I would not mooch a van off him. His secretary took my name and I had to tell her it was an emergency to get the guy on the line. When I explained what I needed, he allowed he could free up one of his busy vans, and for only a modest percentage of the fee I was getting. Only he and I had different ideas about what modest meant, so I passed. I did it nicely, I do not mind admitting, because I had done some legwork for the guy a time or two in the past, and you never know when a little extra work will come in handy. No need upsetting him.

The other man had both his vans tied up on cases of his own, so I decided to rent something and make it do. If you had your druthers, you would go with a van especially rigged up for the work. It would have a quiet-running little blower for ventilation, which is very important in Dallas in August, and special seats with mounts for your cameras, and all the video gear and everything built in. And the windows would be tinted so you could see out but nobody could see in. That would be the way to go. But I called a place that listed itself in the yellow pages under the classy title "Hell on Wheels Party Vans" and took potluck. There was a little trouble about my credit card, but I got that straightened out. It was the only card I had not bothered to surrender on demand after I left the Dallas Police Department and went through my divorce, all of which happened at about the same time and was related in a way that I did not like to think about. All I almost ever used it for was to jimmy door locks, but as far as I knew it was still alive. A little battered, maybe. The lady at Hell on Wheels thought quite a bit less of my credit card than that, but I promised her I would not try to pay for the rental with the card, I would pay cash. The card was just to let me off the lot with the damned van. She sounded dubious, but I figured she would listen to reason when it came right down to it.

Next I called a lady I knew who was in real estate and asked her what she could find out about the house where I had gone to meet Borodin. She made a little show of acting as if she cared why I wanted to know, but not enough to be a nuisance. We had done each other a couple of favors in our time. I try not to be too paranoid about my clients, but Borodin was not exactly run-of-the-mill, and it would not be the first time somebody "borrowed" a vacant house to put up a phony front. The real estate lady said there might be something in her MLS computer if the place had been on the market lately, that she would get back to me. I did not have anything better to do for the moment.

I had plenty of cash, because I had stopped on my way back to the office to cash Mister Borodin's check, just in case Hell on Wheels was legit enough to worry about my plastic. The check had cleared without a whimper, but I had been pretty sure it would. When a client screws you, it usually comes down the line somewhere. So all I had to do was wait for Joe and Speed to get in touch. Hoping that maybe Della was not busy anymore, I walked out of my office in the direction of the coffeepot for a refill.

The guy leaning on Della's desk was not making very much noise. I had not even known he was there. But he was doing quite a bit of talking. And Della was doing a lot of listening. I did not like the look of it.

The boy looked about her age, early twenties, and there was enough resemblance that I thought he might be her brother or something. He had the same corn-silk blond hair and I thought his eyes might be her shade of blue, only they were heavy-lidded and he was talking down across the desk at her so intensely that I could not see much of them. Della was squirming in her little swivel chair like there was a burner under it and it was too hot for her. Her head was ducked forward over her desk and craned up on her neck so that she was looking up into his eyes, and she was doing funny things with her arms. Her shoulders were bunched up under her hair and her elbows were bent out away from her body so she could spread her hands out palms up beside her face to show him that she was sorry, or that she really meant whatever she was trying to tell him, or something disagreeable like that. He was having none of it, though, and kept whispering, making mean hissing sounds like some kind of machinery with steam building up inside, leaking with the pressure of it.

I did not barge in on them, but I did not particularly try to be quiet as I stepped over to the coffeepot either. I wanted her to know I was there if she needed me. There was no way for me to know what this was about and I was thinking the boy might be family, and I am loath to mix in any kind of family business. About the time I put my cup down in front of the urn, I felt the boy look my way. When I half turned to see what came next, I could see his face clearly for the first time. It was fish-belly white and there were two red dots on his cheeks like they used to paint on toy soldiers, because he was so hot about whatever it was. Della saw him look up and turned toward me, leaving her hands the same way as before, turned up to the boy like she was trying to show him something or maybe begging him for something. He had a mean reddish look in his eyes, and I nudged my coffee cup over to one side and poured coffee into one of the Styrofoam jobs we kept for company. My cup was an old blue one I had bought long ago at a Dallas Police Association fund-raiser. There was a design on it, the three kinds of badges Dallas cops had worn since way back in the 1880s. A friend of mine had designed the deal, and I had a big belt buckle somewhere with the same design on it. You could replace a cup like that, but I had had it a long time.

"Who's this?" the boy said.

"Baby, please—"

That was Della, in a soft and timid voice I had not heard from her before. Baby, she had called him.

"I asked you a question!" the boy snapped down at her.

"Jack Kyle," she told him, and then she pleaded with him some more, to do something or not to do something, I could not make it out, with her voice so soft and tremulous.

"O-o-o-oh," says the boy. "The hot-shit private eye I've heard so goddamn much about."

My ex-wife once paid a shrink to imply that I might be some kind of a borderline sociopath, but I had not put much stock in it. Still, I knew that I did not usually react to things the way most people did. Like this boy with his fish-white face with the red dots and whatever misery he was putting Della through. As much as I thought of Della, you would have thought the boy would have pissed me off, but he did not. Not exactly. That is the thing that my ex-wife could not figure out for herself. I was setting my mind on hurting the boy, but not getting mad. That was a boner anyway, you do not fight your best when you are angry. It was better to keep a chill, stay within yourself, and keep your eyes open. The boy did not know that.

"Real hot-shit, ain't you?" he says to me, straightening up so I could see how big he was. He was sizable, thick-chested, and neckless. His nose was thick and lumpy with a knuckle of scar tissue on the bridge of it, where the edge of his football helmet had been slammed down a couple of hundred times. He was a headhunter, a linebacker probably, the kind a coach would have to run out of the weight room. "I said, you think you're hot-shit, don't you, old man?"

Della was looking at me with her mouth open, and I looked back at her to see if I could make out what she wanted to tell me. It looked as if she wanted to say she was sorry about this, but I could have been wrong. It could have been she did not want me to do what we both knew I would if he went on much longer. She had only seen me in one little scrap, but there had been quite a mess out of it, and I remembered that it had had an effect on her.

The boy had a way of smartass talking that made his head wobble on his shoulders a little. That and the way he rolled his hips to make them swagger as he came around the desk toward me told me it had been some time since he had last had his ass whipped, and that the benefits of the experience had worn off.

Della started up out of her chair to stop him or put herself between us, but he pushed her down roughly without looking at her. She sat down hard, and a noise came out of her, a little squeal.

"I'm talking to you, you old fucker," the boy says, swaggering toward me with his red dots shining and his eyebrows up to show me the whites of his eyes. I looked at Della and she was looking back and forth from one of us to the other. I looked beyond her at the top of her desk. There was her typewriter, the telephone with the dozen or so buttons that lit up when somebody on our floor got a call, a coffee cup where she kept pencils and pens, a ceramic pot with ivy in it, and her nameplate. It was a big wooden job. One of the men with an office on our floor, I thought it might be the accountant, had a hobby of woodworking, and he had made it for her for Christmas. It was oak or something and had scalloped edges.

Della jumped up again and threw herself at the boy. She called him Baby a couple of times more and begged him not to. Not to what, she did not say. This time, after he had tried to shirk her off with his arm once, he turned toward her a little and slapped her across her face with his open left hand. That sent her staggering back toward her chair, crying. I did not say anything, just stood there.

"You ain't so goddamn much," the boy informed me. He was about within arm's reach now and stood with his feet spread out and his hands on his hips. He rocked toward me, up on the balls of his feet, and said it again. "You ain't so goddamn much, are you, old man?"

"What are you going to do for your next trick?" I inquired.

"Well, you can talk, can't you, big man?" He was so dumb he turned his head away from me and looked back at Della to make sure he was impressing her, or whatever he thought he was doing.

Actually, that would have been the time to go to work on him, when he looked away like that. And ordinarily I would have, but I did not want him to miss anything that was going to happen to him. I heard Mrs. Farragut's shoes squeak on the floor behind me before she asked what was going on here.

"Personal business, old lady," the boy told her.

"Jack Kyle, this is some more of your mischief," Mrs. Farragut said to my back. Her opinion of me was more or less constant. If there was a problem in the building, it was probably my fault.

Della went at the boy again to try to calm him down and started to say something to Mrs. Farragut, but she did not because she saw the boy draw back his fist to hit her and she flinched.

"Don't," I told the boy, keeping my voice flat.

"Fuck you, old . . ."

He turned on me as I had hoped he would.

"I'm gonna kick yer ass," he promised foolishly.

That was another rule in fighting, don't threaten. If you are going to whip somebody, just do it. He had a lot to learn, and I was in what you might call a didactic mood.

"Uh-huh," I answered, shifting my Styrofoam cup of fresh coffee into my left hand and fumbling in my shirt pocket with my right for my cigarettes.

The boy started his swing from way back there somewhere, and I could see his eyes dip to my right hand. That was why when I threw the hot coffee in his face with my left it came as such a surprise to him. He let out a scream and his knockout punch died in the air between us. He threw both his hands up to his face, to his eyes, where some of the coffee had landed. As I stepped in toward him, he must have caught himself, because he went knock-kneed, slamming his knees together and jamming his left hand down between his thighs to protect his groin. He did not turn away from me though.

As a rule, I would rather fight a big man than a little one, and weight lifters are best, as long as you have a little room to move around in. A man carrying a lot of bulk can still be pretty quick, but as a rule he won't have the flexibility or coordination it takes to fight dirty. And I prided myself on not having been in a fair fight since high school. Freshman year.

I was not in tip-top shape because I had not long been out of the hospital from my recent gunshot wound, but to tell the truth I haven't been in all that good a shape since I got run over by a car back in 1970 in the alleged line of duty. I say alleged because the city still had not come through with a pension over it. So the upshot of my condition was that I did not want to try anything fancy, no high kicks or anything like that. But an ankle is as good as a knee if you catch it right, and the boy was too busy worrying about whether I had scalded his eyeballs and covering his groin to make it hard for me.

The first time I kicked down on his ankle bone, his left one, he yelped and hopped a bit. So I stepped around him on his left side and gave it to him again. This one landed better, and he almost went down. He roared at me and lunged with both hands out in front, wanting to crush me. But the bum ankle did not hold his weight, and he stumbled and went down on one knee. I moved on around him and grabbed Della's nameplate off her desk. Holding it like a police baton, I went to work on the boy. I jabbed him hard a couple of times deep in his ribs, once up on the point of his shoulder when he reached for me, and once I snapped the nameplate sharply across his nose, just above the scar tissue. That one bled like hell, and then he had coffee in his eyes and blood in his mouth. He was not much of a threat after that, but I was not quite through with him. I figured I had scored pretty solid on his shoulder, stunned him, because he could not operate his left arm very well. He clambered to his feet but favored his left ankle so that he had no balance. He went for my throat with his right hand, but I blocked him and he only grabbed my left wrist. I rolled it over so the thumb side of his wrist was up, and then I rapped him there sharply with one of the scalloped edges of the heavy nameplate, thinking I might get lucky and break that little dogleg of a wristbone I knew about because I had broken mine once in a scuffle. He howled again, so loud I thought I might have gotten it.

It was not so much that I liked hurting him, although I

did not mind it very much, but I did not want him to hurt Della, and I knew that if he was able to anytime before his anger settled, he probably would. Men who beat up women are like that, they'll take it out on the woman after another man roughs them up a little. I wanted the boy to take long enough getting well that he would not do that to Della.

He was down to one good leg, with both arms out of commission and his face looked a lot worse than it was, so I was about ready to call it a job. Only, when I realized that Della was right there beside me, trying to wedge in between us again and screaming at me to stop, he called her a bitch. He spat blood on her when he said it, so I kicked his good leg out from under him.

CHAPTER FOUR

THE BOY WENT down in a howling heap and Della landed on my back like a cat someone had thrown from across the room, all feet and claws and fangs. She caught me by surprise and the sudden weight of her landing on me hurt my back so badly that I staggered to the floor and shrugged her off over my head. She rolled over and came back at me as I got to my feet, slamming at my chest with her fists and crying. As close as I could get to standing was a kind of hump-backed stoop, and I threw my arms around her as she came at me and pinned her pounding hands between us and held her and then she just cried and I held her close.

Her boyfriend was making a lot of noise and when I looked past Della I saw Mrs. Farragut standing near the door of the office where she worked, looking at us in an odd way. She was a square-built old broad, with her hair done up in some kind of arrangement that looked a lot like the kind of hard hat they make you wear around a construction site, and she was wearing one of her usual dour gray suits and the thick-heeled old-fashioned shoes that your old-maid aunt used to wear. She was standing with her arms crossed across her chest, one hand up to her face with her thumb and second finger cupping her chin, her index finger laid along her cheek, and I could not help thinking she was deep in thought as she considered the three of us, the blubbering kid on the floor and Della and me. It was not what I would have expected from her.

There were a couple of lines flashing on Della's little switchboard, and now that all the commotion was over I could hear the phones ringing. And I noticed most of the doors on our floor were open and people had their heads stuck out to see what was going on. This was only the second time there had been any trouble on our floor. I usually tried to avoid it. I put my hand on the back of Della's head and stroked her, saying something to her softly. But then she took a deep breath and pushed herself away, and I let her go. She looked at me with a mean heat in her eyes, her face twisted and wet from crying, and opened her mouth but did not say anything. She knelt beside the boy and whispered to him, and I heard her call him Baby some more. Then she helped him to his feet and he put his right arm around her shoulders and leaned on her and she walked him toward the elevator, not minding that he was getting blood on her. The elevator came and went and took them away, and Della did not look back at me.

So that was that. I noticed that one of the blinking phone lines was mine, and I replaced Della's nameplate on her desk and reached across to answer it. It was Speed, and he sounded upset. I asked him to hang on until I could step into my office, and I put him on hold. The other line rang a few more times and then it stopped ringing and the blinking light went out.

As I started toward my office, I noticed out of the corner of my eye that all the curious heads had slipped back inside their doors, except of course for Mrs. Farragut. She would have something to say about this, I knew.

I looked back at the place where I had scuffled with the boy, and thought that we had not made too much of a mess. There was a bit of blood on the floor, but not so much you could not set it right with a couple of passes of a mop. The other time had been worse, because the guy had thrown up. I looked from the blood on the floor to Mrs. Farragut to see what she had to say.

"Yes?" I asked, raising my eyebrows to show I wanted to hear it.

"You pulled your punches," she said.

"Nice of you to notice," I answered, and I could not help smiling.

I stepped into my office and picked up my phone.

"Speed," I said.

"What's up, Jack?"

"What's the matter with you, Speedy? You sound kinda low."

"I don't want to talk about it, Jack."

"Okay. Listen, here's what I called you about—"

"It's that goddamn woman, man. I can't believe it."

"Leslie? What's the matter with Leslie?" I had been afraid it was a bad idea when I had introduced them, but they had seemed to be doing great together the last I had heard of them.

"It's . . . I don't want to talk about it, I really don't."

"Okay. So, listen, I've got some work. Are you—"

"The two-timing bitch!"

"Take it easy, Speed. You knew she was a whore when you took up with her. You said you liked that about her."

"Former, Jack. She was a former whore. Or I thought she was, anyway."

"Old habits die hard, Speed. You know that. Listen, why don't you come on over here to my office and I'll fill you in on this job. We can talk about Leslie then."

"Thanks, Jack. But I really don't want to talk about it."

"Yeah, I can tell. So how long will it take you to get here?"

"I already got a job, Jack. This piece I'm working on, see. That's what started the whole thing."

"What whole thing?"

"With Leslie, man! That's how I tumbled onto her. See, it's all about this new surveillance photography, all the new gadgets. I'm doing a piece on it, see, so I strung up this—"

"Save it until I see you, Speed. What kind of a piece?"

"You know, my usual stuff. Fifteen thousand words and pix."

"No, I mean is it on assignment or spec?"

"Spec."

"That's what I thought. I've got a job for you that ain't on speculation, Speed. So get your butt over here and bring whatever camera gear you have handy."

"What is it?" he asked.

"It's twenty-five an hour."

"Sounds interesting."

"Get on over here and we'll talk."

"About half an hour," he said.

"It's a deal."

I felt better about the Borodin deal after talking to Speed, although naturally I hated to hear that he and Leslie were on the outs. Speed and I between us could handle the tail on Mrs. Borodin if we had to, so I felt like I was off to a good start on the deal. I wanted Joe if he was available, because he was the best I knew at tailing a car. He rode a motorcycle usually, and he would scare you to death the way he worked in and out of traffic, but he stuck to somebody like a tick once he was on them. He was tenacious and smart, and had nerves. I had seen him talk his way out of some tight spots with a bullshit smile and an attitude. He was tops in an undercover job too, and that was where I had met him.

But if it had to be just Speed and me, we could make do. One in the van to keep an eye on things while Mrs. Borodin was at the town house, the other in a car to go with her when she left. It was skimpy, but it beat the hell out of trying to do it solo. Once we got her pattern down, we could tuck her in at night and then probably Speed would take the night shift and I would come on in the morning to keep tabs on her if she went anywhere. I needed to swing by Mrs. Borodin's little hideaway pretty soon, while the light was still good and before she was supposed to be there, to get the lay of the land. But I decided to wait a while longer in hopes that Joe would call.

My real estate friend called back to say that the Borodin

house had been on the market, up for sale until about a month ago. Now somebody with a foreign-looking name had leased it for six months with an option. She thought the name had been Bolino, or something like that. I thanked her, said I owed her one. She said I could bet my ass I did.

While I waited to see if Joe would call, I smoked a cigarette and worried about Della. I did not like any part of what had happened but most of all I did not like the way she had called the boy Baby and the picture that put into my mind of the two of them. I had always been of two minds about Della. Looking at her, I thought of her one way and imagined how it would be. You could not help thinking along those lines when you saw the way she looked and how she moved. But when I talked to her, or rather when she talked to me, there was that kind of kid quality, that blue-eyed, sweet-voiced "Gee" kind of an attitude she had, that made me feel like her big brother or something. Okay, I was old enough to be her father, but big brother was more like how I felt. Maybe not even that, maybe just like an older friend. She needed a bit of seeing after, I had always thought. Now I thought about her and the boy being together, and I did not like it because of how he would be with her and even more because it would be because she wanted it. It felt like there was part of her I had not seen before, even suspected. I wondered for about the millionth time why we can't be smarter about who we fall in love with. With whom we fall in love. Whatever.

Finally Joe did call, about the time the custodian I was sure Mrs. Farragut had called finished mopping up in the lobby.

"What's up?" he asked.

"A little work, if you're free," I said.

"When?"

"Tonight."

"Can't make it."

"When could you?" I asked.

"Tomorrow maybe, the next day for sure."

"It should be for several days. Call me when you're available."

"You got it. Anything else?"

"That's about it. How've you been doing, Joe?"

"Maintaining. You?"

"Can't complain, you know how it is."

"Yeah. Be talkin' to you."

"Right."

And that was that. Joe did not waste time or words. He would be along when he could, and he knew I would be fair on the money. What else was there?

It was a little after four o'clock, and Hell on Wheels Party Vans was open till seven. Borodin had said we needed to be in place at the town house by around eight. I had checked out the license numbers on my way back to the office from Borodin's, after cashing his check, and that left me plenty of time to drive by and look Sylvia's place over before I picked up the van. I dug into the jar in my desk drawer and came up with half a dozen quarters, which I dropped into my pants pocket for pay phones, and I reminded myself to call Della later.

CHAPTER
FIVE

THE OAK LAWN address was not hard to find and there were a few landmarks in the neighborhood that meant something to me. The address was in a complex not far from Lee Park, a pleasant bit of greenery with a pseudo-Grecian shell with columns for a band to play in and a statue down by Cedar Springs of Robert E. Lee and some other guy on horses. I remembered in the early seventies when the uniforms from Central used to scrimmage in the park with hippie dopers and half-assed radicals and all kinds of trash on a more or less regular basis.

Oak Lawn, the boulevard, ran within a few blocks of the park and it was not far from there to the Wine Press, a restaurant at Wycliffe. It was a nice place, and I liked to meet clients there.

The location I was interested in was on one of the side streets that ran off of Oak Lawn near Lemmon Avenue. Once I figured out within a block or so where the place was, I circled the general area, working my way in toward the place. That way I could get a look at the neighborhood without showing myself around the complex itself any more than I had to. I did not want to be obvious because not only did I have to be concerned about Sylvia seeing me, there was all that Crime Watch business. Maybe it was a good deal, the police always after people to be good neighbors, keep an eye on the place next door and all that, maybe it stopped a crime or two. But it could be a pain in the butt for somebody like me, whose business consisted largely of lurking.

Circling in toward the location let me refresh my memory on how all the little side streets were laid out in this old part of town, how the alleys were, things I would need to know. Once you are on a tail and they go mobile, there is not much time to figure out that kind of stuff. And the driver you are trying to follow, it stands to reason, knows the layout better than you most of the time. Plus, he or she knows where they are going and you do not. You would be amazed how oblivious most people are to a tail most of the time. The problem is usually not that they spot you or that they are doing things on purpose to avoid being followed, it is just that they know some bullshit little shortcut and unintentionally they put you in a bind and you end up losing them. Also, since you cannot always tail someone by just driving along behind them like on TV, especially if traffic is light, you many times need to cut over one street this way or that and parallel them. One-way streets can really screw you up then. So I took the time to look things over on my way in.

In the process of cutting the odds against being able to keep tabs on Mrs. Sylvia Borodin before I even pulled into the apartment complex where she was supposed to show up sooner or later, I happened to drive by a couple of places, a fast-food restaurant and a street corner, where friends of mine had been shot. Most cops and ex-cops that I knew had places like those filed away in their memory banks. The ones who did not had it to look forward to.

Easing into the parking lot of the complex itself, I made one slow circle and satisfied myself that none of the cars on Borodin's slip of paper was there. It was early yet, not quite five in the evening. Borodin had said his wife probably would not be home before eight.

There were some parking spaces marked for visitors and I left my car in one of them and went for a walk through the complex. I wanted to see exactly how Sylvia's place was laid out.

On my way in along a walk that led up between hedges with flowers that were still pink and white in spite of our long August, I met two ladies walking out. They were dressed like maids, with plastic bags on their arms, the bags heavy and gouged into corners at the bottoms by the stuff inside them. The two women, both of them probably in their fifties, were talking in low voices to each other as I stood aside almost in the hedge and let them pass abreast. They did not look up or take any notice of me, and I caught bits of what they were saying. They were talking a Spanish I had heard a few times before, the way it was spoken in Central America, as opposed to most places in Mexico, for example. The town house complex where Mrs. Borodin had made her hideout was that kind of a place, where even the domestics were imports. I had already noticed that most of the cars parked in the residents' spaces were foreign jobs, Mercedeses, BMWs, a couple of Acuras. That did not make me feel any kinder toward the people who lived there. I had the notion that it ought to be a Class B misdemeanor for a U.S. citizen to buy a foreign car, and that meant a thousand-dollar fine and six months in the county jail. But I was full of wrong-headed stuff like that. It had been pointed out to me a number of times.

The whole condo/town house/apartment thing in Dallas was hard to keep up with. The market on them, whatever you called them, had gone about like a roller coaster in the last ten or fifteen years. From when nobody knew what one was and everybody just bought houses up until a few years ago when the oil business rolled over on one wing and flew into the ground, you could not go wrong. One of these things you might have bought for thirty thousand ten or twelve years ago had been a hundred grand five years later, twenty a couple of years ago, and nowadays I heard you could not give them away. There was no mortgage money for them, and you had to pay cash or buy them like cars, on a short note. I had always wondered what kept Dallas going, exactly what held the thing up, because as far as I could see the town was made of real estate, oil, and insurance, with some high-tech stuff coming in the last few years. With a few exceptions, nobody seemed to be making anything that anybody else needed. They were all just servicing one another, and I never understood where the money came from that all the high rollers passed around among themselves. With what they liked to call the energy downturn, real estate had "softened" to quicksand, and I was curious what there was left to keep the town open. There was not anything to insure. Banking and insurance had always been there, backgrounding the flashy stuff, but with our oil and real estate problems, banks all over Texas were going under, and savings and loans were in even worse shape. Things had changed drastically from the optimistic "Sunbelt" boomlet of the early eighties and out-of-staters were buying up Texas banks and businesses, a lot of them from so far out of state that they ate with chopsticks. The insurance companies always made theirs, of course, and they had enough hacks bought down in Austin to make sure it stayed that way. But nowadays we seemed to specialize in "fronts," guys and gals with foot-long smiles who wore thousand-dollar suits and twenty-thousand-dollar watches and drove fifty-thousand-dollar cars and all of it was leased or borrowed except maybe the smiles. They'd nurse a glass of white wine at happy hour so they could eat the free munchies because there was no food in the showcase houses they lived in, also leased, and they all scampered around like cranked rats on treadmills trying to hold the whole bullshit deal together. That was what Dallas was getting to be, and I thought that this little village of town houses in Oak Lawn where Sylvia Borodin slipped away from her husband to do whatever it was that she did looked like it might be part of all that.

There were a dozen of the units, four to each of the three buildings. Each building had two downstairs and two upstairs, and the buildings were laid at angles to the street so that all the units faced the interior, where the hedges and the rest of the landscaping surrounded a pool with a sauna at one end and plenty of deck chairs scattered around for everyone to work on a tan at one time. There were a couple of built-in grills for outdoor parties, and overall the place looked very sociable.

The number Borodin had given me belonged to a downstairs unit on the far side of the third building, the farthest one from the street. At first it had the appearance of offering some seclusion, a little privacy. But when I had walked around the back of the place and come back to the pool, I wondered why Mrs. Borodin had chosen a place that did not have a back way out. There was an alley in back, but a stockade fence ran the length of the lot and there was no way to get a car out except through the parking lot onto the street by the way I had come in. It would make my job a little easier, but I could not help wondering about it. Of course, everybody is not as paranoid as I am, but I had to think that Mrs. Borodin was too sure that her husband did not suspect her of anything. I thought it was dangerous to take a man like him lightly. Maybe Sylvia was not as smart as she looked in her photographs.

We would not have to go on the property at all to keep an eye on Mrs. Borodin's car, to know when she came and went. I found a spot across the street where an old restaurant had been torn down and the lot cleared. The little six-space parking lot was still in good shape, and there was a building going up next door, an apartment complex that apparently meant to use the lot where the restaurant had been for parking. We could put the van in the little parking lot and nobody would think much of it, especially after they got used to its being there. There were always cars and equipment left near a construction site like that. But when I pulled in there in my car to check it out, I discovered we would not be able to use it because it did not look like we could see the door of Mrs. Borodin's unit. Then I backed up a bit on the rise that led up from the street to where the restaurant had been, and there it was, a clear view of her door. We would try it there to begin with at least.

The lady at Hell on Wheels Party Vans looked a little

better than she had sounded on the phone, sweet-faced except for the hard lines at the corners of her eyes and the over-bleached blond hair that looked like it felt like straw. There was a lot of debate about the status and general repute of my long-suffering old credit card, and the upshot was that I had to leave a thousand dollars of Borodin's money behind with the lady, who wasted no time telling me she had heard it all before, before she would let me drive the beast off the lot. She gave me a receipt and promised I could have the thousand back less my charges when I returned the van, and smiled for the first time when I left. She had not minded that I wanted to leave my car at her place, after she had made sure I understood that she would not be responsible if anything happened to it.

It was not a van I would have picked for the job, but it was the only one on the lot that did not have some kind of goofy paint job or something else that would make it too conspicuous. It was plain, a dark chocolate brown that might look like anything from black to gray under artifical light at night. It was one of Ford's models, and I was glad at least that it came without bench seats in the back. I figured it had been some-body's delivery van before Hell on Wheels got their hands on it and they had not had time to screw it up yet with all that carpeting and seats and crap they seemed to like so much.

So that was it. All I needed was Speed and I was ready to go. I would pick him up at my place, run by Hell on Wheels for my car, and then follow him over to the address in Oak Lawn. I knew where I wanted to stash my car, somewhere close enough to get to it if Mrs. Borodin left so I could follow her, and somewhere it would not attract a lot of attention.

CHAPTER
SIX

SPEED WAS PITIFUL. He was in such bad shape, so heartsick and especially so loquacious about it, that I wished I had not brought him in on the deal. I had shown him the layout the first time through, and then I had taken the first shift. Ten minutes to midnight, right on schedule, he came tapping softly on the back door of the van and I let him in. I had all the photos of Mrs. Borodin taped to the van wall beneath the side window through which we were watching her place. I had laid a thick blanket doubled on the bare van floor to muffle any noise my two aluminum folding lawn chairs might make, and Speed had set up one of his cameras on a tripod. It had a hellaciously big telephoto lens that made you think you could put your hand out and touch Sylvia Borodin's door when you looked through it, although it must have been a hundred yards away. That was all of our gear, that and a plastic cooler with soft drinks and a couple of sandwiches, and of course an empty plastic milk jug to piss in so we wouldn't have to get out of the van to do that.

"I left your car in the same place," he assured me as he climbed in beside me in the van.

"Good."

"Anything happening?" he asked.

"No. She came in about half past eight, driving that Mercedes," I told him, pointing at the card I had taped up alongside one of our photographs of her, with the three license numbers Borodin had given me and the information that went with each car, according to their registrations. "She parked over there, see it? That's the space reserved for her unit. She walked in and shut the door and there hasn't been another sign of her."

"Good," he said, shaking his head about something else, the thing with Leslie, I imagined.

I hoped he wouldn't start in on that again because I wanted to get away from him and go home and get some sleep. If Mrs. Borodin left between now and daylight, Speed would be on his own to try and keep up with her in the van, but I didn't think she would go out, and I wanted some sleep because I would be on it all the next day, and maybe longer depending on how things worked out with Joe. I had had a pretty long day already, and was too old and stiff in the back to miss a night's sleep if I could avoid it. I was in no mood for Speed's sad tale, I had things on my mind, but Speed started in almost as soon as he settled beside me.

"You were right all along, Jack. You can't trust women, any of them, the goddamn, sorry—"

"Take it easy, will you?" I interrupted him, thinking that I had never told him you couldn't trust women in particular. It was my long-held view that you couldn't trust anybody. I didn't discriminate.

"I would never have believed it, Jack. Swear to God, if I hadn't seen it myself. My very own eyes. I'd like to tear 'em right out of their sockets, swear to God."

He was low, no question about it, and he had been drinking, which I did not particularly care for when he was on a job with me. Speed could not exactly handle his liquor and I was generally opposed to that kind of thing on principle. I made exceptions now and then, of course, but on principle I was against it. That part about his eyes worried me, and rather than take the chance he might do something oedipal, I cursed under my breath and made up my mind to hear him out for a bit. Maybe then he would settle down and I could go get some sleep. Or maybe I would have to do my sleeping there in the van so I would be handy, although it would not be my first choice.

"Tell me about it, Speed," I said to him, trying to sound as if I really cared about his trouble. Thing was, I did care, but I don't often sound that way, even when I mean it.

"I don't want to bother you with it, Jack."

"You dumb son of a bitch, you've already bothered me more than a goddamn 'nuff. Now stop whining around like a kicked dog and tell me what the fucking deal is. You're cutting into my sack time, asshole."

"Okay. Here it is." He rubbed a hand across his face and took a deep breath to begin.

"Christ," I mumbled. Why is it people don't take me seriously until I abuse them?

"I was working on this story I told you about," he says, and I could see he was dying to tell me the whole thing, would have cried all night if I had not insisted.

"The one about surveillance photography," I said to encourage him that I had been listening.

"Right. See, there's just some fantastic stuff out. Like fiberoptics."

"What?"

Well, if I had hoped he would make short work of his story, I never should have asked about this fiberoptics crap. He got off into that and went on like there was no end to it. The upshot was you could take some amazing pictures with this stuff. It was basically, if I followed Speed, a hot new technology that would let you shoot video through a wire, or something like that. Doctors had used it for a long time to see into people's bodies without cutting into them. They would insert this little fiberoptics wire and there was some kind of unbelievably tiny lens in the wire that would send back pictures of the insides of a vein or artery, stuff like that. Hell of a deal. Now, the stuff was on the market for "counterintelligence" work, which is how a lot of magazines refer to the snooping business, my business more or less. I began not to mind listening to Speed around this point, because I could see how this stuff might come in pretty handy.

Speed loved this kind of thing. He was a real nut about gadgets and science, especially if it had anything to do with taking pictures. That was his main thing, although he was not shabby when it came to audio recording either. In some circles, he was considered one of the top sound men in this part of the country, but photography was his first love. I watched him as best I could inside the dark van as he went on about this stuff, and thought that he might have forgotten about Leslie altogether.

Speed, and if I ever knew his whole righteous name, I had long since forgotten it, was a lanky guy, who would have been tall if he hadn't been so stoop-shouldered. He had big feet and big hands, as far as length goes. But his fingers were skinny like a bird's bones and looked like he should have played the piano or been a surgeon or something. He wore glasses sometimes, I think when he remembered where he had left them, and he was wearing them tonight. They were the big kind, round, with wires for frames. His hair, which was a sandy brown and long in the back, fell over his forehead and he was constantly doing something about it, either flicking his head around to swing his hair out of his eyes or pushing it up with his hand. I don't know if he remembered to eat when I wasn't around, but he didn't look like he did. He did not smoke, and carried so much stuff in his shirt pockets that he looked like he had tits. He was one of those guys everybody makes fun of for having the little plastic pocket liners full of all kinds of pencils and pens, and also in his pockets he kept all the notes he had written to himself, a lot of them on bar napkins because he could never remember where he had left his notepad, which was usually in his hip pocket. Every time I had run into him since I first knew him he had been the same, totally wrapped up in something and very excited about it. The last time he and I had been together, it had been nuclear weapons. Now it was this new fiberoptics stuff. It seemed to be whatever he was working on at the moment, but I didn't know if he wrote stories about what caught his eye or if he just got obsessed by whatever stories he was doing.

There was a lot of technical stuff that was over my head, but then Speed got down to the case at hand. He and Leslie Armitage, a lady I had known since my days working Vice, had been together for quite a while, since I had introduced them to each other, more or less, at Red's Bar one evening. They had even worked on my last case for me a little, and they had looked as happy as a couple of kids. I had been worried because Leslie was a whore, or had been one. But Speed knew about that, said she had told him, and it did not seem to be a problem. The last I knew they were playing house in his place, a small but terribly cluttered apartment in East Dallas. Then I had been out of touch for a while, what with getting shot and recuperating and one thing and another. It seems that in the meantime Leslie had talked Speed into moving in with her in an apartment where she had been living alone in a much nicer part of town. It was somewhere in Carrollton, a suburb north of town out near the DFW airport. So far so good, but just the other day he had rigged up a little camera at her place to see for himself how the new technology worked. And he wanted to take some pictures of Leslie without her knowing it, kind of surprise her. He launched off into how you can get still photos from the fiberoptic videotape if you know what you're doing, but I didn't pay much attention to that because I was wondering what had made him think she would be pleased about having her picture taken that way. But after all, he knew her better than I did, and I had no doubt his intentions were good.

Well, the crux of it was that Leslie shooed him out of her apartment one weekend and gave him a story about having company and she would see him after a couple of days. That would have made me suspicious already, but he didn't think anything of it until later when he got a look at his videotape. He had rigged it up with a wall spike and a remote recorder, some more technical stuff I didn't wear myself out listening to, but the bottom line was when he saw the video, there was Leslie, up to her old tricks. Speed did not know the guy, had never seen him before. That was what all the whining was about. He had not seen or spoken to her since. I told him it was a hell of a deal, and let him make me promise we would look into it as soon as this Borodin thing was wrapped up. He seemed to feel better after that, and I checked my watch. I could still make it to my office in time to get a few hours sleep before coming back to relieve Speed, and I was trying to decide if sleeping in the army cot I was used to, the one I kept stashed behind the filing cabinet in my office, was sufficiently better than curling up on the van floor to be worth the drive when something happened.

I was looking past the camera, alongside the big lens, out the window of the van toward Mrs. Borodin's front door, and I saw it open and someone step out. When I looked through the camera, I saw that it was her, Sylvia. I cranked off half a dozen shots of her, the motor drive of the camera grinding noisily, as she made her way down the walk between the low hedges toward the parking lot. Then I told Speed to watch to see if anyone followed her, anyone else, I meant, and I grabbed his other camera and scrambled over him and out the door of the van, which I tried to close without making any noise. I looked around the corner of the van and saw her walking toward her Mercedes. And then I jogged away to the place where Speed had left my car.

When I had the car up and running, and I had pulled it into a spot where I could see the driveway leading out of the town house parking lot onto the street without being seen myself, I took a moment to check my watch. It was twenty minutes past midnight. She turned to her left, my right, and drove away in the direction of Oak Lawn, the street. When she had gone most of a block, I eased out into the street behind her and turned my lights on. This may not take long after all, I thought to myself.

CHAPTER
SEVEN

Mrs. Borodin handled the Mercedes pretty well, but she did not seem to be in any particular hurry. She turned right onto Oak Lawn and slipped through the traffic without taking any chances. There were more cars out that time of early morning than you might expect, and I wondered as I usually did who all these people were and where they were going. Most of the clubs closed at two, in just over an hour. Some of these people out on the streets were on their way home, or on their way for a bite to eat after a little partying, or maybe just on their way to anywhere to keep from going home.

She made the jog at Cedar Springs and continued on Oak Lawn toward Stemmons Freeway. As I cleared the intersection a couple of cars behind her, I looked to my right and saw smoke and the whirling red lights of police cars and a couple of fire-trucks, and from the location I guessed somebody might have torched the headquarters of the local gay advocate group again. When Mrs. Borodin switched into the left-hand of the two lanes on our side of the street as we came up on Maple Avenue, I hoped she was not on her way to meet somebody at Riverchon Park. She did not impress me as someone who would, but a left at Maple would take us in that direction. Riverchon used to be a nice place, there was a decent baseball stadium there which backed up against the Dallas North Tollway. But nowadays it was no place to be at night unless you were looking for trouble. A friend of mine, a Dallas police captain no less, had been shot in the park a few weeks earlier, working some kind of undercover decoy deal. He had been Vice captain then, and I thought how much that did not sound like the guy I had worked for when I was in Vice. That character would only come out at night for a banquet.

But she did not turn at Maple, only used the left lane to get around a drunk who could not decide what to do next, and I had to stall a second or two so I would not be directly behind her, and she scooted through the intersection and disappeared down the hill past the minimum security county jail unit on the right, in the direction of Stemmons. I hurried a bit so I could see if she took one of the freeway entry ramps, but she did not. She kept going, under Harry Hines and Stemmons, and I followed her all the way through until we were on Industrial Boulevard.

Industrial was its own little neighborhood in a way. You could say it had its own charm. Out past the point where it split with Irving Boulevard, which continued parallel to Stemmons into the suburb of Irving, where the Dallas Cowboys played, Industrial was mostly hotels, motels, and a couple of cafés. It hooked up with Stemmons in a stretch that was nicer hotels and all the marts, the Trade Mart, Apparel Mart, and some other stuff that drew crowds of various types according to the particular type of trade show that was in town on a given weekend. The city fathers, or mothers, or whatever we were calling the shot-callers nowadays, had tried to dress the place up a little by changing the name of the street from Industrial Boulevard to Trade Mart Boulevard, or some crap like that. That was how we handled a lot of our problems. We did not solve them, we just changed the name of something. Like in South Dallas where I used to work in Patrol, they had changed old Forest Avenue to Martin Luther King Boulevard. Same thing.

Industrial Boulevard originally got its name because of the industrial types of businesses located there, and there was still a lot of that: truck companies, warehouses, various light manufacturers, wholesale outlets of all kinds. It was one of the few parts of Dallas where anybody seemed to be making anything. Down below where Industrial split with Irving, back toward downtown, it had gotten to be mostly bars and cafés, with here and there a business in between.

Only a block or so after she passed the Industrial-Irving split, Mrs. Borodin stopped in the street with her turn signal flashing for a left-hand turn across the two oncoming lanes. I rolled to a stop a safe distance behind her, so that the two cars between us screened me from her in case she was checking her rearview mirror. I looked in the direction her flashing signal was pointing and tried to figure out where she was going. On that side of the street I could see a couple of "nude modeling" joints, a café that had been closed for quite a while, and a strip joint. I knew the strip joint, it had not been a bad place years back when I used to go in there to watch a particular dancer when she was in town. Mind you, that was in the old days when they still had strippers. The women would come out from backstage in evening gowns, and there was a live band. It took about three numbers for each dancer to tease and flirt her way down to a G-string and pasties. They had to wear pasties in those days. And then they would actually dance, some of them better than others. The one I liked in particular was a hell of a dancer. All of them worked some kind of a circuit in those days, so many weeks in Houston, then somewhere else, and then so many weeks in Dallas. That was before I got into the Vice business, but I understood there were half a dozen guys, most of them from Chicago and other places, who ran the whole business in town. It was a system, and maybe it had its faults, but it suited me a lot better than the way things were now, when instead of real strippers you got these kids who just yanked off their T-shirts and showed you all they could remember from their high school gym class.

Mrs. Borodin got her opening in traffic and whipped across

the two facing lanes and drove into the strip joint parking lot. I watched her get out and lock her Mercedes and walk toward the door of the place as I let a pack of cars go by, and then I followed. She was in the door and out of sight by the time I found a place to park.

As I stepped inside the front door of the club, the noise hit me first, the booming rock-and-roll thunder that blanketed the place and made it impossible for me to hear what the woman just inside was saying to me. But her universal gesture with the open palm extended was clear enough. I gave her a five and she smiled and mouthed thank-you. I had expected change.

There were three stages lighted and occupied, one big one with seats around its edge and two smaller ones out among the tables. There was considerably less than a capacity crowd, and it was not hard to spot Mrs. Borodin. She was the only woman in the place who did not work there. She had found a table off to one side and was deep in conversation with a guy who looked like he would have preferred a seat much closer to the action.

The girl on the main stage was working harder than I would have expected so late in the night, but without any pretense of dancing. To the music roaring back and forth across the joint from speakers the size of footlockers, she was doing a series of splits, each of them ending up in a kind of somersault into another split. She had her fans, three guys probably my age, in dress shirts with their ties pulled loose at the collar. The other two kids on the table stages were just going through the motions, and one of them seemed to be carrying on a conversation with a nasty-looking guy standing nearby, one of those biker types you see everywhere these days, with plenty of tattoos showing on his arms where they stuck out from his black T-shirt that had a logo of some heavy metal rock band. This place was full of stories, but I had business already.

Mrs. Borodin's friend was fiftyish, with a toupee that almost matched the color of his real hair. He was fat, too, and wore the cheap-looking GI kind of glasses that servicemen get for nothing on base. They did not fit very well anymore, if they ever had, and he was constantly jabbing at them with the middle finger of his right hand to get them up off the tip of his nose.

I found a table off to the right side of the place as you go in, where there was nothing behind me but a couple more empty tables and where I could see the front door and Mrs. Borodin and her friend without being too obvious. When I turned to look at Sylvia, one of the table stages was almost between us and a little to my left, so I could pretend to be watching the dancer in case Sylvia looked over her shoulder in my direction.

I had almost hit my chair with my butt before the waitress appeared and asked what I would be drinking. I told her a light beer would be nice and she said I'd better take two, because they would stop serving in a couple of minutes. We communicated all of this by screaming back and forth at each other over the wind-tunnel volume of the music.

As I waited for my beers and smoked a cigarette, I tried to come up with a story that would explain Sylvia Borodin and the guy at the table with her. Romance was out, unless somebody had completely redefined the concept without my noticing. Sylvia was a looker, much better in person than in her pictures. She was late twenties, with a lot of hair, and she had a way of moving inside her clothes that spoke volumes without being obvious, if that makes sense. For instance, the outfit she was wearing there in the club was nothing but a blouse and skirt with a tasteful amount of jewelry sparkling here and there, nothing gaudy. But I had seen her walk a bit, and she did a hell of a job of it. I thought she was like little Della that way, she just had it, that special way of being put together that can drive a man crazy, and it showed through whether they meant for it to or not. Which got me thinking about Della and her boyfriend, and it worried me that I had not been able to reach her. I had tried her home phone four or five times earlier in the evening, before doing my time in the van, but I had only been able to talk to her answering machine. She had a chirpy, cheerful little message on the thing, but I was worried she was not feeling very chirpy anymore. She was probably still mad at me, but then I remembered how she had laid her head on my chest when I had held her and made her stop fighting me. I did not know if she was mad at me really for hurting the boy, or at him for making it necessary, or maybe even at herself for being involved in the whole thing. Besides, I was not worried about her being mad, whether it was at me or anybody. I was worried that she might be in some kind of trouble. The boy might have done something to her——. I should have really put him out of commission, but I had held back because of her. Like Mrs. Farragut had said, I'd pulled my punches. I had hurt him, but I did not think I'd broken anything, and that had probably been a mistake. I wondered a little about Mrs. Farragut, too. She had a pretty good eye for the rough stuff, and I wondered where she had picked that up. I'm inclined to think I may not be a good judge of women, the way they keep surprising me.

Sylvia Borodin had a real drink in front of her, I noticed, when she moved a little to her right to get her cigarettes out of her purse, which she had stashed in an empty chair. The guy with the glasses and the bad hair was sucking his drink through a straw. It was one of those technicolor jobs that comes with a little umbrella and has fruit on the top of it. Jesus, I thought, if this nerd is getting any of that, there is no God.

She blew her smoke out of one corner of her mouth so she wouldn't get it in the nerd's face and then leaned toward him to say something. He leaned toward her, and their heads were close enough they might have been kissing, but I did not think they were. The music in the joint was so loud you had to do that just to be heard.

When Stefan Galipolus came in the front door and sauntered over to their table I was almost glad to see him. He smiled and even bowed a little at the waist, and took Sylvia's hand in his and gave it one of those ultrasuave Continental-type moves where he put his face down over it and almost kissed it. She smiled up at him and the geek with the fruity drink sat looking up at Galipolus with his mouth open.

Galipolus was tall and very handsome, in a dark and somehow oily way. He wore his hair a bit long and brushed straight back all around, not blow-dried like the local studs. He was clean-shaven, tanned, and well rested. His clothes were tasteful, and I guessed expensive, from the look of them. I did not see any jewelry on him except a smallish watch on his right wrist. After he had made quite a fuss over Mrs. Borodin, he turned his charm on the geek, who responded by curling the corners of his open mouth up into a grin and nodding energetically enough that his glasses slid down his nose again. He shook hands with Galipolus and then the tall handsome man sat down in a chair between Sylvia and the geek. I noticed that he chose the chair that would put his back toward a wall, even though he had to hand Sylvia's purse to her to do it. Maybe he just wanted to watch the dancers while he and the other two talked.

They had not been at it long when the lights inside the club flashed off and back on a couple of times. An amplified voice from somewhere announced last call, and then we went back to the normal level of darkness and the deafening music came at us again.

Galipolus was doing most of the talking, leaning toward the geek and paying Sylvia Borodin very little attention, which struck me as more than a little odd. At one point, the geek actually talked, and Galipolus listened. The geek pointed at Sylvia with an open palm and said something, then shook his head up and down a couple of times for emphasis. Galipolus's shoulders went up in a question, and then the geek shook his head vehemently from side to side to say no to something like he really meant it.

I was so taken with trying to figure out what they might be saying to each other and how they all three figured in on the deal, that I did not realize there was something wrong until the girl with the camera came around. She went from table to table, skipping over mine because I was alone, apparently asking people if they wanted their picture taken. That was new to me, I would not have thought there would be any takers, that this was the kind of place where you especially would not want your picture taken. But I was wrong again. Of the three businessmen on the barstools alongside the main stage, two of them did want their pictures taken. It was not hard for them to persuade a dancer who was not onstage at the moment to pose with them, and the girl who was onstage bent over the two men and posed with a bare tit aimed at each of their heads for good measure. It struck me as a bonehead move, the kind of thing a man would wake up worrying about the next morning, but there is no accounting for people. Next the camera girl stopped by the table where Sylvia and her two friends sat. She said something to Galipolus and smiled back when he smiled at her, and then they both said something and everybody at the table laughed a little. I got the impression the camera girl knew him, or had seen him before at least, and then finally it came to me. The photograph Borodin had given me of his wife and Galipolus, the one he said had been taken at some kind of social event. It was from this dump, and that must have been where he got the address. I had not checked to make sure, but I had a pretty good idea that this place was the address he had given me along with the photos and the license numbers. I could not figure out why he had lied about where the party pic had been taken if he was going to turn right around and give me the address of the place. Husbands can be pretty irrational animals, I knew only too well, but he must have known I would figure this out. I made a note to ask him about that, and I also made a bet with myself that when this little party was over and we all went outside I would find a couple of cars with the other two license numbers Borodin had given me. If I did, if Galipolus got into one and the geek got into the other, Mr. Borodin would need to explain to me why he had held out on me. I had thought we had a better understanding than that.

There was no point in waiting until they turned up the lights and threw us out. I finished my second beer and left a couple of ones on my table for the waitress and went outside.

I looked over the cars waiting in the parking lot and found that I had been only half right. In addition to Mrs. Borodin's Mercedes and a few others, there was only one with a license number Borodin had given me. It had come back to some kind of leasing company, which was a blind, and I guessed it was Galipolus's car. What the geek might be driving, I could only guess, although there was a Volkswagen Rabbit I thought likely, largely because it had a compass suction-cupped onto the dash so the driver would always know which way he was going. There were also a couple of motorcycles off to one side, and a couple of tough-looking characters lurking near them. One was the tattooed boy I had seen talking to one of the dancers. I had not noticed the other one, but they looked as if they might belong to the same club.

Without making any eye contact or giving off any other kind of signal that I knew they were there to the motorcycle riders, I cranked up my old Chevy and pulled it back into the shadows of the building next door to the parking lot and waited.

The geek came out first, only a few minutes later. He walked kind of heel-and-toe, without swinging his arms more than a little, like a man who spent most of his life sitting down somewhere. I did not know how many of those sissy drinks he had drunk, but he was grinning as he fumbled in the pockets of his polyester pants and I could hear his keys jingling. But he did not get in the Rabbit I had figured him for. Instead, he climbed into a Chevrolet Caprice station wagon, but not before I had taken enough shots of him with Speed's camera to think at least one of them would come out. There was some light in the parking lot, but not enough for me to be overconfident with the camera. Speed had loaded it with some kind of high-speed film with a brand name that sounded French and set the controls of the camera on automatic to make it easy for me. He had assured me that not even I could screw it up. We would see about that.

I made sure I got at least one shot of the rear end of the station wagon as it drove away, just in case I forgot the license number, which I did not think I would. I did not turn on a light or even try to scrawl the number down in the dark, because I did not want to miss anything and I did not want to make myself obvious with the light. The two characters with the motorcycles were still there, but they did not act like they were paying me any attention.

The three businessmen were next, loud and happy, and they stumbled over to a Chrysler K car, probably rented. They had the fun-time look of salesmen on a trip. Maybe they were in town for some kind of show at the Trade Mart. They were still screwing around getting into the Chrysler and arguing about who was the designated driver when I saw Mrs. Borodin and Mister Galipolus walk out of the club, arm in arm. I took some more pictures.

CHAPTER EIGHT

THE WAY THEY behaved made me wonder if they had spotted me. Galipolus had his arm around Sylvia's waist and he was looking down at her. They were talking, but she was not looking up at him. She was looking where she was going. He walked her to her Mercedes and stood beside her as she unlocked the driver's door. From where I was sitting in the shadows I thought it would make a perfect picture. He would kiss her beside the car and I would get it, with the front of the club in the background. Maybe he would get in the car with her and worry about his own car later. That would be good too, because I knew if they got in the Mercedes, even if it was just to say good-bye for the moment, he would not pass up the chance to show her how he felt about her, and that would make a good picture too. But they did not behave that way, which was what made me wonder.

When she had her door open, she turned to Galipolus and gave him her hand, like for a handshake. He took it, looked into her face for a long couple of seconds, and he kissed her hand the same way he had before. Then he stepped back and she slipped into the Mercedes, closed the door, and drove away.

It did not figure. I had let the geek go his way, thinking I had his license plate number and I could track him down later if it seemed important. And I had hoped Sylvia and Galipolus would leave together. That would have simplified things. But if they left separately, I had made up my mind to stick with him. I was reasonably sure where she would be going, and Speed was on her place. I figured it was worth more to see what Galipolus might be up to. More than likely, he would go to Sylvia's hideout anyway. If they were headed for his place, I could pick her up again there. So far the one I knew least about was Galipolus, so he was the one I would tail. This was a part of a one-man tail job where it was easy to make the wrong call, but that was all a part of it, and that was one reason I had worked it out with Borodin ahead of time to understand that I might lose track of his wife somewhere along the way. That gave me the latitude I needed to play my hunches, and that is the best way to work, all in all.

Sylvia left the parking lot and turned right, going back the way she had come. I watched Galipolus watch her go and then he walked away from me toward a couple of cars parked beside the club. A man from inside stepped through the front door and looked over the lot. He was making sure nobody was hanging around outside, I guessed. They handle a good bit of cash in a place like that, and had to be on their toes. He did not say anything to the two motorcycle types, so I figured they were regulars of some kind. More than likely, they were with a couple of the dancers. That is the way it is a lot of the time. The girls work in the clubs to support the sorry bastards, whose only known livelihood is peddling dope. Some of them are even too lazy to do that. Go figure it.

It occurred to me that the man in the door of the club might spot me and walk over to run me off, but if he saw me he did not wonder about me enough to come out into the lot looking for trouble. If I had been smart in picking my place, he did not see me at all, or may have just thought mine was a car someone had left behind.

Galipolus drove out of the next lot, and I had been right

about him at least. He was driving a BMW with a license number that was the second of the three Borodin had given me. He also turned right out of the lot and headed north toward Oak Lawn. I hoped Speed was awake and that he had put his video camera together, because I wanted stills and tape of Sylvia and Stefan walking into their love nest. It would mean the job was done in a day, and that would cut into the proceeds, but I had the feeling that Borodin would not quibble about the advance, and then I would have some time to see what was going on with Della. And, I had almost forgotten, to see if there was anything I could do about Leslie for Speed. Like a soap opera, these people.

Galipolus did not play along with me and make short work of the case. He only went Sylvia's way as far as Stemmons, where he took the northbound entrance ramp and blasted off about as fast as his little BMW would go. I flogged my old Chevy as hard as I thought it would stand and managed to keep him in sight most of the way. I was not surprised there were no police cars on the freeway. Two in the morning, there was a bit too much going on around the joints for Patrol types to spend their time lurking out on the interstate, and Traffic officers did not work late nights unless there was some kind of special DWI deal on.

So Mister G. was free to drive as fast as he liked, except for here and there he had to shut it down when he topped a hill and came roaring up behind a slow-motion drunk trying to make it home. That happened a couple of times, and if it had not I might not have been able to stay close enough to see him take the Royal Lane exit. By the time I got off I-35 at Royal and rolled up beneath the light at the foot of the ramp, he was gone. But I could see quite a distance to my left, west toward Las Colinas, and did not see any traffic at all. To my right, toward Harry Hines, the next light had caught a little pack of late traffic, so I turned that way.

It was not hard after that, because there was enough local traffic and occasional drunken driving going on that even Mister G. had to be careful. Royal was three lanes in each direction, and I made it a point to stay one lane over from Galipolus, with a car or two between us whenever I could. He did not do any of the things you should do if you think you are being followed, or even if you think you might be, and I reminded myself every once in a while to check behind me, to make sure I was not being followed. You'd be surprised how easy it is to miss a tail on yourself when you're tailing somebody. I did not know anything about Galipolus or his line of business except for what Mister Borodin had told me, and I had even less reason than usual to believe everything he had said. But I knew that some people in certain businesses made it a practice to have friends of theirs follow them from a long way back just to see if anyone else is following them tight.

Thinking along those lines, as I followed Galipolus east on Royal Lane, I could not help wondering just what kind of business these two might really be in, Galipolus and Borodin. Borodin had said it was investments, "a little import-export." That was not a terribly reassuring way of putting it. Ask any gangster what he does for a living, he'll say "investments." Ask a drug smuggler, "import-export." There *were* legitimate import-export businesses, just like there probably were some squares somewhere who really were in investments. But I did not think Borodin had been very convincing, except for his scotch and cash. I knew part of it was my xenophobia. I had a thing about foreigners, and I could not help it. I had not always been that way, only in the last few years, when there seemed to have gotten to be so damned many of them in town. If you have a weekend to waste some time, come to Dallas and try to find a 7-Eleven clerk who speaks English, for Christ's sake.

A couple of streets west of Inwood, Galipolus turned right without bothering to slow down nearly enough, and squealed his tires around the corner, then fishtailed back under control going south. I took the corner much less dramatically, and spotted his lights two blocks south of me, signaling a left turn, so that the Cadillac directly behind him would not run over him when he slowed, which it almost did anyway. That was all right, it meant that he had enough on his mind that he would not notice me. Galipolus survived his turn into a side street and I followed him at a safe distance.

I cut off my lights and drifted to a stop alongside the curb, using my handbrake to stop myself so that my brake lights would not call attention to me, and watched Galipolus whip his BMW into the driveway of a house in the middle of the block ahead. I saw his dome light blink on when he got out and when he stepped onto the front porch of the house I saw a light come on and the door open. Someone had been waiting up for him.

After about five minutes, during which time I figured he probably would not be looking out his front door anymore and it was not likely he would remember something and come walking back out to his car and see me, I turned my headlights on and drove by Galipolus's house, or at least the house where he had gone. It was the fourth house down the block, and I made a note of the number. His was the only car in the driveway, and the garage door was down. There were no lights showing to the front of the house, and it looked as if he was in for the night.

Two houses beyond Galipolus's, I passed a van parked at the curb on the opposite side of the street. Once past it, I almost stopped and went back, because there was something about it. I did not stop, I only slowed down and looked at the street behind me in my rearview mirror. There were cars parked here and there at the curb in the stretch that lay behind me, but only a few. And there was only the one van. It sat in front of a house with a front drive like Galipolus's, and there was one car in it too. So what? Somebody had a van, and they parked it on the street so they could put their car in the drive. Maybe they did not drive their van every day, maybe it was just for weekends. Yeah.

I went on through to Inwood and turned right. It was less than a mile to Walnut Hill, a left there and past the North Dallas Tollway, and then the next light was Preston Road. A right there, and then south until Preston turned into Oak Lawn, and I would be back at Sylvia's town house. Borodin's big house was about two blocks south of Walnut Hill. It was a curious thing. He and Galipolus had taken up residence within a couple of miles of each other, but I had the impression that Borodin did not know that.

It was half past three when I tapped our signal softly on the rear window of the van and Speed let me in. I was glad to see he had his video camera all ready to go, but he said there had not been much to take pictures of. Mrs. Borodin had come home about half past two, parked her car in her space, and gone inside her unit. End of report.

I told Speed he was doing a hell of a job and to keep his eyes open. Then I curled up on a blanket on the floor of the van and I was asleep before he could get started with any more about Leslie Armitage and his personal problems.

CHAPTER NINE

I AWOKE EARLY the next morning, before six, because my back hurt so badly. The floor of the van was no place for a man in my condition to sleep, and I felt like I might never walk again if I did not get out and stretch my legs while I still could. I asked Speed if he would mind sticking around while I went for some things, and he said he did not have anywhere to go anyway. He wanted to talk about Leslie again, but I managed to clamber out of the van before he could do much more than sigh forlornly.

There was a gaggle of men next door at the apartment complex under construction, getting an early start before the hot part of the day. Some of them saw me get out of the van, but if they thought anything of it, none of them let on. I noticed most of them were Latinos, and as I walked to the place where I had left my car I heard a couple of them speaking Spanish back and forth, one asking the other if he thought I might be with Immigration.

I took the car and gassed it up, being careful to keep my receipt, and used the service station rest room to change my socks and skivvies and wash up. Then I found a doughnut shop with a pay phone outside. There was a 7-Eleven next door.

Nobody answered the phone at my office except Della on tape. I left a message for her that I would call back a little later and that I hoped she was all right. Then I called the number for my pal Joe and the same lady answered. We talked in Spanish from the start this time, and she told me Joe had left word that he expected to finish up the thing he was working on this morning and that he would be at that number by noon or a little after.

I told her that was good, that I needed his help, and that I would call back later. Then I bought one each of the local daily newspapers and went into the doughnut shop to buy breakfast. I got a couple of apple fritters, my favorite, and a dozen assorted doughnuts because I was not sure what Speed liked. I tossed the papers and the doughnuts into my car and dug out the thermos I kept there and went next door to the 7-Eleven to fill it. I got several packets of artificial sweetener and two plastic cups because I liked my coffee sweet and Speed took his black and straight, and I took the nice Iranian at the register up on his offer of three packs of ultralight cigarettes for only four bucks. Big deal.

Back at the van, I was thinking it was time to send Speed home when he finished his two doughnuts and the last of his coffee and made me listen to the whole thing about Leslie again.

Half an hour later I had to interrupt him to tell him it was time to go. He looked hurt, but I wanted him to get a little rest before he had to pull another night shift. That started him on the business about having no place to go. I knew better than that, that he had kept his efficiency in East Dallas, and I told him to go there. I don't think he appreciated my attitude, but I was not in top shape myself, and I had enough on my mind. Finally, he said he would see me at the same time as last night and I promised him I would call if anything came up. I gave him the film I had shot the night before to develop for me, peeled a couple of our photos of Mrs. Borodin off the van wall, hopped out of the van, and watched him drive away in it.

I hiked over to my car, opened the trunk, removed the wooden rod and wedged it into place in the back of my car, over the backseat. There were rings in each end of the rod that fit over the hooks mounted above each rear door for hanging clothes. I pulled out half a dozen shirts and some other stuff on clothes hangers, and hung all that on the rod. These were not clothes you would wear, unless you were impersonating a bum Just stuff to hide in. Then I took out the empty cardboard box that just about fit on the ledge behind the backseat, tossed in a clean plastic milk jug for emergencies, and that was that. I changed into a clean shirt out of my bag in the trunk, then got in the car and pulled it around to a shaded curbside spot up the block from Sylvia's town house, where I parked it and crawled into the backseat, pushing half of the clothes hanging from the rod to either side of me. The box up in the back behind me made it so somebody in back of me would not notice me, and the hanging clothes hid me from the sides. From the front I would not make a silhouette because of the box and because the hanging clothes made the inside of my car dark there in the shade at the curb, with everything else around bright and sunny. I had my coffee thermos, Speed's camera, and my cigarettes, with which I would have to be careful not to start a fire. I was set for the day shift.

Only nothing happened. Except that the August sun rose and the day got hotter and hotter. I had my car windows down to catch a breeze if there was any, but there was none. The inside of my car got so hot and airless that if I had had a dog with me the ASPCA would have busted me for cruelty. The crew across the street worked steadily without hurrying around, and I could not blame them. As a matter of fact, they were getting more done than I would have in their place. Maybe they were used to the heat.

From time to time I looked through Speed's camera with the lens run out to top power just to make sure Sylvia Borodin's town house had not evaporated in the heat shimmering off the concrete around her pool. The lens on this camera was nothing like the monster Speed had mounted on the one in the van, but if I could figure out what the numbers meant, it went up to two hundred millimeters, whatever that meant. Anyway, it was about like looking through binoculars, and Sylvia's place was still there, all right. So was her Mercedes. Until a quarter to two in the afternoon.

Sylvia came bouncing down the walk to her car and I was damned glad to see her, and not just because she was wearing a little sundress that you could see through when the sun hit her just right, although that was worth waiting for. I had been slumped in the backseat of my car long enough, and my back was bitching at me again. She was going out, and that suited me fine.

She turned left out of her driveway again and drove past me, back toward Oak Lawn. I slid over the seat under the wheel and watched her in my rearview mirror until she signaled a right turn on Oak Lawn and I saw her head turn, the profile of her head as she looked to her left at the oncoming traffic. Then I made a U-turn and went the way she had gone.

Things were not going badly at all, because she was going to a place I was more than a little fond of myself, the Wine Press.

I made sure I caught the light at the cross street when I saw her pull into one of the spaces in front of the restaurant so she would have time to get to the door before I passed by. Of course, there was a chance she was going somewhere else, to the little shop next door maybe, but my luck held and she went into the cool darkness of the bar. I drove past her car and turned right to park in the lot behind the little bank there. But I noticed someone had put up some signs threatening to tow my car away if I was not a customer of the bank and whoever else had offices in the squat little building that sat on the corner. They probably wouldn't, and for all I knew I wouldn't be there long enough for them to call a wrecker anyway, but I did not want to take the chance. That could play hell with a surveillance, having to track your car down. I made a Y-turn and only had to wait for a couple of cars to get out of my way before I was able to pull out onto Oak Lawn, make a right into the far lane, and turn at the signal back to my left and into the strip shopping center parking lot across the street from the Wine Press. I found a spot at the west end of the lot that would be out of sight of anyone in the Wine Press and parked at the side nearest the street. Back into my trunk where I kept a garment bag for a jacket, and I would be set. I had worn my navy blazer the night before, so I went with my other jacket this time, a light-colored plaid that looked okay with my khaki slacks and the clean blue shirt. I wished I had the camera Speed had meant to bring along with the rest of his gear, the one that is built into a briefcase so that you can point the bag and take pictures by pressing a button on the handle, but he had left it at his place. I could not complain. He had furnished more equipment already than I could afford to rent, much less buy. I would just have to see who Sylvia was meeting and then try to leave first and get their pictures on their way out.

I pushed through the door and took the place in. It was a narrow, long room with two staggered rows of tables on your left as you went in and a bar on your right. In back there was a kitchen on the right, and the phones and rest rooms on your left. In the center, a flight of stairs led up to a half-floor loft and a hallway led past the stairs to an outdoor patio area where they had some tables set up. I was glad that Sylvia and her friends felt the way I did about that—they had opted for the air-conditioned part of the building. The three of them were sitting at a table on the left in front of the high wall that was taken up with shelves full of bottles of every kind of wine I had ever heard of. Which does not necessarily mean a hell of a lot, except that there had to be something like a thousand bottles of wine there.

They were about halfway between the door and the little alcove where the phones and rest rooms were, and they had one of the two tables that were occupied. There were a couple of guys at the bar on my right, and two women were sitting at the first table on the left. I looked to my right toward the bar as I walked past. At the blackboard someone had written out the specials of the day, and I told the young man who inquired that I would like a table for two because I was meeting someone. There were only a couple of tables for two, and they were along the wall behind the table I was really interested in. He showed me the way like I couldn't see them myself and I picked the one farthest back, the last one before the alcove. The young man, who was wearing a white tuxedo shirt, black slacks, and some kind of black hiking shoes, asked me if I would like a menu and I said no, so he cleared my table of the napkins and silverware and I told him I would like a tall glass of ice water and a Pinch on the rocks. He smiled and headed for the bar.

Sylvia had two friends at her table. One looked like business. He was a black man wearing a serious gray suit and a very serious navy tie with a perfectly round knot that was smooth and looked as good as you would ever see one done on a stiff in a funeral parlor. His shirt was white, with the kind of generous, soft collar you got when you spent a lot of money on your shirts. He was talking and Sylvia was listening.

The other man at the table was thirty-five, I guessed, maybe only thirty with a lot of mileage. He did not look very businesslike, in his pink polo shirt with the collar up and his fashionably baggy khaki pleated slacks. His shoes were some kind of very low-cut leather loafers that looked like house shoes but were probably Italian and very expensive. He wore glasses, the kind with big round lenses and brown-speckled frames. He was listening to the man in the suit, but he was looking at Sylvia. He could not take his eyes off of her. I could understand that, because Mrs. Borodin was doing a lot with that little white sundress, even though she was just sitting there.

They still had their silverware, so I guessed they had told the young waiter that they would be eating. That would make it easier to gauge when they would be leaving. Once I had gotten a good enough look so that I could describe the two men and would recognize either of them if I saw them again, I didn't look their way anymore. I pulled the *Times Herald* crossword puzzle out of my hip pocket and went to work on it. There were a couple of tables between me and them, and if I did not look at them, there was no reason to think they would pay any attention to me. I turned my chair to put my back to the shelves of wine bottles on my right and focused on my crossword, trying to listen to everything they said.

The waiter brought my water and my scotch, and I drank the water first, straight down. Then I took a sip of my scotch and checked my watch, which was what I would have done if I really were waiting for someone.

Sylvia and her friends were mumblers, and I was on my second scotch by the time their food came. They all had salads, and I noticed the businessman was drinking iced tea. Sylvia and the pink polo shirt were having white wine.

I was not getting much from the conversation, and there was not much left of their salads by the time my third scotch arrived, so I stepped into the alcove to make a couple of phone calls. When I called Joe's number, he himself answered for a change and said he was available. I made sure nobody was around and then told him where to meet me and when. It was twenty to three, and he said he could make it by six-thirty, no problem. That meant I could brief him, and he could handle the evening shift, giving me a bit of time off. I would come back and spell him around ten or eleven, then hold Speed's hand for a while on the late shift, probably sleep in the van again if I had to.

Next I called the office. Della answered, in person this time, and I asked how she was doing. She said "fine," in that clipped way people use when they are doing anything but fine. I asked her how her boyfriend was, and she did not say anything for about half a minute, which seemed like a long time while I tried to figure out if there was anything else I could say that would help. I could not think of anything except maybe to say I was sorry, which I was not. She finally said something about the boy's daddy. I asked her to repeat it.

"He said he's going to make charges against you."

"He doesn't have the terminology right, kid, but never mind that. What did he say those charges were going to be?"

"Aggravated assault."

"I see. What's the deal with your boyfriend, is he a juvenile with some kind of a gland problem or something? How old is he?"

"Twenty-two," she said.

"That's what I thought. So he's old enough to make his own trouble, isn't he? What's Daddy got to do with it?"

"You don't understand, Jack."

"No shit. Tell Daddy this for me, Della. Tell him two things. One, if his shithead kid ever slaps you again I'll kill him. Two, if Daddy goes anywhere near the DA with this, I'll find his little sweetums and do the job right this time. I may not kill him, I may just fuck him up so goddamn bad he'll crawl off somewhere and kill his goddamn self. You want to read that back to me?"

"Jack . . ."

I waited, but she did not finish. I thought I could hear her crying.

"What?"

"You're not helping."

"Maybe I shouldn't have mixed in at all, kid. I didn't know you got off on being slapped around. You didn't look like you were having fun. What did you want me to do?"

"It's not you, Jack. It's Ronny. He has problems."

"Wrong, kid. Ronny . . . is that the boy who slapped you or the daddy?"

"The boy, I mean, Ronny is my boyfriend, the one you beat up."

"Yeah, well, he doesn't have a problem, Della. He is a problem. He's a little shithead who beats up women and goes crying to his daddy when a grown-up treats him like a man needs to be treated who does that. What the hell are you doing screwing around with trash like that anyway?"

"You don't understand."

"Of course not. That's why I asked."

"I can't explain it. You don't know Ronny the way I do."

"I can just imagine."

"Well, listen, Jack, you don't have any messages, if that's why you called in."

"It's not and you know it. I called to see about you. That's

82

why I called your place last night, but I never got an answer. Where were you?"

"I was at home, I just didn't answer the phone."

"Yeah, I guess you were busy nursing Ronny back to health, so he could whip your—" I tried to catch myself, not get mad. "How did it go? How did he treat you afterward?"

"Don't worry about it, Jack. It's not your problem."

"It's not yours either, kid. Don't let him use you, that's all."

"Listen, Jack, I know you're trying to . . . I know your heart's in the right place, but—"

"Della, just play back to yourself all that stuff you told me about my ex-wife, all right? All that 'she's no good for you, she doesn't love you or she wouldn't do you this way,' remember? I know I didn't listen to you, but you were right, and you're a lot smarter than I am, so wise up, okay?"

"Yeah."

"You know you can count on me, kid. If there's anything I can do—"

"I know, Jack. But, listen, my other lines are ringing. I'll talk to you later."

"Yeah. Bye."

Women. Go figure them.

All of which took too long, and Sylvia and her friends were getting up from their table when I stepped back into the main room. I tossed too much money on my table for the drinks and made it out the door trying not to look like I was in a hurry, which I was. I got to my car in time to get Speed's camera out of the trunk, and I held it down alongside my leg as I went around and got in the car so Sylvia and her two friends would not spot it as they came out the front door of the restaurant, which they did just as I slid behind the wheel of my car. I was far enough away and the angle of the sun cast my front seat in shadow, so I did not think they could see me or if they could that they could tell what I was doing. The clothes and stuff in the back of the car helped make it hard for anyone to tell if my car was occupied or not.

The guy in the suit did not dawdle. He nodded rather curtly

at Sylvia and the pink shirt, then strode off to a car parked at the curb. It was an Olds, a four-door with a maroon vinyl roof over a white body. I didn't think the car matched the man, but maybe it was a company car. He backed out and caught the light green as he drove by where I sat in my sweltering old Chevy with no air-conditioning and in a moment was gone westbound on Oak Lawn.

Snap, grind. Snap, grind. Snap, grind. I took a few pictures of them as quickly as I could, then settled down to make sure I got some I could use.

The pink shirt lingered. He walked Sylvia to her car and when she had sat down behind the wheel, he stood in the open door and looked down at her, still talking. Then after a minute or two of that he did me a favor and leaned down and kissed her. It was a little too quick for me to get a picture of it, but when he did it again I was ready for it. He lingered over her the second time, and I saw her left hand come up out of the car as if she would push him away, but she did not. She just laid her hand on his pink polo shirt and kissed him back. He lowered himself beside her and reached in with his left hand to touch her. I was banging away with Speed's motor drive and thinking maybe I should pace myself a little so I would not run out of film before he got her clothes off, the way the two of them were going at each other.

Finally, she drew back and shook her head, but I did not get the impression she was saying no to anything. I got the impression that she was just trying to catch her breath, or maybe cool herself off a bit. He was insistent, and while she was shaking her head I saw him lean forward and put his hand on her knee, and then his hand was not there anymore, and her knees weren't together either. She had stopped shaking her head. She arched her neck and laid her head way back, and I could see that her mouth was open, like she was gasping for air. I figured it was even hotter in her car than it was in mine.

This went on for a while, and I really started thinking the two of them might disappear into the Mercedes and then all I would see would be feet in the air, but finally they broke the clinch and she closed her door. He rapped on her window with a knuckle and down came the window so he could kiss her some more. And then she laughed and away she went. He stood watching as she drove away. I hoped he was not driving one of those little sports cars, because he had a hard-on I could see from across the street, and I did not think he would be able to get it under the wheel of one of those little things.

When she had gone, he jogged across the street to the same parking lot I was in, but it was a long strip shopping center, and the car he jogged to was half a block away. He disappeared for a couple of seconds as he climbed into a car that was blocked from my view, then reappeared at the wheel of an El Dorado. Good for him, I thought. Plenty of room in that. He backed out of a space and I got a clear shot of the rear of his car to record the license number, and then he pulled out of the lot at the light down the street and turned right. I did not think I would have to tail him very far. I thought I knew where he was going.

CHAPTER
TEN

I WAS RIGHT. Pink Shirt whistled down the road in his El Dorado and took the shortest possible route to Mrs. Borodin's town house complex, where he practically hopped out before the big Caddy stopped rolling in one of the visitor's spaces and then he literally danced up the walk toward her door, which opened before he knocked, and if I was not mistaken a pair of lovely female hands may have grabbed him by the front of his pink polo shirt and yanked him inside. I was curious if maybe he'd left his fancy little Italian shoes on the porch the way he flew through the door before it closed. That was three forty-five. Nothing else happened, that I could see, until it was time for Joe to show up. I was a little disappointed that I couldn't hear Mrs. Borodin singing, "Ah, sweet mystery of life, at last I've found you!" like Madeline Kahn in *Young Frankenstein*.

Joe was on time and in the right place. I laid it out for him, the story and the photos of Mrs. Borodin, and left him to look after things.

It was a little after seven when I got back to my office, because I had stopped on the way and picked up a couple of barbecued beef sandwiches and a pair of quart cans of beer. I did not have a refrigerator of my own, and if I left beer in the little community job in the closet behind the coffee urn, it was always gone the next day. I suspected Mrs. Farragut.

I had not expected Della to still be in the office, and she was not. I also had not expected her to answer when I called her apartment, but she did. She sounded a little tired, but better than earlier.

"How are you, kid?"

"I'm doing okay," she promised.

"Where's Ronny?"

"He's not here."

"Good. How is that going?"

"It's not, right now."

"I'm sorry to hear that, Della."

"You are not."

"I am if you are."

"I don't believe you, Jack."

"I mean it. It's your call, kid. If you want the bum, that's your problem, and I want what you want. What's the deal?"

"I don't know. He was supposed to call, but—"

"So that's why you answered." I laughed.

"Don't pick a fight, Jack. I'm not in the mood for any more."

"Hey, don't worry about me. I didn't call to give you a bad time."

"So why did you call then?"

"To see how you were doing, that's all."

"Well, I'm doing okay. So thanks for calling."

"Did you tell Ronny's daddy what I told you to tell him?"

"No, I haven't spoken with him since we talked."

"Good, because I've got a better message. Want to hear it?"

"Sure."

"Tell him these two things instead of the other two. One, he doesn't have a case, because an old broken-down bum like me with a bad back and a trick knee is allowed to use whatever's handy, like a nameplate off a desk, which is not exactly a deadly weapon, to defend himself against a big young bruiser like Ronny, who let's not forget did throw the first punch. Second, Ronny assaulted you, which is aggravated assault because you're a girl, and if anybody's going to do any charging, I'm not disinclined to do a little of my own. And I have the witnesses."

"Do you?"

"Three at least. You, me, and Mrs. Farragut."

"Farragut. Are you kidding?"

"I don't think so. And I know what you're thinking, kid. You wouldn't want to tell on Ronny. But under oath in a courtroom, I don't think you'd perjure yourself for him, either."

"Probably not."

"Make it three things. Tell him Ronny needs help," I said.

"Maybe I'd better write all this down."

"Better than that, give me the old man's number and I'll call and tell him myself."

"I don't think that's a good idea," she said.

"Then you shouldn't have told me he was going to 'make charges.' I can't afford to wait around if he's serious about that."

"I don't think he is, really."

"Then where's the harm in my talking to him?"

"I don't know, Jack, I just . . ."

"You don't want me to stir anything up, because then Ronny might throw another tantrum and you'd catch hell for it, is that it?"

"Something like that."

"Well, Christ, kid, how can anybody help you if—"

"Don't help me, Jack. You've done enough already. I got myself into this, and I'll handle it."

"Then what the hell good are friends?"

"There's someone at the door, Jack. Will you be in the office tomorrow?"

"I don't think so, but I'll call in. Take care of yourself."

"You too."

I held the phone for a while after she was gone, and tried to imagine what was going on at her place, if that was Ronny at her door. I had given up trying to imagine how she got mixed up with the creep in the first place. I did not like to think that her tastes ran that way. I figured she thought she could change him, or something dopey like that.

While I ate my dinner, I called Mister Borodin to let him know how things were going. A soft and sultry female voice answered and told me he was not in. He was expected back later that night. She did not know where he was. After all that, I could not think of anything else to ask Sasha, or any reason why she should talk to me anymore just so I could remember how she looked at the pool the day before, so I said I would call back later. She asked me if there was a message, and I said there was none. Borodin had not said anything about letting her in on the deal.

After the two sandwiches and one of the beers, I felt better and I had convinced myself that Ronny's old man probably would not try to have me thrown in jail for spanking his rotten kid, and I went down the list to my next problem. I found Leslie Armitage's phone number among the list of numbers I had for Speed and gave her a call.

"What's the matter? What's happened to Speed?" was the first thing she said when I told her it was me. It was I. Whatever.

"Speed's fine, Leslie, more or less. Take it easy."

"He's with you, isn't he?"

"He's working on something with me. He's not here with me at this very minute."

"Is he hurt?" she asked, like she thought she already knew the answer.

"No, he's fine. Stop worrying about him and talk to me for a second."

"I thought you said there was nothing wrong."

"Speed is safe and sound, Leslie. He's not wounded or injured or anything like that. He is a little upset."

"I know that. I haven't heard from him in days."

"Yeah, since right after last weekend when you turned a trick at your place after you shooed Speed out with a cock-and-bull story about having company."

"What? Who told you that? Did Speed tell you that?"

"Don't worry about that. Just explain to me why you've gone back to work, or why you had to do it at your place, or why you didn't tell Speed what you were up to, or your side of the story, or some goddamn thing. The guy is driving me batty with this."

"Oh, Jack. Oh, Jack."

There was some more after that, but I couldn't understand most of it, all kinds of "woe is me" bullshit.

"I'm a middle-aged guy here, Leslie. I may not live long enough to hear your whole life story played out in real time. Can you give me maybe just a summary?"

"It was the guy I told you about, Jack."

"What guy?"

"The one from out of town. The businessman who comes to Dallas four or five times a year. The one who pays for this apartment."

"Your deal is still on with him?"

"Yes, I told Speed about it. He must have forgotten."

"Speed knew about your arrangement?"

"I told him, I swear I did."

"And he said he didn't mind?"

"Yes."

"And you believed him?"

"Well yeah, I—"

"The guy is crazy in love with you, woman. Have you been faking it so long you don't know the real thing anymore?"

"You mean . . . you mean, he really—"

"Yeah, yeah, that's what I mean. The thought of you with another man is killing him."

"He loves me, you mean?"

"That's the impression I've got."

"Oh my God."

And then nothing for a while.

"Leslie, are you still there?"

"Uh-huh."

"So, now what, Leslie?"

"Jesus, Jack, I don't know."

"Should I tell him it's over, or what?" I offered.

"Don't you dare, goddamn you, I'll—"

"Easy, take it easy, Leslie. I was just asking. You want him then?"

"Of course I do."

"Maybe you could promise to give up the life, even this little part-time deal?"

"I will, I swear to God. I thought . . . it was all I had coming in, I didn't want to be a burden, you know, Speed doesn't make much money, Jack, and . . . oh, my God."

"I sense that it comes as a surprise to you that Speed is crazy about you. Didn't he ever tell you?"

"Well yeah, but . . . I mean, they all say that, you know?"

"Yeah, I guess you're right. Only Speed is just a little bit special."

"Oh, I know, I swear to you, Jack, I know he is. If I've screwed this up, I'll never . . . I don't know what I'll do."

"Call him. He's at his place."

"I will."

"Only, do me a favor and don't get him so worked up he'll try to get out of working tonight, will you? I need my sleep."

"Jack, you're cold."

"No, I'm just old. Tell him you'll be waiting for him at his place when he gets off in the morning, something like that, will you?"

"I can't make any promises, Jack. See ya."

And again the empty phone line hummed in my ear. I put the receiver down and smoked a cigarette with my last beer. What was wrong with this picture, I asked myself. Lately I had been meddling in more affairs than Dear Abby, and where had it got me? For stepping in to save poor little Della, I could have some fairly serious legal trouble, which could very well jeopardize my private investigator's license. Now I thought maybe I had patched things up with Speed and Leslie and all that meant was that I probably would end up working all night by myself. And then there was Sylvia Borodin and Pink Shirt. I was certainly getting ready to rain on their little parade, for which at least I stood to see a little cash. One out of three, maybe.

But that was not the worst of it. Why did I have the impression that everybody out there, behind all those thousands of lights I could see from my office window, all of those people out there were paired off one way or another, and I was the odd man out?

CHAPTER ELEVEN

I SET MY alarm clock and got a couple of hours' sleep before relieving Joe on surveillance at ten o'clock. If Leslie and Speed got back together, he might not show at midnight, and I would have to stand his watch too.

It came as a happy surprise a few minutes before midnight when Speed came tapping on the back door of my van. I contained myself until he was inside and the door was closed behind him.

"Glad to see you, Speed, old buddy." I gave his near arm a squeeze. "I didn't much think you'd show."

"Why ever not?" he asked, his face the very portrait of innocence.

"The bitch didn't call?"

"Of whom are yoom speaking?"

Speed knew I had this thing about who and whom, and he was the only one of my friends who made any effort at all. It was when he had been drinking that he started that "yoom" business. I did not think it was deliberate.

"Of the whom yoom been walking the floor over her cheatin' heart: Miss Leslie."

"Oh, her."

"Uh-huh. She didn't call you?"

"She might have."

"Yeah, like you wouldn't remember."

"As a matter of fact—"

"And here you are shit-faced."

"Am not."

"No, not much."

"Listen here, Turnaround Jack Kyle, I'll have you to understand . . ."

He did not finish right away, whatever it was he was going to have me understand, because he was trying to sit down about a foot and a half short of the lawn chair, and was only managing to hook one bony hip on the arm of the chair nearest the back door of the van. I was afraid he would turn the chair over and make enough noise to be heard across the street.

"Let me help you with that," I offered, catching him by the slack of his britches between his hip pockets. I guided him toward me until he was more or less centered over the seat part of his chair and then let him go. He settled in without too much fuss.

"Listen here, Turna——"

"And I know you're drunk now, Speed, or you wouldn't be calling me that."

"I don't know why not."

"It's a nickname I don't care for, and you know it."

"I ain't afraid of you," he said with his bottom lip out.

"You don't have any reason to be, but you're more considerate when you're sober. I'll just assume that Leslie called and you two've got your problem straightened out."

"Could be."

"And since I asked her not to rev your motor so high you wouldn't work tonight, and since you're both the impetuous type, I'll also assume that you've already had your kiss-and-makeup party and that's why you're shit-faced."

"Am not."

"And why you look like you've had a spinal tap or she's

sucked your spine out the head of your pecker or something."

"Talk that shit, Jack, bless your heart."

"Uh-huh. If you were in any shape to drive, I'd just about as soon send you back to her. I'm not going to get any sleep tonight."

"I'll damn sure leave if that's the way you feel about it," Speed said with his lip out again.

"The hell you will. I'm not having a DWI on my conscience."

"Am not."

"Stop saying that," I said, sounding peevish. "And suck your lip back in before something happens to it."

"Given this attitude problem of yours, I don't suppose there's any point in my inviting you to join me in a toast."

He tugged a bottle out from under his floppy shirttails and grinned. Actually, I was glad he was happy again, and I did not mind it more than a little that he was drunk, although I was as serious as I could be about that drunk-driving business. I felt that if any of my friends had to die it ought to be for a reason.

"Maybe later," I said.

"There you go, partner." He grinned and put one arm around my shoulder to give me a squeeze.

"There I go," I answered.

"I owe you one, Jack," he added, and I could tell without looking at him by the quiver in his voice that he was about to cry.

"Don't get weepy, Speed, for Christ's sake. I'm glad you and Leslie are back together, and I'm glad you're here. Now just hush."

"There you go," he said, and the grin was back on his face.

It was not long after that that something happened. Speed did hush for almost a quarter of an hour, and then stirred himself to assure me that he was in good shape and that I could turn in anytime I liked. It was maybe another ten minutes before I heard him snoring. I shook him awake.

"Huh? Wha's the deal?"

"I don't care if you sleep on the job, but crawl over there on the floor and sprawl out on your stomach, man. I can't stand that racket you're making."

"I have it on good authority—"

"Leslie says you don't snore, I guess. That shows she loves you, right there. Now . . ."

But I did not finish because while I was talking to Speed I was still watching Sylvia Borodin's front door, and I saw it open. Light from inside her town house fell on her and Pink Shirt, only he was not wearing his pink shirt anymore. At first I thought he was not wearing anything, I thought neither of them was wearing anything. But they were.

"S-h-h-h." I held a finger to my lips and shushed at Speed, who had decided it would be better if he crawled over me and lay down on the floor. "Hold it."

"What?"

"Sit down, damnit. They're out."

"Huh?"

"You shit-faced lovesick son of a bitch, sit down and hush. They're coming out."

I watched the two of them, Sylvia and Pink Shirtless, make their way down the walk between the hedges toward the swimming pool. They were walking the way lovers do, ambling in a crooked line. She was holding his left arm in both her hands, and her head was on his shoulder. I could not see her face at first, but I could see that he was smiling.

There was some light in the courtyard where they were, but not as much as I would have liked. Each of the units had a light beside its front door and there were the two electric yard lights that were supposed to look like old-fashioned gaslights at either end of the pool. With that and all the shrubbery that ran along the walk in front of each building, there was a hodge-podge of light and shadows for the two lovers to meander through. I hoped that Speed's hotsy-totsy French-sounding film was up to the challenge as I banged away at them through the window of the van. After I had eight or ten tries, I looked to make sure Speed was cranking up his video camera, and he was.

96

"How's it look?" I asked him.

"Huh?"

"How are you for light?"

"Awright, prob'ly."

He still sounded half-asleep, and I checked to make sure the recording light was on. He was squinting through the eyepiece pretty convincingly, and I could hear the soft hum of the recorder.

Sylvia and her boyfriend sauntered down to the tiled deck of the pool, where there was pretty good light and no shrubbery, and I took some more pictures of them. They kissed, and I saw the man bend a little from the waist as he kissed her and put what looked like a wicker picnic basket on the ground. Then he took Sylvia in his arms and kissed her quite a bit more seriously. Snap, grind. Snap, grind. I was sure there was no way they could hear the camera's motor drive, but I switched it off anyway and started advancing the film manually after each shot. Looking at the two of them through the two hundred millimeter lens made them seem close, made it seem as if they could hear me, as if I could hear them murmuring to each other.

She was wearing a one-piece swimsuit that I thought might be what they call a maillot, a strapless job that clung to her breasts and rose high on her hips. Her legs were stunning, and I noticed she was wearing some kind of shoes, mules I thought they were, like sandals with high heels and no straps on her heels to hold them on. The muscles of her legs had to work to keep her balance on the shoes as she leaned on her boyfriend, her neck curved up to lift her face to his. Her mouth was open the way it had been in her car outside the Wine Press.

The boyfriend was taking his time, nibbling and nuzzling one ear and then the other, working his way down her throat to the hollow her collarbones made, back up and over her shoulder into the places beneath her long hair, and then he would lift his head to look into her face and he would kiss her closed eyelids and her open lips, then all over again, moving a little lower each time until finally he buried his face between her breasts. She giggled languorously as she raised one hand to keep the top of her swimsuit from slipping down any more as he worked it down with his chin, his lips traveling between her breasts and back and forth across the upper slopes of them.

"Damn," Speed muttered.

"What?" I asked, afraid there was trouble with the equipment.

"Nothing, only . . ."

"Oh," I answered. I knew what he meant. Watching them was having the same effect on me, and I did not have anybody waiting at home for me. When I took the time to look at Speed, I thought by the way he was bent to his task that he looked sober enough now.

She was still laughing, softly I imagined, with half-closed eyes and a twisted hungry grin. Her hand moved slowly, everything about her moved slowly, as if she might have been dreaming. When he raised his head and whispered something in her ear, she arched her back to press her breasts against his bare chest and threw her head back and laughed. He put his right hand on her breast and tugged down her suit to reveal for an instant the nipple of her left breast before his hand closed on it. She tugged away, still laughing, but his other arm held her to him. She kissed him quickly, shaking her head as if to say no. With both her hands she outfumbled him and tugged her suit back into place. He answered her quick kiss with one of his own and released her. She stepped back and I noticed how her legs were, one knee bent and the other straight. She ran her hands through her hair. That reminded me of Sasha beside her husband's pool, and I thought they had a lot in common.

As the boyfriend busied himself with the contents of their picnic basket, I tried to compare the wife I was taking pictures of with the naked woman beside her husband's pool. I could not find anything wrong with either of them, but I thought that each had her own way of being beautiful. Mrs. Borodin's hair was probably brown, with a reddish look to it, and it looked fuller than Sasha's but not nearly as long. And Mrs. Borodin was more voluptuous, with hips that rolled as she moved. Sasha's body was more angular, slimmer, like a tempered spring.

It was not as if I presumed to judge either of them, and it had been a long time since anyone who looked like these two had taken an interest in me certainly, it was just that my mind worked that way.

While her boyfriend was busy squatting beside their basket, Mrs. Borodin stepped out of her shoes. Twisting her hair up on top of her head and leaning her shoulders to her right for balance as she went, she waded down the steps at one end of the pool until the water was up to her waist, and then, with a look back at her boyfriend, she brought her hands together in front of her and pushed off to stroke lazily into the deeper end. He must have heard the noise she made in the water, because he turned to look at her and said something. By the time she pulled up at the opposite end of the pool from him, he had two tall long-stemmed glasses full of what looked like champagne and he walked around the edge of the pool to join her. She reached up, holding herself up at the side of the pool, as if she would take the glass he was offering her. Instead, she ran her hand up his leg, inside the leg of his trunks, and touched him. He made a funny face and bowed his knees, laughing, as she moved her hand inside his trunks. She lifted herself and playfully kissed his trunks where they hid her hand and his cock, then she laughed and slithered away back under the water.

Speed and I could see her in the pool, could see into the water, because we were sitting in the van on the rise where the old restaurant had been.

The boyfriend set the wineglasses on the side of the pool, and with a couple of looks over his shoulders like he was afraid someone might be watching, went to the light pole at the deeper end of the pool. He tampered with it for a moment—he must have unscrewed the bulb—and the light went out. The deep end of the pool was in shadow, with the light at the other end of the pool casting only the faintest glow there.

"It's okay," Speed assured me.

I was worried that the boyfriend had made it too dark for me to get pictures, and Speed knew what I was thinking. But he had gear I had not seen before mounted on his video camera, and he was telling me that he was still in good shape. He had tried earlier to explain his rig to me, but I had not been interested. I did not know if he was using infrared or what, and I did not care. I trusted Speed on this, if on nothing else. So I just tried to keep my eyes on the dark end of the pool and hoped that I was getting something for all my snapping.

The boyfriend eased himself into the water. I saw the silvery turbulence of the water's surface as he lifted Mrs. Borodin and pinned her to the side of the pool. I strained to make out their two bodies, but it was not easy. They seemed to have melted together. I did see Mrs. Borodin rise from the water and arch her back over the side of the pool. Her hips rolled at the surface of the water in glistening froth. I saw what must have been her swimsuit flutter in the night air and settle into the water behind him. He wedged himself between her thighs and her eyes twinkled with the soft light from the other end of the pool.

CHAPTER
TWELVE

MRS. BORODIN AND her boyfriend carried on like that longer than you might have thought they could, until they both had to be pruney. Finally they fished their respective suits out of the pool, dressed each other, tossed their empty wine bottle back into their wicker basket, and wobbled arm in arm back up the sidewalk between the hedges and disappeared through the front door of her unit. It stood to reason that neither of them would be going anywhere for a while, and I did not mind then that Speed crawled over me and made a nest for himself on the floor of the van to get some sleep. He did not sleep very well though. He tossed and mumbled until sunup, and I thought he might be having dreams, the nature of which I could imagine without much trouble. There would be no point in denying that I ran Speed's videotape back a couple of times so I could watch it in the camera's little viewfinder. The first time was so I could assure myself that he had gotten all of it and that you could tell who the two people were on the tape. The second time my motive was considerably less professional.

Joe showed up punctually the next morning, and I kicked Speed awake and sent him home to Leslie with high ambitions and instructions to develop the pictures I had taken. I told Joe I thought we had about all we needed, to take it easy on the tail if Mrs. Borodin went mobile, not to get burned if he could help it. He grinned at that, but then he took a lot more pride in his talent for tailing people than I did.

Sleep was what I needed, a couple of hours stretched out horizontal on something not too soft and not too firm so my back could unkink itself. But the squares in my neighboring offices would be open for business, and I was not sure what mood Della would be in. It was my custom when the need arose to hang a sign on my office door that said IN CONFERENCE so I could catch up on my sleep, but that was best done in the swivel chair with my feet up on the desk, and that would not do as much good for my back as a lie-down in my nice army surplus cot. It seemed like too much trouble to drag the cot out from its hiding place behind my file cabinet anyway, so I decided to brace myself with a cup of hot 7-Eleven coffee and get a few things done.

This guy from the strip joint on Industrial interested me, the geeky one with the pocket protector and all the pencils. And I needed to see what I could find on Mrs. Borodin's two friends from the Wine Press, the Brooks Brothers black guy and Pink Shirt. The best place to start was down at the County, with registrations on their cars.

From a pay phone in the first-floor corridor of the old and endangered Dallas County Courthouse Annex, which if it was not a historical monument sure as hell should have been, I called the office. Della's voice was cool and a little strained. I did not ask her about her boyfriend or his litigious old man. She said there were no messages, and I made myself a note to give Mister Borodin a call before noon to let him know I had something. I had not earned all of his two grand yet, but there was no point in dragging it out much longer.

The old courthouse annex building looked like something out of a Vincent Price movie, with filigree, gargoyles, and I did not know what all staring down at the pedestrians on their way to work or court or whatever. It was not as big an attraction as the Old Red Courthouse across the street from it, but it had something to say. That was a weird thing about being divorced in Dallas County. The official address where you sent your child support check every month was Dallas County Child Support, Old Red Courthouse, Dallas, Texas. As if Dallas were some tumbleweed crossroads hamlet where addresses were unnecessary. The annex and the red monster had been built eons ago, sometime in the 1800s, and they both needed work. The new courthouse, where county and district courts actually met and the sheriff had his offices, was on the south side of Commerce Street, a white thing with lots of glass on the lower floors and elevators that almost did not work. The red one was across Commerce, between it and Main. Across Main, running all the way to Elm on the north, was the annex, where you checked license registrations. All three of them were bounded on the west by Houston Street, and across Houston the three streets, Commerce, Main, and Elm, fell away toward the underpass that ran beneath railroad tracks on their way toward Stemmons Freeway and Industrial Boulevard, the "triple underpass" there was so much to be said about. Diagonally across the intersection of Elm and Houston from the annex stood the Texas Schoolbook Depository, where this or that group of Dallasites always seemed to be haggling about putting in one kind of museum or another.

The ladies behind the counter who ran registrations were in no rush to start their day, but the good part of it was that they were still relatively fresh, and it did not take long to find out that the car I had seen the geek drive away from the Industrial Boulevard strip joint was registered to a Bernard L. Teckmann with an address in Richardson. It went downhill from there. The Brooks Brothers man from the Wine Press had a car whose registration had not been reported, whatever that meant. The lady at the counter explained that maybe the car recently had changed hands and the title transfer had not been processed, or three or four other possibilities. This I did not care for, along with the way Borodin's license numbers had come back to leasing companies—dead ends. Pink Shirt's tag came back "out of country—not in file." I wrote it all down to keep from paying the two bucks each they charge you for a copy of their printouts and thanked the clerks. They watched me leave as if they did not know where I might be going but wished they were going with me. By the time I left a line had begun to form.

On my way to Richardson I stopped at another 7-Eleven, one on Fitzhugh Avenue, a few blocks off Central Expressway, and got some more coffee. I was hungry, but the junk food in the plastic case beside the coffee machines did not appeal to me. I thought that after I ran by Teckmann's Richardson address I might stop in somewhere and treat myself to a regular breakfast, the kind that included eggs and some kind of bread. On my way out of the store I called Borodin from a pay phone. It was after nine o'clock, and I thought I'd rather risk waking him than missing him again.

A sleepy woman answered the phone, and I wondered if Sasha slept in the same outfit she swam in. When I told her who I was, she at least did not say anything derogative, only asked me to wait. I did, and she came back on the line in a couple of minutes, about thirty seconds before she would have reached my time limit for holding a phone, and said Borodin was "not available."

I asked her to have him call my office and she said she would. I did not ask her exactly what "not available" meant.

CHAPTER
THIRTEEN

I HAD NOT meant to do anything more than drive by the house in Richardson where Dallas County said the car the geek had been driving belonged. But on my first pass I saw the woman in the front yard and I stopped. Call it a hunch.

There are at least two parts of the town of Richardson. A hell of a lot more than that, of course, if you know anything about it, but at least two. The new part and the old part. If you were any part of the great influx of outlanders from the "Rust Belt" or wherever who descended on the Dallas–Fort Worth Metroplex in the last ten years or so, you would have heard about Richardson. The "Metroplex" was something the media insisted on calling Dallas and Tarrant Counties, even though as far as anybody could determine by combining dictionary definitions, the word probably only meant something like "plaited womb." Or at least you had heard of the Richardson Independent School District. It was much, much better than the Dallas Independent School District, and friends of mine, mostly ex-cops who had gone into real estate, had told me over many a late-night glass of hooch in this or that bar that they had to marvel at how this news had circulated among the thundering herd of families coming to town. (They had come at a rate of something like a thousand head a week for several years before the bubble burst, oil prices slipped, real estate quivered, and a hell of a lot of our banks wound up beached like paddle wheelers on Red River sandbars.) The thing was, the Dallas schools had gone under a desegration court order, something I knew a little about from my days with the police department when we had spent a lot of time waiting for the kind of anti-busing riots we had heard about in Boston and elsewhere to break out. They never did, for a lot of reasons. The Richardson schools, as far as I knew, never even anticipated a problem, even though some of the schools in the Richardson district actually were located within the city limits of Dallas. Anyway, the Richardson schools had a hell of a reputation. Whether they deserved it I was never in a position to form an opinion about. One result was that a hell of a lot of newcomers had settled in the Richardson area, which was due north of Dallas, astraddle North Central Expressway. When Richardson was full, they built more houses and spread up into Plano, and wherever else they could find in Collin County, Dallas County's neighbor to the north. Dallas the city even expanded as far north as it could to get in on things, so that now part of Dallas was in Collin County and the Dallas cops who worked in the new North Central Patrol Division wound up having to file a lot of their cases there instead of with the Dallas County District Attorney's Office. It was a hell of a deal, all of which was to say that for a lot of people for a long time Richardson was one of Dallas's northern suburbs that enjoyed an affluent, high-techish reputation. (Texas Instruments had its main operation there.) The old part was pretty much what was left of the little country town that twenty years before had been quite a ways up the road from Dallas, far enough away in those days that you could catch a Greyhound or Continental bus at one of the downtown Dallas bus stations and pay to ride all the way north to Richardson. Of course that was in the days when Greenville Avenue actually was the road to Greenville and Lover's Lane meant what it said. Bernard L. Teckmann lived in the old part of Richardson, and the woman in the front yard of his house looked old enough to remember when it was a bus ride away.

"Morning." I smiled out my car window at her.

She straightened from whatever she had been doing in the flower bed that ran across the front of the squat brick tract house which I knew would have three tiny bedrooms and a bath and a half, tops. She was wearing a wide-brimmed coarse straw hat, the kind with a green plastic visor built into the front of the brim and two ends of twine dangling that she had not bothered to tie in a bow underneath her chin. Also a long-sleeved man's old white dress shirt, gray now, with the cuffs unbuttoned, and a biggish pair of white cotton gloves with fingers that dangled loosely around the handle of a trowel in one hand and a long-handled open-ended basket in the other. She was wearing slacks, and they were green and dirty at the knees. She rose to her feet and took a couple of steps toward me onto the remnants of a lawn that had succumbed to too many Dallas summers and only here and there featured greenish tufts that probably were Johnson grass instead of Bermuda. I could see her red toenails where they curled up out the front of her straw shoes with silly built-up heels and no straps at the back. Mules, I thought, and remembered Mrs. Borodin the night before.

"Yes?" she answered, her right arm bent across her face beneath the brim of her hat. The sun was behind me, but I had not thought it was still so low.

"Would you be—Mrs. Teckmann?" I sang out, pretending to check something beside me on the car seat. "Mrs. Bernard L. Teckmann?"

"Somebody has to be," she answered without a hint in her voice that it was meant to be funny.

Ordinarily, the last thing I would have been interested in doing would have been to make contact with anyone involved by association or otherwise with my investigation. If Bernard Teckmann was of interest, the first step ninety-nine times out of a hundred would have been to tail him first, for as long as circumstances allowed, to get a picture of him, set his routine, find out all we could about him. Maybe then I would have actually made an approach like the one I was about to make. Maybe, but probably not. But my business is not a science, and a lot of the good stuff comes from playing your hunches. Teckmann's house was in the middle of a block on a pretty narrow residential street. A lot of his neighbors parked their cars at the curb in front of their houses because they had expanded their dens into the space that had originally been their garages. It was the kind of neighborhood where they would do that because they could not afford bigger houses. Or because their nerves, aside from their finances, could not bear another long-term debt. It was a neighborhood where people were just now paying off thirty-year mortgages with monthly payments of only a couple hundred dollars, when any newer or bigger house anywhere in the Metroplex would come with a monthly nut of at least seven hundred. They were stuck like bugs on flypaper, so they knocked down walls and built out into their garages, financing it all with second mortgages that only meant another couple of hundred a month for five years or so.

If she had not been in the yard, I would not have stopped. But she was, and she was the only one out from all the empty yards I could see in either direction. So you could see what I meant by its being a hunch.

"My name is—" I started to lie, fumbling in my glove compartment through my collection of business cards. Never in the last decade or so have I been in a business of any kind that I have not tried to capture at least half a dozen of the business cards people like to display on their desks or front counters. There were two hundred cards in my glove compartment, without exaggeration, and I was ready to be anybody from Alex Abel, Appraiser, to N. W. Zeigler, Taxidermist, but none of that was necessary.

"Don't bother, it'll only upset me when I forget it."

The woman was ten feet away by this time, having trudged from her flower bed to the sidewalk.

"Okay." I smiled at her, not wanting to upset her.

"I guess you'll want to come inside, look it over," she added, tugging off her gloves.

"If you don't mind," I said, still smiling.

"Wouldn't matter if I did. I know how you people are."

With that, leaving me to wonder what people she meant, the woman in the hat turned her back to me and plodded away toward the front door of the house. When it came clear that she meant for me to follow, I shut off the engine of my battered old Chevy and stepped out onto the crumbling and inhospitable gray dirt of her yard. Almost jogging, I followed her into the house.

She held the front doors, the screen door that opened outward and the faded white wooden one with the diamond-shaped windows. I nodded as I sidled past her into Mister Teckmann's home.

"It's down the hall, second door on your left," she informed me, in a flat and matter-of-fact tone that really made me wonder who she thought I was. "It's locked, of course, but I have the key."

"Oh" was all I could think of to say, and I could not help wondering if my hunch had played me foul.

"Here," she groaned, and I turned to see her standing on tiptoes to reach up on top of the avocado-colored refrigerator. The little kitchen opened off the dining area that was only a space on the plastic-tiled floor, linoleum made to look like ceramics. A fake wooden table with fake brass legs stood amid four plastic-legged chairs with synthetic foam pads on their backs and seats, off-white pads whose seams were cracked like dry skin. There was an avocado-colored range, too. A lot of people had fallen for that color scheme, but I thought most of them had come to their senses.

After a teetering thirty seconds of suspense she managed to come down up-right with a key in her hand. It had an oblong plastic name tag attached to the head of it with an avocado-green string I thought might have been fishing line. On the tag, which looked like it was meant to be affixed to luggage, were the words LAB and PRIVATE scrawled atilt in some kind of Magic Marker.

"There," she exhaled, as if it had been a hell of a chore but now her duty was done. "Help yourself."

"Thank you very much," I told her, taking the key from her.

Down the hall I went, all of the twelve or fourteen feet from the dining area to the second door on the left. Without concerning myself with what might lie behind the first door, I plugged the key into the slotted knob of the second and twisted it until there was a click. Looking back over my shoulder, I saw the woman standing in her little kitchen in front of the green refrigerator. She was taking off her hat. Without saying anything to her, I went inside the room.

What I expected to find, I could not say. But what was there was disappointing: a smallish desk, a folding chair that should have been at a canasta table somewhere. A computer stood black-eyed and smartassed, daring me to get anything out of it. I did not bother it, knowing that I had no chance of guessing which keys to fondle to tease it into telling me anything. Computers and I did not get along at all, my only experience with them being limited to surreal spats with one or another utility company over their allegations that I had made too many calls to Bombay or might have flushed my toilet a million times a day for a month.

Beside the computer were a printer in harness and a plain white notepad. I bent down to study the surface of the top page of the notepad at an angle to the overhead light, but I could not make out any impressions of what might have been written there, even though I could see that several sheets had been torn off the pad.

As I stooped to study the pad, a speck of color caught my eye, a sly and out-of-place smudge of red beneath the computer keyboard. I lifted the keyboard gingerly to find a rumpled brochure from an airline, one that advertised its flights and tourist packages to Mexico. On the cover was a blonde in a bikini on a white tropical beach, awash in a gentle surf. And that was all, just the cover, torn raggedly off the brochure itself. Odd, I thought.

There was a file cabinet in the corner farthest from the door, a green army surplus job that showed signs of having been banged around. A bar ran down through all four of the drawer handles. Through a hole in the top end of the bar and a hasp welded onto the top of the cabinet was a padlock. I tried the lock and found that although it was closed it was not locked. I used to have one like it on my locker down at the Southeast Sub-Station, which I guess nowadays they call the Southeast Patrol Division. I lost and forgot my keys a lot in those days and finally gave up and pried my lock open one day. After that, I did not get around to getting a new lock for a long time and just kept the old one on my locker door. You could close it so that it looked secure as could be, but all you had to do was tug on it to open it. That was the way Mister Teckmann's lock was.

Doctor Teckmann, rather. Before I pulled the rod up through the drawer handles and looked inside his files, I stepped back to the door of the room and checked to make sure Mrs. Teckmann was not lurking in the hall. She was not. In fact, when I stepped through the door and looked both ways, I did not see her anywhere, or hear her either, for that matter. So I went back into the room and was pleased to find that there was a knob switch lock on the inside of the door so that Doctor Teckmann could lock himself up in his room and do whatever it was that he did. I locked it, and that was when I took the time to look at the stuff on his walls. There were three degrees in dusty frames, cheap jobs from a drugstore, fake wood plastic frames with yellow plastic strip that was supposed to look like brass. A baccalaureate, a master's and a doctor's degrees, in variations of specializations that boiled down to one kind or another of electrical engineering. The dates were from twenty to almost thirty years old, and I figured he must have been in on some of the first of the computer business in the country.

Aside from the degrees, there were only a couple of photos, one of a youngish fat man already losing his hair standing beside a tall, slender woman who was striking in a way, allowing for the primitive quality of the black-and-white print. The other looked like a photo for a school annual, a girl who might have been in high school, taken so long ago that she had her hair up in a do I had never seen in real life. That one looked as if it had been in black and white too, but someone had tried to tint it to make it more lifelike. It had not worked; in fact it had made the girl look like a corpse.

The file cabinet was a disappointment. The top drawer was empty, whatever had been kept there scooped out to leave only the piddling debris that accumulates in the drawers of file cabinets; tattered corners of papers and the odd paper clip. The second and third still had stuff in them, but all of it was so old the manila folders had turned brown and the papers inside looked like parchment. I could not make much out of the labels on the folders, combinations of letters and numbers run together like serial numbers or something. And the few pages I tugged out of their files at random were speckled with handwritten notes that might have been mathematical formulas. The ones that had dates were no more recent than the early 1970s.

In the bottom drawer I found stuff that made an intruder of me, the kinds of sentimentalities that even I have managed to hang on to as I've moved from place to place. There were several Father's Day cards, handmade by Teckmann's kid, the tinted girl smiling down at me from the wall above his desk, on sheets of crumbly art paper with crayons. A couple of newspaper clippings, one announcing that Texas Instruments was pleased to welcome its new employee, Doctor Teckmann, into the corporate family. That one told of his degrees and mentioned his "commendable and impressive" service in the U.S. Air Force. It did not specify what that service had been. The rest of it was just old and long-lapsed insurance policies, copies of stories from magazines that had been out-of-business for years. I closed the last drawer and put the rod and the padlock back the way I had found them. Having saved the best for last, I took a look at Doctor Teckmann's trash basket. It was a plastic one, square and beige, in which he had not bothered to put any kind of a bag or liner.

There was nothing in it but paper, the computer kind with perforations running down either side. Its being neatly printed did not make it any easier for me to understand, and I almost did not bother to take any of it. But it occurred to me it might mean something to somebody, and I picked up about half of the tight little wads just in case. I opened each of them, smoothed them across my knee, then folded them and slipped them into my jacket pocket. It was too hot for even the summer-weight sports coat I was wearing, but I had gotten into the habit of wearing one when I was a cop so nobody could see that I had a revolver stuck in the waistband of my pants. Now that I did not carry a gun anymore, I wore a jacket so somebody might think I did. Of the eight wadded sheets in the trash, I had taken four, pretty sure he would not notice any were gone. But in doing so, I uncovered the bottom of the plastic basket, and that was when I saw the part that worried me: black ash, curly blackened shards, and matching corners from three white sheets of paper lying nestled in one corner of the basket, that the fire had not destroyed.

I had no way of knowing what it had been that Doctor Teckmann had done for the U.S. Air Force, or for Texas Instruments, or what his connection was with Sylvia Borodin or Stefan Galipolus for that matter. But what I knew I did not care for. I knew that Doctor Teckmann had written something on his notepad and that then he had taken the trouble of burning the next three sheets from the pad because he wanted to be sure that nobody found any tracings to figure out what that had been.

I did not care for that at all.

CHAPTER FOURTEEN

I SAID GOOD-BYE to Mrs. Teckmann, who was back at her work in the flower bed. She took such little note of me that I took a chance and asked her who she thought I was.

"I know who you are," she said, amused with me.

"Do you?"

"Good heavens, young man, you've got it written all over you. You people haven't changed since the Korean War."

"Haven't we?"

"Not enough to matter. You're not as clean-cut as most, and if you don't mind my saying so, you're a little old for the work, but you can't hide that look you all have."

Now I was curious.

"Who has?"

"Is this part of the clearance thing, asking me questions? It didn't used to be. It used to be just take a look in his study, make sure he had locks and all that, passwords on his computer, and everything—"

She stopped without finishing, letting her voice curl up into the hot morning air without making it mean anything. I saw in her eyes that she was remembering something, or trying to. I did not say anything, and after a bit she went on.

"—of course, it's been a while since the last time, come to think of it."

"How long?"

"As if you didn't know," she said, looking sideways at me with a conspiratorial grin that showed yellowed teeth. "As if you didn't have it all down in his file somewhere."

"I see."

She had told me what I had wanted to know, and I turned to go. But she came after me and put her hand on my arm. When I turned I was looking into her eyes and I thought from the way they searched my face back and forth that I was seeing a little panic and something else, a bit of confusion. It was as if she was trying to remember when her husband had last been investigated for a security clearance but she could not make any sense of what time had been up to. At the same time she was afraid that by not remembering she might be queering it for him. She held tightly to my sleeve and I thought that I had seen something like it before, the way she looked at me—the way you look at a cop or a clerk or some other petty official for whom you cannot muster much regard, but who might out of malice or indifference screw things up for you.

"I can remember," she promised me. "Just give me a second."

"It's not important," I assured her. "That's not part of it."

"Are you sure?"

"Yes, ma'am. I'm positive."

"Security," she whispered, stepping close to me. "One of those alphabet jobs, the anagram jumble. Mister Teckmann used to kid about that, said he was going to write a book someday and call it 'The Anagram Jumble.' Like *The Asphalt Jungle*, get it?"

"Yes, ma'am." I smiled at her joke and gently took her hand off my arm. "I like it." I made a noise like a laugh and grinned broadly at her as I backed away toward the street and my car.

She was standing at the curb as I drove away and I watched her in my rearview mirror until I turned a corner. I stuck my arm out my car window and waved at her, but she did not wave back. She turned and dashed back toward her house. I figured she was going to make sure her husband's study was locked and the key was where it belonged on top of the avocado-green refrigerator.

Teckmann was a case. There had not been anything in his study newer than about 1969, except for the computer stuff. His daughter must have died about then, and I did not think that Mrs. Teckmann had been paying much attention since. What Doctor Teckmann himself had been up to, I wondered about. Import-export, Borodin had said. Investments. I had liked the whole deal better when it was a case of infidelity, without the embellishments.

Rather than retracing my route back west on Belt Line to Preston and then south to LBJ, I took a chance and wheeled my old Chevy around the pillars of the underpass and trundled up the ramp onto Central Expressway. Surprisingly, nobody was doing any work on it that day, and both southbound lanes were open. There was not even a grid lock under way, which was newsworthy, and I made good time, south on Central and around the big curving ramp to west on LBJ Freeway. I got off five minutes later at the Preston exit and pulled into the driveway of the Denny's that fronted an off-brand motel I could never remember the name of. Which was not usually the case. From my days working Vice, I knew most of the hotels in town pretty well.

It may be revealing, and it's probably some kind of indictment, but I actually liked Denny's and some of the other chain twenty-four-hour eateries for much the same reason I had an affinity for 7-Elevens. From my days in Patrol, they were part of my twenty-four-hour world, part of the drill that went on all the time without worrying about what time it was or if it was some kind of holiday or whatever. The plastic, functional utility of places like that appealed to me, the frank and disillusioned but undefeated air of a divorced mother working to feed her kids or some guy who was new in town and the country too, for that matter, who was still learning the language and making a living and damn glad to be there. Something like that.

I walked in and sat down, knowing what I wanted, one of the breakfasts pictured on the menu, and that was the way I ordered it, eggs and all. I liked that the waitress put a little pot of coffee on my table and then didn't bother me until my food was ready. I looked over a *Dallas Morning News* that somebody had left behind, but there was not much in it of interest. When I thought about calling my office, I thought about Della and decided to wait and have my breakfast first. It was exactly what I expected, which is nothing to sneeze at.

Della was typing when I stepped off the elevator and she looked up to see who it was and when it was me she only bounced her eyebrows up and curled the ends of her lips for a hello and did not say anything.

"Any messages?" I asked.

"Mister Borodin called, said to tell you he would be at home until one o'clock, if you had anything to report."

"Okay."

Della did not ask me if I had anything to report, or say anything about my case at all, which was a bad sign. A terrible sign. As a rule, she took an interest in my cases. This time, there was nothing, what I have heard referred to as a stony silence. Things could not go on for long like that, as far as I was concerned. But before I saw what could be done about it, there was some business to take care of.

Sasha answered when I called Borodin's home number and said something about his being indisposed. It was the second time she had told me something like that, and when she assured me she would be happy to relay any message, I almost spent the energy it would have taken to explain things to her. But I did not. I had been up all night. So I only told her I was in my office and to have her uncle call me. When I said "your uncle," she made a noise that was probably the Cypriot equivalent of "huh?" so I reminded her that Borodin had passed her off to me as his niece, and then she snapped. Maybe when you look like she did you don't have to be quick.

Without asking Della, I deduced from the absence of any notes on my desk that Joe had not called in with anything. He was tailing Mrs. Borodin during most of the daylight hours for me, but I had not expected any movement out of her until much later in the day, after the evening she had put in. For the record, I had all I really needed, all that a jealous husband would be interested in. But I had told Joe to stay on it anyway. I had told him, in fact, that the one I was most interested in today was Mister Pink Shirt. I wanted to know who the hell he was, where he went if anywhere.

What I had in mind was a nap, at least until Borodin called back. Whether to go full bore was the question, put the IN CONFERENCE sign on the door and break out the cot, or to make myself as comfortable as I could in the old swivel chair. My back was tight and crotchety, enough so that I thought for a bit about calling my lawyer. The thing with the disability pension had dragged on to the point that I would not have minded a firm no, as long as I could close the books on it. It was like the divorce that way, went on forever until you got to a point that you did not even care, as long as you did not have to think about it anymore.

Della's voice on the intercom, chilly and professional-sounding, cut into my musings to tell me that Mister Borodin was on line one. Another bad sign. Ordinarily, she would have said, "Your client," and I would have acted busy and said, "Which one?" and she would have come back with, "How many do you have?" This thing with me and her boyfriend was going to have to be worked out.

"Good morning," I said when I answered the phone, grinning again to make my voice sound that way. When I don't grin, people on the other end always think I've just woken up, for some reason.

"Good day, Mister Kyle" came the well-rested voice of my client over the line.

A bit condescending, I thought.

118

"Sorry to hear you've been indisposed," I said.

"What?"

"Your . . . niece. She said—"

"Oh. Never mind that. Have you anything to report?"

I liked the sound of that. Have you anything. It sounded British.

"As a matter of fact, I have," I said, having considered saying "actually" and decided against it. With my Texas twang, it's ever so hard to sound English.

"What?"

"Not over the phone, naturally," I chided him, getting back for his "good day." "I could drop around within the hour, if that's convenient."

"By all means. I'll be expecting you."

He hung up before I said that would be fine, and I was left wondering why I let myself be influenced by people I met. Character flaw, I imagined, that and too little sleep.

CHAPTER
FIFTEEN

FIRST THINGS FIRST.

Like when I was working Patrol. One balmy summer evening I had what you could call an epiphany, if you were so inclined. My partner and I were on our way to a man-with-a-gun call, and I had just unwrapped a cigar and was about to light it. When we got the call, I had just finished licking the cigar, which you could still do in those days because they hadn't started using the tar-paper wrapper they use now, which, if you dared to lick it would not only make your tongue bleed but would leave you with a taste in your mouth like you had eaten a bug off linoleum. So I had licked it but instead of lighting it I just put it in the car ashtray because we would be code six in a minute. I would just wait until after we had handled the call and then I would fire it up. That was when I had my little epiphany. In a chilling, pulse-flickering moment it occurred to me that I very well might get out of that squad car and never, ever get back into it. It was a man-with-a-gun, after all. So I went ahead and lit the cigar and smoked it as much as I could before we got there. As it happened, I did not get killed or even hurt, but anyway, there you are. First things first.

"Della," I said, standing in my office door.

"Yes, Jack?" she answered, not looking up from her typing.

"You want to step into my office for a minute?"

"No."

Okay, that was plain enough.

"Good," I said. I was getting a little sore myself, and I had things on my mind. "I was hoping you'd say that. Because what I want is to clear the air around here and get this thing with your boyfriend settled. And I think it would be better if we did it out here in the lobby, where there's plenty of room to pace up and down and scream or whatever comes up. Good thinking. Let's do it out here."

"Jack—"

"Now, the way I see it is this: Your boyfriend is an asshole. I am your friend. At least your friend. At the very least. Mind you, I'm not in a position to know all the whys and wherefores of your relationship, so I'll just have to start with the part where I came in, which is when this asshole was mistreating you."

"Jack—"

"Now, it is my experience that young men like your boyfriend behave the way he was behaving here in the lobby with you for only one of two major reasons. One, he's afraid he can't get it up, or, two, he can't get it up. Now—"

That was all it took. Della hopped up and ran at me like a terrier and before you could say it we were in my office with the door closed which was where I wanted to have this conversation in the first place.

"Jack, goddamnit!"

You would have thought that was the kickoff to something big, but then she stopped. Della did not curse much, as far as I knew anyway, and it was as if saying that much had taken something out of her. She did not slump against me, which I would have liked because then I would have taken her in my arms like a father or a brother or just like an old friend at least. She did sink a little against my closed door, and she did not say anything else.

"Della," I said, trying to put everything I felt about her

into the way I said her name, even though I was not sure what exactly I felt about her.

But she only lowered her head and raised her hands and hid her face with her fingers. I thought she might be crying.

"Kid," I started again. "I don't . . . how in heaven's name can you be mad at me? I don't know this guy from Adam. I hear what's going on, I walk out, and he's giving you hell. That ain't enough, then he starts in on me. What did you want me to do?"

"Jack, you don't understand."

"No shit," says I, which was as natural as breathing, but a mistake nonetheless.

"Forget it."

With that she threw open my office door and stalked out, and after a moment's consideration I decided I did not have the time to keep after her. To hell with it.

Borodin's house looked about the same when I pulled into the circular driveway half an hour later, but I did not remind myself of Raymond Chandler's boy anymore.

CHAPTER SIXTEEN

I WAS NOT half as crisp and chipper as I had been on my first visit, having been up all night. My clothes and my attitude all had a pretty rumpled air about them, and that was one reason I did not bother to go to the front door at all this time. I skipped the part where the little ramrod guy in the white jacket cocked one eyebrow and looked up his nose at me, and walked around the corner of the house and down the side into the big backyard with its patio and pool. The pool was empty this time, but the patio was not. One chaise longue in particular was far from empty. Crowded, even.

If Sasha was Borodin's niece, this was a very close family indeed. She was the one who saw me, finally. And she must have seen me upside down. Her long pretty neck arched down off the foot of the chaise so that her long hair spilled on the patio beneath her. She was making faces with her eyes closed until she opened them and saw me. Whatever she said was in some other language, and I could not make it out, but it meant something to Borodin, because his head shot up from her breasts and he pushed himself up off her and looked at me with his eyes bugged out and his mouth open for a couple of seconds. A camera would have been nice, because Sasha's legs stuck up on either side of him like the two sides of a rabbit ear TV antenna.

"Hope I'm not intruding," I said.

"Mister Kyle" was all Borodin could think to say.

"You were expecting me, weren't you?" I asked.

He and the girl had recovered enough from the surprise of my being there that he unplugged himself and she swung one leg over him and rolled off the chaise and into a kimono that she pulled closed and tied with a black sash. Borodin turned his back to me and stepped into a pair of shorts.

"I was expecting you at the door," he said over his shoulder, but if he meant it to sound as if he was scolding me, it did not come out that way. He was still panting, so he could not get much authority into his voice.

"Sir?"

I turned to see the butler, Anton, poised at the back door of the house. Poised for what, I did not know, but he was looking at me in a way I had seen before from other men and a few women, and I did not care for it.

"It's all right, Anton," Mister Borodin assured him. "Quite all right, thank you."

"Yes, sir."

Anton nodded that stiff little nod he had done before.

Sasha was looking at me too, but it was hard to tell what she had in mind. I did not think the reddish flush of her face and her throat had anything to do with being embarrassed, more likely with the inconvenience of having been interrupted.

"I could come back later," I offered.

"No, that won't be necessary," Borodin assured me, standing now that he was more or less dressed and waving me toward a chair. "Sit down, make yourself comfortable, Mister Kyle."

"Inside would be better," I said.

"Oh?"

"Yes. You have a VCR inside, don't you?"

"What? Yes, of course."

"I have a videotape you'll want to see."

"Oh? Good. Very good. Come in then."

Anton stepped to one side and held the back door of the big house open for us, while Sasha stood beside the chaise longue and pouted or whatever she was doing. Mister Borodin smiled graciously and showed me inside. I expected him to say something about what I had seen, him and Sasha, but he did not, meaning that he probably figured it was my word against his and hers, and Anton's too, if it came to that, and it was better left as it was. It was not any of my business, technically, and I could not say I was surprised. I could not even say I blamed him, and it did not offend me that Sasha felt that way about older men. Rich older men, I reminded myself.

The videotape went from me to Borodin to Anton, who loaded it into a player that occupied most of one of the shelves of a cabinet. The den was roomy and furnished very nicely. Due largely to an earlier experience with people of whom Borodin reminded me a little, I had half expected the big fine house to be empty inside, a front for whatever kind of operation he was running. This was decidedly not the case. Borodin's house, from everything I could see, was for real. I remembered my friend had said he had leased it, but I could not recall if she had said anything about an option to buy. For a man with a lease, he had moved in a hell of a lot of very nice things. He even had photos on the wall, with him and his two friends Sasha and Anton, him and some other people I did not know. There were not any pictures of him and Mrs. Borodin, I noticed.

Borodin would have had Anton play the videotape right away, but I told him to wait. The tape was the big closer, and I wanted him to get the full effect. If he saw the tape first, the photos would be anticlimactic, and I wanted him to feel that he was getting his money's worth. He was pretty eager for the tape, but he humored me.

How you package the photos you shoot for a client can mean a lot, and there are any number of ways to do it. Some PIs like slides better, and they do a whole slide show, presenting the client at the end of the show with the slides arranged on a lighted viewer display, or in carefully arranged sleeves.

Some of them put their prints into photo albums, with key shots enlarged to cover whole pages. It is all a matter of taste and salesmanship when it comes right down to it. I had not gone to that kind of trouble for Borodin, because he had impressed me as the kind of man who was interested in results over style. All I had done was arrange the best of the photos in chronological order in the pocketed kind of plastic sheets that fit into an album and put them in a manila envelope. All the rest of the prints and all the negatives were bundled up in a second envelope, and I showed him that one first. Then the album pages, one at a time, in order. There was a written report too, but only because the State Board required one, and it mostly had to do with the hours we had worked and our expenses, with one paragraph of narrative on the second page that summed up our findings. As I had expected, Borodin paid no attention to that and went right for the sheets of photos. He nodded his head and smiled as he went through them.

"Very good, Mister Kyle," he said. "Very good."

It was not what you would expect from a suspicious husband necessarily, but then you get all kinds in this business, and I had stopped expecting anything in particular.

Borodin gave me the impression that he would have been happy with just the photos, and I thought he lingered a bit over the ones I had taken of his wife and Pink Shirt in her car outside the Wine Press. But I had whetted his appetite with the tape, and it was not long before he was ready to see it. Anton punched on the machine.

It would have been much better if I had given Speed time to clean up the sound. He had wanted to dub something in that sounded professional instead of what was on the tape as it was, our comments back and forth across the videocam. You could shoot video like that with no sound at all, but it was best to let the mike run, because you could keep a commentary that way, like taking notes, without having to write anything down or trying to remember the sequence or timing of things, and without having to look away from the camera. Normally, you would clean it up later, before you showed it to the client. But

I had not taken time for that. I had begun to want this case to be over.

"Remarkable!" Borodin exclaimed when we got to the part where his wife and Pink Shirt were in the pool. "Very good indeed, Mister Kyle."

When all was said and done, I left the Borodin place in better shape than I had hoped. He was impressed with our results, and far from quibbling about the bill and my advance, he had paid me a bonus. Ten clean, crisp hundred-dollar bills. That was how much he had liked the job we had done for him.

Which was good news, all the way around. He had paid me what amounted to six hundred dollars a day. Joe and Speed had worked eight hours a day at twenty-five dollars an hour, for two hundred a day apiece, leaving two hundred a day for me. And Borodin had not quibbled about expenses, happy to pay for the rent of the van and incidentals. A thousand-dollar bonus on top of it put me almost two thousand dollars to the good, for less than a week's work. It was the best week I had had since opening the agency, which was not saying a hell of a lot. Most of my business so far had been legwork for other PIs, and a couple of insurance deals that had turned out well enough that they might lead to something better down the road. There had been the one big case, and I had seen some money out of that, but with getting gutshot and having my arm broken, I had not come out ahead, certainly not if you figured the downtime for healing.

So that was that. The Borodin thing had worked out better than I had expected, and the fact that something was wrong did not enter into it. It should not have entered in, anyway, because I was a businessman and my part was over. On my way back to my office, though, I worried about it. About Borodin and Sasha and Mrs. Borodin and Pink Shirt, and Doctor Teckmann and his distracted wife and the tinted photo of the young girl with the toothy smile on the wall above Teckmann's computer and the notepad he had been so careful about. I worried about it, which is what I seem to do best, but I told myself I was well out of it and tried to focus on the money. I had uses for it.

Back at the office, I thought it would be a good time to get things straight with Della, but when I stepped off the elevator she was not at her desk. She had left a note taped to the back of her chair that said she was ill and had gone home, that she had called the service for a temp to fill in for the afternoon.

I called Della's place but there was no answer. Joe called in not long after that. He told me he was still on the condo, that there had been no sign of Sylvia Borodin or Pink Shirt. He said he guessed they were sleeping in, and I told him I didn't wonder. That led him to speculate about the tape he must have heard about from Speed, and I assured him it was pretty hot, all right. He said he had confidence in me, that he knew I placed too high a value on employee morale to have handed the tape over to the client without making a copy for him to see. For training purposes, he said.

No dice, I told him. The client gets everything, and no copies get made. He was crushed, but felt better after I told him we had gotten paid and offered to treat him and Speed to dinner that evening. Joe said he would get word to Speed and I asked him and Speed to put their heads together and get the van back to Hell on Wheels and tell the lady there that I would be in that afternoon to settle up with her. Joe said no problem, and I called Della at home again, but did not get an answer that time either.

The smiling temporary swiveled all the way around in Della's chair as I walked from my office across the lobby to the coffeepot and poured myself a cup. I could not tell if she was friendly or if there was something about me to make her not want me to get behind her for some reason.

When I had my coffee sweet enough, I turned, getting still another smile from the temporary, and went to the office in the corner of the lobby where Mrs. Farragut did whatever it was that she did. Mrs. Farragut was not a fan of mine, but I knew better than most that she kept a close eye on everything that went on on our floor. Not that a lot went on. I was pretty much the black sheep of the group, which was probably why Mrs. Farragut seemed to pay so much attention to me.

"Excuse me," I said from the doorway of her office. "Are you busy?"

"Yes."

She did not say it with any particular venom, just a head-on kind of blunt indifference that let you know where you stood, which was somewhere that meant you were not worth very much of her time.

"What's the matter with Della?"

"She said she wasn't feeling well."

"How bad was it?"

"Not bad. She'll be in tomorrow, I imagine."

Mrs. Farragut looked up at me from whatever she was working on and I was surprised to see that it was a computer. It did not go with the way she looked at all. From the way she looked, she should have been dipping a quill pen in an inkwell.

"I called her place, but she didn't answer," I said.

"She may not feel like taking calls, Mister Kyle."

"I guess you're right. Thanks."

I went back to my office feeling surprised and a little disappointed that Farragut had not snarled at me the way she usually did. She had not been solicitous by any stretch, but she had been almost decent. I did not care for that somehow. I liked people to be constant, but it seemed they were always changing on me.

Back at my desk, I devoted myself to closing out the paperwork on the Borodin case. That did not take long. It was just a matter of putting my copies of my written report and receipts for expenses into the same file folder with my copy of the contract, and then a little housekeeping with the agency ledger, including posting the payments and writing a check apiece for Joe and Speed, and taking my time the way I did I still was through in about half an hour. Then there was nothing left to do but run by Hell on Wheels and get back my deposit less whatever I owed them.

One more try at Della's, with the same result. I thought

about running by her place while I was out. All of which was on my mind, so I was not sure myself why I did what I did next, which was to call the Teckmann residence.

Mrs. Teckmann answered and said her husband was not in. I told her who I was and although I could not be sure because she sounded as dazed as she had in person, I thought she remembered me. I told her I was the guy from the "alphabet jumble," and if that meant anything to her she did not let on.

"When do you expect Doctor Teckmann back?" I asked.

"I . . . I'm not sure, exactly."

"I see," I said, as something I did not care for occurred to me. "When did he leave?"

There was silence on the line for long enough that I was about to ask her again, when finally she answered, in a way.

"It was . . . yesterday, I believe," she said.

Which meant it might have been any day that week. Probably any day but today, if I was any judge of Mrs. Teckmann's state of mind.

"I see. Thank you," I said.

"Is anything wrong?" she asked.

"No, ma'am," I assured her, thinking I was probably lying.

"Is he . . ."

She did not finish her question, and I tried to finish it for her in my mind. Had she been about to ask if he was in any trouble, or if he was really working on something for somebody in the alphabet jumble?

"Everything's fine, Mrs. Teckmann. Thank you very much."

"You're quite welcome, I'm sure."

CHAPTER
SEVENTEEN

EVERYTHING WAS TAKEN care of. I had settled up with Hell on Wheels and got most of my deposit back, I had paychecks in my pocket for Speed and Joe, and Kyle and Associates was practically solvent. I had written and mailed checks to the property management office for this and last month's rent on my office, and to my in-laws in Paris, up near Oklahoma, for two months of child support. Mom and Pop did not want any money from me, and I knew they put whatever I sent them in a savings account for the kid, which was just as well with me. It was not that they had anything against me particularly, that was not why they did not want my money. They did not want anybody's money, because that was the way they were. They lived simply as they could well afford to live and did not want anything they did not need. I thought it was the way everybody should operate, and I did not know why my ex-wife had not learned that from them. There was a hell of a sore spot, but that was another story.

We were all set for an evening on the town. I was to meet Joe and Speed at Red's Bar at seven for drinks, then dinner at the eatery of their choice, to celebrate the wrap-up of the Borodin case. Speed would bring Leslie, and I knew I could count on her to come up with some place expensive. But that was all right, it was not often that I was in a position to treat, and they were friends of mine.

By quarter past six, everyone else had gone home on my floor and I had the place to myself. That was when I went down to the men's room to freshen up and change clothes. I put on my one suit, which was navy blue. The jacket to that suit went well enough with my three pairs of pants, the two tan ones and the gray one, so that I could give the impression of having a wardrobe. I had a sport coat, a couple of light blue dress shirts, the button-down-collar kind, and one white shirt, if the cleaners had managed to get the stains out, and that was about it. A couple of conservative ties, and one pair of cordovan shoes, because they went with anything. Except for the way my mind worked sometimes, my life was simple.

When I was dressed, I meant to leave, but I did not for a while. Instead, I dragged my chess set out of one of the drawers of my file cabinet and set up a problem. It was from one of the Karpov-Kasparov championship games, and I had photocopied the game notations out of one of my neighbor's newspapers. My chess set was one of those electronic ones that let you play against a computer, but the damn thing cheated, so I seldom turned it on. I moved the pieces by hand, and tried to re-create games from the notations. This one interested me, but as soon as I had the pieces in place I did not want to work it out anymore. I had flattered myself by thinking I had seen a way Karpov might have saved a tie the last time I had looked at it, but this evening I looked at it for a couple of minutes and then pushed the set to one side of my desk blotter. I had other things on my mind.

I called Della's number one more time, but still there was no answer. It occurred to me again to go by and check on her, but I had walked in on one couple that day, and I did not feel like pressing my luck.

The thing was, Sylvia Borodin was on my mind. She meant a hell of a lot less to me than Della, nothing in fact. I had done my job and been well paid. Next case. Only, there was something about the whole thing that kept humming around in my head, buzzing around like a fly. Something about Mrs. Borodin, something about Mrs. Teckmann. Doctor Teckmann worried me, with that business about the notepad. His wife worried me, with her air of loss and confusion. One thing I have never cared for in private eye novels was the way these guys keep working on a case after they've been fired. Private eyes are businessmen and businesswomen. The point is to make a living. Chandler was right when he had Philip Marlowe tell somebody that there was not much money in it if you were honest, but the idea was not to make much money, just a living. You could do that, if you did not have your heart set on living very well.

Still, there is a reason why the business is not easy, a reason why so many of the best of the PIs are ex-cops of one kind or another. You could call it the hunch factor. Good investigators make their livings with facts, like engineers. But it goes beyond facts sometimes, or else it involves facts that are so small, so subtle, that you can't see them, they don't get factored in to anybody's equations. A good investigator gets hunches, and it is bad business to ignore them. I had a hunch about the Borodin case, one you could best describe as a kind of a smell. It was not that business with my client and Sasha on the chaise longue. A husband whose wife was behaving the way Mrs. Borodin was might act that way. Given the way Sasha looked, a husband whose wife wasn't cheating might act that way. That was not what bothered me, not even that Borodin had been careless enough to let me walk in on him, although that made it worse than if he hadn't.

After wasting almost half an hour mulling things over, I noticed it was almost seven and called Red's. Red answered and I left a message with him for Joe and Speed, who were not there yet. Leslie took forever getting ready, and I imagined she was holding them up. I asked Red to tell them I would be late, that if they wanted they could leave word with him where they had decided to have dinner and I would join them there.

Then I locked up my office and took the stairs down to the ground floor.

The lobby of our building was no more elaborate than usual for an office building built in North Dallas around 1980. It had its share of plants and a low fountain along one wall that ran all the time, dribbling water down a concentric pair of flagstone walls a couple of feet high. The stairs opened onto the lobby from the wall opposite the fountain, with the outside door to your right and the two elevator doors to your left. In the same wall as the stairway door, a twisted set of stairs led up to the second floor for some reason. As a rule the lobby was well lighted all the time, but it looked dim as I stepped through the door from the stairs. I saw the one standing beside the elevator doors, waiting, a tallish slender figure wearing gray coveralls that made whoever it was look like a serviceman. Only there was something about the body inside the coveralls that was all wrong.

I did not see the other one at all, because the lobby really was darker than usual and he was partially screened by the door when I opened it. The door had one of those hydraulic sleeves on it so it did not open all the way back against the wall, and it closed by itself.

The one by the elevators turned toward me when I stepped through the door. The face was expressionless, or rather, it was fixed in an inane big smile that reminded me for a moment of the temporary who had filled in for Della that afternoon and who smiled at everyone and everything but did not speak very much English. This one was much taller than the temporary and came toward me with a sense of purpose that could only mean trouble.

But it was the other one who made trouble for me first, the one I had not even seen.

I was looking at the one coming toward me from the elevators with the idiot plastic face and the dark blue ball cap that was too big, swallowing much of the head and the top third of the face, when something hit me in the ribs beneath my right arm. I thought it was a gun at first, because it had that cool hard feel to it, but it was not a gun.

It felt like I had grabbed a live wire and sounded like a

light bulb popping, and the electrical charge knocked me off my feet. There was a sound that went with it after the pop, a sizzling and a fluttering hum that ran together, and I hit the floor hard. It was a stone floor, and I curled up around my ribs when the charge hit. I had fallen onto the floor so hard that the jolt of it took what breath the shock had left me. I felt like some kind of fish, lying on the floor rolled up into a tingling tight ball with my mouth open, gasping for air. What kind of a fish curls up like this, I asked myself, as if I had nothing else to worry about. An eel, maybe.

They were in no hurry, either of them. They were not worried about me, that was for sure. I was down and would have been better off if I'd been out. As it was, I was having no luck trying to make my arms and legs do what I wanted, which was to roll away and get up quick. The charge I had taken had tensed every muscle in my body, and nothing I could do would make them do anything else. It wasn't easy, but I looked to my right to see what was going to happen next, and I saw the second one leaning down over me. I could not tell much about the size of this one, because of the angle and because I wasn't seeing very clearly, but the face and the ball cap looked the same as the first one. I saw the thing the second one had zapped me with, a stun gun of some kind, one of those gizmos that operates on the same principle as a cattle prod, only you use them on people. The Dallas cops had tried them because they were looking for a way to put people down without killing them. The cops had passed on them after field tests because there was some trouble keeping the batteries charged. This guy leaning over me did not have that problem. He hit me with the gizmo again, and I heard myself screaming. Somebody kicked me over with a boot, and the third time the stun gun fired off in my chest I thought my heart had started fibrillating, the way it does when you are electrocuted.

Then they kicked the shit out of me, the two of them working at it with black boots I could see clearly until one of them kicked me in the face, and then I did not see anything for a while.

CHAPTER
EIGHTEEN

IT MIGHT HAVE been midnight for all I knew when I woke up. The lobby lights were working fine again, and it was pitch-dark outside. Everything hurt.

After a couple of minutes, I had myself sitting upright, leaning against the wall beside the stairway door. It spooked me bad when I looked down at my blue dress shirt and saw blood on my stomach, because I was afraid they had kicked open my bullet hole. But they hadn't. It turned out the blood on my shirt was from my nose, which was broken again, pretty good this time. My ribs ached and my chest felt as if someone had hacked it open and reached inside with both hands and yanked out a lung. But other than that, I was not in bad shape. Nothing seemed to be broken, although my two visitors had worked on both my legs well enough that it was a wonder. I hadn't remembered either of them rolling me over, but somehow they had managed to get at my hamstrings with enough authority that I was not sure I could walk. I've taken my share of beatings and dished out a couple along the way. This one had carried a message with it. I was receptive as hell at the moment, but I couldn't figure out what the message was exactly. Except for my nose, they had worked me over in a way that wouldn't show unless I stripped. That meant something. They had banged up my legs better than I had ever seen it done. That meant something too. What any of it meant, I couldn't figure out, but then it occurred to me that a concussion was not out of the question, and maybe I would be able to come up with it later.

Before I went to the trouble of getting up, I took advantage of my position to look over the floor as closely as I could. That was when I noticed that my right eye was swollen almost shut. I put the fingers of my right hand on it gingerly, and it felt like the knot was about softball-size. I left my hand there to make sure my eyeball didn't fall out and slid around the floor for a couple of minutes hoping I would spot something one of the two hitters had dropped. Nothing. The only debris on the floor was me.

Then I stood up, using the knob of the stairwell door for all it was worth. I made it to my feet, but that was not the hard part. If you've ever tried to limp on both legs at once, you get the picture I must have presented as I headed for the elevator. I didn't fall, because I knew that would hurt worse than what I was doing, as hard as that was to believe.

The elevator came and took me to my floor. From the elevator to Della's desk to my office door, I made the trip in little hops, teetering and cursing for all I was worth. My phone was ringing.

I got my door unlocked and made it to my chair, leaving some blood on my desk in the process. Not until I had sunk into the swivel chair and let my legs hurt all they wanted did I remember that the only first aid stuff on the floor was the little kit Della kept in her desk somewhere. She had insisted once on patching up a little nick on my cheek, something I got from a guy's pinkie ring. Where was she now, when I needed her? To hell with it, I said aloud. Before I would get back up and walk again, I would rather bleed to death. My phone kept ringing.

The nose could have bled all night for all I cared, if all it meant was ruining my shirt. But when I managed to drag the bottle out of my big desk drawer and got the cap off, the taste of the blood in my mouth fouled the scotch. Wouldn't do. So I took off my navy blue jacket and peeled off my shirt and used it as a compress to see if I could get the bleeding to stop. After a while, it did. Then, holding my wadded shirt tightly over my busted nose, I tried the scotch again. It was better that time.

The phone quit ringing then for a while, and I sat at my desk with my shirt on my nose and drank scotch and smoked cigarettes until I was good and drunk and there was only about a pint left in the big bottle of Johnny Walker Red. I tried to clean the blood off my watch to see what time it was, but there was blood on my hand by then and it didn't work. I dialed one of those numbers where you can find out what time it is if you don't mind listening to a bank commercial, and the recorded voice informed me it was 9:42 P.M. I had bumped into my friends in the lobby around seven and must have been drinking for most of an hour. That meant I had been out for an hour, and my laborious treks from the lobby floor to the elevator and from the elevator into my office had taken a long time. I had a concussion for sure, and that explained the way my head felt, which was like the top of it was standing up like a kick-pedal trash can lid.

I made up my mind to get up. I would hobble down the hall to the men's room and clean myself up. That would help some. And then I would . . . do whatever came next. I didn't know what that would be exactly, but it would come to me when I was more presentable. My phone rang again, sounding as if it were far off, and that was all that happened for a while.

I woke up sometime later when Fast Eddie Cochran and the Brooks Brother walked into my office and made a fuss.

Fast Eddie Cochran was a homicide lieutenant with the Dallas Police Department and a good friend of mine. The Brooks Brother was the black man I had seen Mrs. Borodin with at the Wine Press.

Eddie and the Brooks Brother did not belong together. They were from completely different parts of my life, and that was why I thought I was dreaming when they walked into my office and woke me up.

"What happened to you?" Eddie asked.

"Hiya, Eddie," I answered.

"I'd better get you some medical attention," Eddie said. "Are you up to moving? I can take you in my car or call for an ambulance."

"Hiya, Eddie," I answered.

"Let's make it an ambulance, Jack. No sense in you bleeding in my take-home car."

"Look at this, Mister Kyle," the Brooks Brother said rather pointedly. He had something in his hand.

It began to occur to me that this was really happening, and I started paying more attention. I blinked my eyes a couple of times, but I didn't shake my head to clear the cobwebs the way they do in the movies. With a bad head, the last thing you want is any shaking.

"What's up?" I asked, to either of them who wanted to tell me.

"You want an ambulance or not?" Eddie asked, my phone in his hand.

"If I haven't died yet, I ain't gonna," I said, trying to smile. One of my eyes would not open, and I tried to remember why.

"Fine," said the other one, the black guy in the Brooks Brothers suit with the thing in his hand. "Look at this."

"What's the deal, Eddie? Who is this guy and why is he showing me pictures of his kids?"

"Smartass," says the black guy, sounding like he's coming toward me.

"Take it easy," says Eddie, like he might be getting between us.

"What's the deal?" says I again, wondering.

"The usual, Jack. You're in big trouble."

"Oh."

Somebody took hold of me then, and when I looked up I was glad it was Eddie, because I had not cared for the tone of the other one's voice.

"Get on your feet, Jack. Come on."

Eddie got me on my feet, with considerable effort, and then everything about the preceding evening came back to me.

I hurt everywhere I had then, and now all my muscles were stiff too. My back hurt about as much as I would expect after spending a night in my swivel chair, but this morning it just went with the package. Everything hurt.

"Where are you taking him?" the black man asked.

"I'm going to see if I can clean him up a little, get a better idea of where he's hurt. Why don't you put on a pot of coffee."

The other one did not say anything to that, but at least he did not start any rough stuff. He put whatever it was in his hand back into an inside pocket of his well-made suit and Eddie took me down the hall.

The cleanup helped, and I told Eddie where I thought Della kept the first aid kit and he found it after a brief search. He did all he could for me and I closed my office door long enough to climb into my last set of clean underwear and put on my gray pants and white shirt. When I came out, Eddie handed me a cup of hot coffee the way I like it, with about a third of a dose of artificial sweetener, and lit a cigarette for me. I almost felt up to a little breakfast, Eddie having informed me that it was about a quarter to five in the morning, and tried not to think about the way I had looked in the men's room mirror.

"That's better," I said, leaning back in Della's chair. We were not in my office anymore because there was still quite a bit of blood in there. The lady who cleaned the place would love that. This was the second time I had made a mess, but the first time that it was my blood.

"Good," said the Brooks Brother. "Now, take a look."

He held out the thing again, and now I could see it better. It was not a picture of his kids at all, it was something else entirely. I had seen them before. It was an official-looking laminated card in a leather folder, with two or three colors on it and some kind of a seal, with the Brooks Brother's photograph that showed him scowling, the way he was now. When I squinted my good eye, I could make out the big letters, which spelled out U.S. CUSTOMS.

"Oh," I said. It was all that came to me.

"Now, Mister Kyle, I have a few questions."

I have been called a son of a bitch plenty of times in a nicer tone of voice than the Customs guy called me "Mister Kyle." My head still hurt, but it was clearing a bit now, and I could tell he was not just rude, he was pissed.

"Me too," I shot back, keeping my voice low but making a point, or trying to. I looked at Eddie. "You two have business with me?"

"I'm afraid so."

With Customs? What the hell did I have to do with Customs? What did Eddie have to do with them for that matter? Customs and Homicide. Like I didn't have enough trouble of my own.

"Okay, let's have it," I said.

"Do you recognize her?" the Brooks Brother, whose name was really Agent Thompson, asked, showing me a photograph he took out of his jacket pocket. I knew her all right.

"Yeah," I answered. "Who is she?"

"Do you recognize her or not?" Thompson demanded, raising his voice.

"Her name is Felicia Adams, Jack." Eddie told me softly. He understood, about my head and about my question. "She's a Customs agent. She was working undercover on a big case, and now she's disappeared."

I did not say anything, but I heard the noise I made, some kind of a moan.

"She disappeared, Mister Kyle. Do you understand?"

"What happened?" I asked, afraid I knew.

"Something went wrong," Thompson answered, his voice rising. "Somebody blew her cover."

"Jesus," I said.

"Jack, talk to us," Eddie said.

"We don't have much time," Thompson said, trying to control his temper, but not having much luck. He moved toward me and shouted at me. "Goddamnit, talk!"

"Partner, put me in jail if you want," I said. "Take out your gun and kill me if it'll make you feel any better. But I'm asking you nice, please don't yell. My head—"

141

With both hands I held my head, because it had begun to hurt worse than ever. I leaned forward and put my elbows on Della's desk and squeezed my head with both hands to try to make it stop hurting, but it didn't, because I was looking at the photograph Agent Thompson of Customs had put in front of me. She was attractive in the photo, in a different way, more civil service somehow. But I recognized her all right. It was the woman I had known as Sylvia Borodin.

CHAPTER
NINETEEN

I TOLD EDDIE and Agent Thompson my story as we went. It was going to be a hectic day, and a hell of a long one, the way things were looking. The house in the country, where I had watched Anton, the butler, feeding his Dobermans, did not have an address, and I was not sure of my directions, not 100 percent. When I gave it my best shot, Thompson did not look like he thought I was really trying, but I had pretty well lost patience with him too. You get to a certain point, when you're in it up to your eyelids, and it's not going to get much worse, and you just say to hell with it. That's about where my relationship with Agent Thompson had gotten by the time Eddie pulled his Diplomat into the vacant lot they had decided would be their staging area for the move on Borodin's house. Thompson had no use for me and that was too bad, because I figured he was a decent guy, and I knew he was over the wall about having two people go missing on him. You can relate to that, but at the same time, while I might have inadvertently screwed up his deal, I knew I had not done anything wrong. What was I supposed to do, run a national agencies check on every client who hired me to keep tabs on his wife? Goddamnit, I felt bad enough all by myself about the agents, I did not need Thompson's attitude. Already, even before we got there, I was trying to put it together in my head how I was going to settle up with Borodin and his pals. The American justice system is tops, and I have a reasonable amount of faith in it as a rule. but I did not think it provided for somebody to drape Borodin's entrails over a barbed wire fence while he was still alive, and that was what I had in mind for the son of a bitch.

Dallas TAC was already at the staging area and gearing up when we pulled in. I had friends in the Tactical Section once, particularly a captain of theirs who used to be a drinking buddy. But, like everything else, most of the people I knew had moved on to other assignments, or retired, or died or something. Of the two teams busy getting ready for whatever awaited them in the Borodin house there in the early morning grayness of the row of trees across the back of the vacant lot, I only recognized two men. One was an old-head troop with thinning hair and a shuffling gait that I knew personally to be one of the coolest gunmen in a tight spot that you would ever want to see. The other was a sergeant. They looked us over when we pulled in, but they had no time for small talk; they had their game faces on.

They were all in black, their special outfits with the baggy pockets for this and that and the ballistic vests with all kinds of straps and pockets for whatever the hell gear and high-tech gizmos they were using these days. With all I had on my mind, I could not help taking in their weapons, it's a habit that's hard to break. I was impressed. There were several of those ugly little German submachine guns, the kind with a barrel so short the Krauts stuck a handle on the bottom of it so you wouldn't slip and get your off hand in front of the muzzle and lose a couple of fingers. The old breech-loading grenade launchers I knew from Vietnam, although I could never remember the model number for them because I always got it mixed up with the machine gun, all the M-60s and M-79s and the other Ms running together on me in the haze of memory. Short-barreled pump shotguns with pistol grips, the whole thing not much bigger than a pistol, and I knew they were loaded with double-O buckshot, nine pellets to a pop, each of them a pellet the size of a small handgun round. The shotgun had always been my choice of a weapon, when I had a choice, which I most often didn't due to working the more or less undercover way I usually worked. The boys were up for it, whatever it was, and I could not help thinking I was glad I was not holed up at Borodin's place, whatever else was going on.

Eddie and Thompson left me in Eddie's car with orders from Thompson not to "wander off" and went over to the side of the TAC van to huddle up with the TAC lieutenant and make their plans. That suited me, I did not want any part of them for the moment because I had enough on my mind already. It probably did not take me much more than a minute to drag myself out of the Diplomat, and the backs of my legs felt as if somebody had left knitting needles sticking out of them. Who the hell beats people up that way?

When I finally made it out of the car, I leaned against it and smoked a cigarette. The early morning air did not feel bad, better than the boozy, smoky air of my office, and I made myself stretch my legs, first one and then the other, and pretended they felt better for it.

There are no words to describe how bad it is to blow another cop's cover. Okay, I was not a cop anymore, but that was only the official view of it. Once a cop, always a cop, and don't let anybody tell you any different, not if your outfit was any good at all, and by God, the Dallas PD was one of the best, whatever you or I may find to say about this or that one who was in it and shouldn't have been. It is just the very worst thing you can do. One of the first half dozen things my trainer, Charlie Frederick, ever told me was that anytime I was in uniform and saw another officer I recognized who was not in uniform, I was never, never, never to speak to that officer first. I was not to let on that I had ever seen that officer before, not even if we were in the academy together. The reason was that you never knew, the other cop might be working, might be undercover working on some kind of deal, and if you spoke you might queer it for him. I say him, because in those days that was all we had, men, and most of them, like about 90 percent, were white. Things are a hell of a lot different now, and better for it, but that was the way it was then. Not burning somebody's cover was just one of the first things they drummed into you in those days, by which I mean fifteen or twenty years ago when senior patrol officers and trainers had enough experience to know what was what. Nowadays, I understand the cops are so short-handed kids start training by the time they make one year's probation, and they tell me it's not the same anymore. Whatever, screwing up an undercover deal was just absolutely a religious thing with me, only about twice as important as religion. That was how bad I felt about this thing with Felicia Adams or whatever her real name was.

Some of the TAC troops moved out after their huddle, and I was impressed with the way they all disappeared before they had gone very far. You wouldn't have thought there was that much cover in the neighborhood, but where were they? It's called "invisible deployment," and TAC is serious about it. Nothing would happen for a while now, and I did not like the idea of waiting to hear what they found. Better for me if somebody had said I should go over to Borodin's house, kick the door down, and take it from there. I would have liked that better, but I was kidding myself. The way my legs felt, I would have had to be on roller skates to get down the hill.

Long before it was time for TAC to have got inside the place and reported anything, Eddie came stalking back toward me and his car with a worried look on his face.

"What's up?" I asked.

"Thompson's people are having trouble finding the place."

"What place?"

"Where the guy fed the dogs."

"Jeez, you just go out Preston to where it turns into Two-eighty-nine, and then you . . ."

"Save it, Jack. You're going to show us."

"Okay, let's go."

"Hang on, we're going to have company."

146

"Thompson?"

"Nah, he's going to stay here until they have entry. He's sending one of his boys."

"Okay. Anything on Pink Shirt?"

"Who?"

"The guy I told you about in the car, Eddie. The guy who was shtuppin' whatshername in the pool, the one in the tapes."

"You weren't kidding about that?"

"Come on, Eddie, would I joke about any of this shit?"

"That's weird, Jack."

"You're telling me? So, what's the deal on this guy?"

"His name's Jerry Sykes."

"What was that about Sykes?" asked a burly young man who appeared beside me as if out of nowhere because I had not been paying attention.

"Jack, this is Agent Welsh."

"Welch," the kid corrected him.

"Welch," Eddie said. "He's going to run out there with us."

"How do you do," I said.

"Get in," said Agent Welch, with a c.

I got in, in the front seat beside Eddie, and that did not seem to bother Agent Welch a bit. From the look of him, I got the notion that he preferred sitting behind me, in case he got clearance from somebody to wring my neck.

"What's that about Sykes?" Welch repeated as we backed out of the lot into the street.

"I was about to tell Jack about him," Eddie said.

"Is that a good idea?" Welch wanted to know.

"Jerry Sykes is a Customs agent too," Eddie told me, not giving a shit whether Welch thought it was a good idea or not.

"You're kidding me," I said. Pink Shirt was a cop too?

"One of their best, from what they tell me. Just transferred in here from California. Been working in Silicon Valley."

"He's a legend," Welch informed me with the same tone of voice I've heard hard-shell Baptist deacons speak of Jesus or segregation.

"So how come he and whatshername were bare-assed out in the moonlit night before last fucking like a pair of trout instead of . . ."

Instead of covering their butts, or something to that effect, was what I would have said if I had been permitted to finish. But I wasn't, because in the blink of an eye there was no more air for me to breathe. This kid Welch was about twice as quick as you would expect by the size of him and the kind of bovine way he carried himself. His hands were about the size of catcher's mitts, and it did not take him long to crank down on my neck hard enough that I could feel my eyeballs bulging.

"Think about it, Welch" was all that Eddie said.

While I would have liked a little more from him, that little bit seemed to do the job. Welch loosened his grip on my throat, and I could almost hear him thinking. Finally, he turned loose of me altogether and slumped back into his seat.

"Watch how you talk about Jerry Sykes," he said.

That I would, I would have said, but I was busy getting my breath. So there was not much more in the way of conversation as Eddie drove north on Preston out past LBJ and waited for me to tell him where to turn.

"Hey," Welch said as I was looking for landmarks. We were out beyond the ranch with the buffalo and the longhorn cattle. "Hey, they got something."

"What is it?" Eddie asked.

"They're in the house."

"Borodin's house or . . ." Eddie started to ask.

"Yeah, yeah. Wait a minute."

When I turned in my seat to look, I saw Welch had one thick finger of his left hand shoved into his left ear. There was a slim plastic cord running from his ear down inside the lapel of his jacket, and I noticed something wrapped around the thumb of his left hand. There was another cord running down out of his hand and then up his left jacket sleeve. He had one of those nifty radio rigs like the Secret Service use, the kind where you see all the guys standing around with what look like hearing aids in their ears, and they talk into their fists all the time. Welch was talking into his fist now.

"She's okay," he announced at last.

"Sylvia . . . I mean, whatshername, the lady agent?" I asked.

"Yeah. No sign of Jerry though."

"What about the other house, the one with the Dobermans?" Eddie wondered aloud. "Have your people found it yet?"

"Up at that next road," I told Eddie, pointing. "Turn right. It's not far."

Welch talked into his fist some more.

"How far, Jack?"

"A couple of miles, I'd say."

"It's on this road?"

"Nah, you take a left, it's really out in the sticks, Eddie."

"They're on it," Welch announced. "They're taking care of the dogs now."

What that meant exactly I did not know, but to tell the truth I did not care if it meant they were machine-gunning the goddamn hounds. Sykes had not been in Borodin's house with whatshername, and this dump in the country was the last place I knew to look. I wanted it to be over.

"They're going in," Welch told us.

"How much farther?" Eddie was in a hurry too.

"Up there," I said. "Take a left on the little road that runs down that fence line. You can see the house from here."

"That's it?" he asked.

"Yeah."

There were a couple of cars parked at the house, one in front, the other on one side. The place was near the top of a long gentle hill, and except for the road that followed a row of trees and brush that ran up a line where a fence had been, all the land around the house was in pasture or tilled ground. There was no cover to speak of, and the men in the cars had not had much choice except to roar right up on the place.

"Jesus!" Welch whispered.

"What?" I demanded, but the big man did not answer right away.

Eddie did not waste any breath trying to get an answer out of the big man in the backseat, who sat with his hearing aid in his ear and stared dumbly at his fist as if he had heard something that did not make any sense. Eddie skidded the Diplomat to a stop behind one of the feds' cars and we all scrambled out. They had a man posted at the gate in the fence that ran around the house and he had his eye on us. Eddie was first out, and Welch rallied enough to be second. I was still not moving that well and placed a poor third. When the man at the gate saw Welch, he seemed to relax a bit, and Welch made a motion with a hammy hand to say that we were all right, we were with him.

Welch and Eddie got a sign from the fed at the gate, a move of his head toward the house, that it was okay to go in, and they went quickly through the gate and into the house. I hobbled after them as best I could.

The two Dobermans were in a small pen that stood at one corner of the house and they were both asleep or dead. Asleep, I assumed, since if they had been in the small pen there would not have been any need to kill them, and if they were dead, the feds would not have bothered putting them in the pen. They must have used dart guns on them, I thought, but then I caught the smell from the house and I forgot about the dogs.

The house showed no sign of it from the outside, but I knew at once, as soon as I caught a whiff of the smell, that something terrible had happened inside. Something or somebody had blown up.

CHAPTER
TWENTY

IT HAD NOT made much of a fire, just enough so that as I trailed into the house after Eddie and big Welch, I saw right away that there was a place on the facing wall of what I took to be the living room where the wallpaper had been scorched. It looked like a wound, a gunshot wound in the flesh of the paper that had probably been white once but had turned to something shabby and stained, a yellowish-brown like smokers' teeth. About six feet up from the floor, in a circle the size of a basketball that was flat across its bottom, the hole was black and whatever it was had burned right through into the slats behind the Sheetrock wall. As it stretched up and out from that part, the wound went grayish until it faded into a jagged edge that ran almost to the ceiling. At its edges, the wallpaper was crisp and crinkled and smelled of cordite.

There had been something, a small table or maybe a stool, near the wall when the thing had exploded. You could tell because there was an almost ruler-straight horizontal line about waist high at the wall, just beneath the darkest part, the center of the wound. Beneath that line, there was less damage to the wall. That was the flat bottom of the round core of the blast. I stopped just inside the door and looked between Eddie and Welch as they went gingerly forward, to see if I could spot the table that had been there. Maybe I did, because knocked toward me, toward the front door and away from the wounded wall, a pair of wooden legs lay splintered on the floor. I thought I could make out some more wood around on the floor, about enough to account for a rather long-legged table with a top maybe a foot across.

Beneath the splintered wooden legs lay what I knew had been a man until pretty recently, but that was based more on my experience with these things than with the way the thing looked.

"Who is it?" Welch asked, looking at the two Customs agents who were standing to one side. They had shotguns in their hands, and I thought one of them looked ill.

"How the hell would I know?" the other one answered. He looked as if he was handling the sight and smell of the thing better than his partner.

"What's this?" I asked, bending to take a better look at something that lay against the yellowed baseboard of the front wall, about a foot to my left inside the door.

"Don't touch that!" one of the feds ordered, although I had no intention of touching anything and had not made a move to disturb it. This wasn't my first murder scene.

But I did not make a big thing about it when one of the Customs men strode over to me as if it mattered, or maybe he thought I hadn't heard him.

"Who's been notified?" Eddie asked.

"Uh . . . nobody, yet," said the one who looked ill.

"We just walked in on it a minute ago ourselves," his partner said, turning from me toward Eddie. Then to the sickly one he said, "Get Thompson on the radio, tell him to get out here as quick as he can."

The upset-looking one did not have to be told twice to step out into the fresh air. I heard him talking into his fist as the screen door twanged shut behind him.

"Jack, where the hell are we?" Eddie asked.

He knew where we were as well as I did, but I knew what he meant. This place was probably outside the Dallas city limits, but since the city had annexed Renner and slopped over into Collin County a few years ago, it was not easy to be sure anymore.

"Beats me," I told him.

"I'll check with North Central," he said, and he went out to his car.

That left me, Welch, and the bossy Customs man. If they had been on their game, they would have run me out. I had no business there, but I figured they didn't see much of this kind of action, and since I'd come with Eddie, it didn't register with them. Even big Welch forgot how much he did not like me, because he was trying so hard to guess who the dead man was.

Thompson wouldn't waste any time getting rid of me, I knew, if Eddie didn't do it first. I did not mind that Eddie had left me inside, which meant at least that he was not worried that I might have had anything to do with this. It had not been that way on my last case, and I was glad we would not have to go through all that again. He knew me well enough to believe my story, which was true after all, and I had the notion that he was in on this deal about as much to look after me as anything else.

People would be coming soon, I knew, and the whole thing would get very official, so I took advantage of whatever time I had in the house to see what I could see.

Since the officious one had taken it upon himself to guard the little dead critter beside the baseboard, I moved away toward the scarred far wall to take a closer look. When I got almost within arm's reach of the wall, I put both hands behind my back, just so my friend with the shotgun would not have to worry I might tamper with the evidence. What I found there was pretty hard to look at, but it told me something.

In about the dead center of the burned and blasted circle on the wall, well above the line that showed where the table had stood, something about the damage was different. From across the room, it had looked as black as the rest of it, but from up close I could see it was wet and oddly textured. There was stuff embedded in the wall there.

"They're en route," Eddie announced as he came back in through the screen door.

"Who is?" the bossy agent wanted to know.

"Everybody, the usual."

"Thompson?"

"Yeah, him too." Eddie looked at me but did not say anything.

"What do we do now?" Welch wondered aloud.

"Depends," Eddie said, taking charge of things. To the bossy one, he said, "Did you check the rest of the house?"

"Yeah, there's not much to it."

"There's enough for somebody to hide in. Are you satisfied there's nobody else here?"

The bossy one thought that over, and I knew he did not want to commit himself in case there turned out there was somebody stashed away under the floorboards or behind a secret panel or something. But he did not want to let on that they had not been thorough with their search either.

"No," he said. "There's nobody else."

"Then we might as well wait outside till the crime scene guys come. Let's go."

I followed Jack out the front door onto the porch, and Welch and the other Customs guy followed me. Eddie suggested to the one who had looked sick that he might ought to keep an eye on the back of the house just in case, and he went away around the corner of the house. Then Eddie suggested that we might as well have a look around outside until everybody else got there, and reminded us not to step on any tracks if we found any.

"What do you make of it?" Eddie asked me when we separated from Welch and the bossy one to look around the gravel driveway on the far side of our cars outside the fence.

"The bomb was in the telephone."

"Yeah."

"That's not all," I said.

154

"Isn't it?"

"No. The bomb killed him, whoever that is. But I don't think it did all that damage to the body."

"What do you mean?"

"It would be a small shaped charge probably, in the earpiece of the receiver. C-4 would do it. Maybe they hollowed out the whole phone, to make room for a bigger charge, but I'd say it was just a small shot in the earpiece, easier that way to fix it so the phone would still work."

"So?"

"So that's why he doesn't have a head anymore. But I don't think that accounts for the shape the rest of him is in."

"They torched him?"

"Yeah. I'd bet you'll find when you pick up what's left of him that there's not much fire damage to the floor underneath. I think somebody came in after he was dead and set fire to the body."

"Why?"

"Same reason they used a bomb instead of a gun in the first place."

"So he'd be hard to identify."

"Makes sense to me, Eddie. What do you think?"

"I think I hope we find enough teeth for a dental."

"He wore a toupee," I said.

"Who, the stiff?"

"I think so. I think that's what that thing was I spotted on the floor, the thing that looked like a fried hamster."

"Funny that didn't get burned too," Eddie mused.

"Probably blew off of him. When whoever it was came in after and burned him, maybe they didn't notice it. Maybe it was dark."

"Why couldn't it have come off somebody else?"

"It may have, but if somebody else dropped their hair, I think they would have noticed that and picked it up. Your lab guys should be able to tell if there's any powder or brains or whatever on it."

"Yeah."

I had a hell of a lot on my mind. Part of it was worrying about who the two jokers were who had waylaid me in the lobby of my building. Part of it was the feeling that I was somehow to blame for all this, the lady agent and whatever she had been through before the cavalry came to her rescue at Borodin's house and the disappearance of her loverboy Pink Shirt, Agent Sykes. But I think the worst of it was I was pretty sure I knew who that thing in the house used to be.

"How many characters do you know, Eddie," I asked, "in this deal who wear toupees?"

"You're asking me? I just got here." Eddie took a fresh toothpick out of his shirt pocket and worked it in the corner of his mouth. "Why? How many do you know?"

"Just one. Guy by the name of Teckmann."

Doctor Teckmann, I reminded myself, and I remembered the crooked smile on the kid's face in the photograph on the wall above his desk. I asked Eddie if he had anybody who could run by the Teckmann house over in Richardson and see if Mrs. Teckmann knew where her husband was. He said he did. I gave him the address and he went to his car to take care of that.

Agent Thompson drove up maybe three or four minutes before the first marked squad car. It turned out the house was in the county, outside of the Dallas city limits. It would be the sheriff's department's case, but my guess was they would not mind if Eddie stuck around. The uniformed deputy who got out of his car to find half a dozen federal agents with a story about a bomb killing looked like he would take all the help he could get. It was not long after that that a crime scene team from the Dallas Police Department showed up. I figured Eddie had offered their services to the county too. There was enough work to go around.

The technicians had been inside the house for a while when the ambulance pulled up, code one. There was no hurry. The deputy medical examiner came next, then a couple of plainclothes deputy sheriffs who would take the case. That was when Eddie was called to his car to take a radio message. It was a terse one, and I saw him throw the radio microphone down in the seat of his car and look at me. He stalked over to me and with one hand on my sleeve tugged me to one side.

"Anything you're not telling me on this one?" he asked.

"Not this time," I said, and I meant it. I looked into his eyes and did not blink until he did. "What is it?"

"This Mrs. Teckmann, in Richardson."

"Yeah?"

"She got the same treatment as the one in there." He jabbed his thumb toward the house and I had a picture of the old woman lying in a smoldering heap on the fake tile floor of her kitchen, pieces of her brains splattered on her avocado-green refrigerator. "Richardson's on the scene now. My guy called 'em as soon as he spotted her through a window."

"Anybody else in the house?" I asked.

Eddie shook his head no, and with another long look into my eyes, he turned away to go and find Thompson.

I knew then who the killer was. There was a hell of a lot of other stuff I was not sure about, and what I knew did not make any sense yet, but there it was. It was long odds I would ever be able to prove it one way or the other, but then I was not a cop anymore. I didn't have to prove anything. The thing was, I knew. Only I was not sure what I was going to do about it.

They wasted most of what was left of my day, another hour or so at the scene, then down to the county where the sheriff's investigators took my statement, then the whole gang of us loaded back into a small fleet of cars and drove the four blocks east from the county building in the seven hundred block of Commerce to the federal building in the eleven hundred block. The feds officed in a tall and very businesslike building named after a former mayor of Dallas who had gone on to serve as a congressman. His name was Earl Cabell, and I remembered him from television and from his being one of the local heavy hitters who greeted President and Mrs. Kennedy when they landed at Love Field in November of 1963. Other than that, I only remembered once when I was a kid living in Paris my dad had come to Dallas to see about getting a job. He had interviewed with a company called Cabell Dairies or something like that, that ran a chain of stores. He did not get the job, or else they may have offered it to him, but he decided not to make the move. Either way, he came back with stories about the man who had done the interviewing. It had not been Earl Cabell, but it had been someone who was ambidextrous. My dad had been awfully impressed with that, said the guy could write with both hands on different forms at the same time. It was the first time I had ever heard of anything like that, and I remember wondering if that was what it took to get on in a big town like Dallas. All of which has nothing to do with Earl Cabell unless he was connected with Cabell Dairies one way or another, but certainly had nothing to do with my being led to an elevator and somewhere into the bowels of the federal building to a small and Spartan room free of distractions like windows, ashtrays, or telephones, where Thompson glowered at me and left me in the care of Agent Welch and another of his men to give my statement all over again.

I was not holding back any information this time. Borodin had played me pretty cheap, but I knew I had not done anything wrong. I had made sure he was who he said he was and I had checked him out the best I could, considering my limited resources. The cash had moved me, and so had Borodin's scotch. Sasha, the skinny-dipper, had been a nice touch too, but I had not exactly stumbled headlong into anything. If a man wants you to do some dirty work for him, it's hard to spot the angle going in. If you are too careful about things, you wouldn't make much of a living in my business. I mean, I'm only as careful as I have to be, and I'm not doing all that good.

When they had asked me everything they could think of to ask and I had gone over that and my statement twice, Welch and his pal more or less excused themselves and left me to stew in my own juice. Only I did not have anything to stew over, and all I wanted them to do was quit wasting time on me and get on with it. I had not told any of them that I knew who had done the two murders, because I knew I would not be able to explain why I knew, and at best they would only throw each other a couple of looks and write it off. At worst, they might start thinking I knew more than I was telling, which I did not, and that could really sidetrack the whole deal. As I saw it, my best move was just to answer their questions and not do anything to get them excited, so they would tire of pawing me over and go look for the rat somewhere else. I did not think they would find him though.

I had been alone in the little room just long enough that I had stopped trying to decide whether I should light a cigarette and had started thinking how nice a tall scotch would be when Eddie came in with coffee in a plastic cup, the kind with no handles.

"How's it going?" he said, smiling but looking tired.

"It's not. Your friends out there doing anything worthwhile, or are all of them trying to figure out a way to hang it on me?"

"They're working it," Eddie answered. He put my coffee down on the little table that, with two straight-back armless chairs, was all the furniture in the room. It was not scotch, but he had remembered I liked artificial sweetener in mine, and it was not bad for office coffee.

Eddie took the other chair and kicked it back so he could put one of his feet up on the table that stood between us. I noticed he had closed the door when he came in and waited to see if he was going to interrogate me. He was pretty good at it, but he and I had learned too much of it together, so he could not put much over on me, any more than I could with him.

"Thompson doesn't like you," he said when he was comfortable.

"No shit," says I. Then I thought about it and added, "I don't blame him. He's taken casualties, and I'm mixed up in it."

That was something I could understand. I had had people under me a time or two in my time with the Dallas PD. Nothing major, my not being a supervisor or anything, just maybe a handful of guys on a deal I had set up or a rookie somebody gave me to break in. There was not much that I could think of that would have been worse than if something had happened to one of them, because I knew I would have gone out of my head replaying every step and trying to figure out if it had been my fault. That was what was eating Thompson, and I knew it. He was not mad at me, he was thinking the whole deal had gone to hell somehow, and since it was his deal it was his fault.

"How's the girl?" I asked.

"Okay. She got roughed up a bit, but not as bad as you did."

Is that so? I thought, and stole a quick look at my friend Eddie over the top of the coffee cup. Not that anything in his face told me anything. Eddie could play poker, as far as not letting his hole card show on his face. But he was pretty stingy with words too, and he had brought that up for a reason, that about the working over I had taken.

It had been on my mind too, naturally. Not up front with the two missing agents and the detonated Mrs. Teckmann and the stiff in the house to be named later. Actually, I was sure I knew who the dead man in the house with the Dobermans was, and that was tied in with my thinking I knew who the killer was, but that was another part of it. So, Eddie wanted to talk about the two characters who had beat me up. That suited me, because evening up that score was also on my agenda, along with settling with somebody for poor old Mrs. Teckmann.

CHAPTER
TWENTY-ONE

It HAD BEEN a man and a woman, I was pretty sure of that. The one near the elevator had been a woman, I had decided, and that was why I noticed something odd about the way she looked or moved, or whatever it was. The second one, the one who had come out of nowhere and zapped me with the gizmo, I had not seen that much of him. But I knew that one was a man, because I remembered his wrists, where they showed between the cuff of a sleeve and a glove. There were a few interesting possibilities, and it would be nice if Eddie were about to tell me something that would settle it for me.

My short list of suspects had consisted of three couples at first: the woman I still thought of as Sylvia Borodin and Pink Shirt, Sasha and the butler, and finally Della and her boyfriend. That was how these things work a lot of the time, you are focused on one thing over here and up jumps something else completely unrelated—that is what gets you. "Sylvia" and Pink Shirt made sense, if she had been Borodin's roving bride and somehow she and her boyfriend had made me tailing them. Della and her boyfriend, I did not like to think they were likely from the get-go, but only because I did not want to think Della would get herself mixed up in anything like that. Of course, I would have said she would never have paired off with an asshole like that in the first place, so that shows you all the hell I know. Sasha and Anton, them I would not have minded suspecting, although at the time I had not been able to figure what motive they would have had. Unless the little straight-backed butler was actually her father or her husband or something, and he had taken some offense at the way I leered at her in the pool. Or maybe my having walked in on her and Borodin knocking off a quick one, if that sort of thing mattered wherever they really came from. Anyway, I had pretty well eliminated "Sylvia" and Pink Shirt upon learning who they really were, and I was still holding Della and the hulk off to one side because I wanted to, so that pretty well left Borodin's cronies. Knowing now that they had been running a game on me, I thought it pretty likely, but I still was not sure why.

Eddie was not volunteering anything else, so I opened with a little question of my own. I had been answering enough of them.

"Not much worse, huh? Maybe almost exactly as much as me?"

"Not so much on the backs of her legs." Eddie pushed his lower lip up like he was making a considered estimate. "Or else she can take it better than you."

"Who can't?" I shrugged back at him. "Stun gun, like on me?"

"Yeah. Two people, she didn't get a look at either of them. She still doesn't know how they got into the condo."

"Hey, the way . . . tell me one more time, what's her real name?"

"Felicia Adams."

"Okay, I got it now. The way Felicia and . . ."

"Sykes, Jerry Sykes."

"Right. The way Felicia and Jerry were going at each other, you could have thrown a wheelbarrow through a picture window and they wouldn't have noticed. Two to one they forgot to lock the goddamn door when they went in after their little swim."

"Could be. They were getting after it, were they?"

"Like I wish I could say I used to do."

"Funny," he said.

"I'd say so, for a couple of cops working undercover."

"No, that's not the way I learned to do it," he admitted.

"When did you ever work undercover?" I jabbed him, almost laughing. But I did not laugh, because I saw a very quick and small thing skitter across his face, something I could easily have missed. But I did not miss it, and it was so . . . furtive that I would have had trouble describing it. He had let something out, with that little crack of his, and I could not be sure what.

There was that about Eddie, something I had known without really knowing for a long time. There was more to him than met the eye, and I knew from my own experience and a couple of things that had happened about what it was, in general. But I had never pushed him on it. Eddie had once been some kind of a spook. I had no way of knowing any more than that, but there had been the thing on my last case, a thing with some old army pal of his, that had triggered a nerve in me along those lines. And something he had said about the CIA once, when I thought he meant somebody in Washington, somebody who was a friend of a friend, only it had turned out that whoever it was had been a hell of a lot closer to home than that. Eddie had never worked undercover with the police department, I knew that because he had come along about the same time I had. I was the one who had "tightroped." If he had done any of it, it was another time and some other place. But like I said, I did not push him on it, and in return he did not prod me any. Like how I knew as much as I did about the way the killing had been done at the house that day. Eddie knew I had pulled a tour in Vietnam, and it was not a secret that most of my time I had been a sniper. But what I knew about improvised demolitions and where I learned it, Eddie had never made it his business to find out. It occurred to me, that if I was right about him, he might not have to find out from me. It was an eerie thing if you dwelled on it.

"I'd say it's about ninety, ninety-five percent that the same ones that took you out did the job on the two agents," Eddie said, giving me something to think about besides when he might have learned how to work undercover.

"Why me?" I asked.

"To keep you out of the way, is all I can figure."

"I was already out of it. Borodin had my report and he paid me off."

"So where were you headed when they jumped you, Jack?"

"I see what you mean."

I certainly did. Because I had been on my way to "Sylvia" . . . Felicia's condo, for one more look. And I had called Red's to leave word that I would be late. So either they had tapped my phone or else they just kicked the shit out of me for drill, just to make sure I didn't get them on videotape kidnapping the two agents. It was something to think about.

"Okay," I said. "So they're pros."

And they had done a pretty fair professional job on me. It was midafternoon by this time, well over twelve hours since the beating, and I was still nowhere near what you would call mobile. But they had not killed me. And that meant something, to me if to no one else.

"They are."

"Okay, Eddie. Get me another cup of coffee and let's play twenty questions, or two hundred questions, or whatever the hell your game is."

"What?"

"Goddamnit, Eddie, you know something, you know the whole spitball thing, for all I know. More than likely, I'm not cleared for any of it, which is okay with me. I'm especially trained to work in the dark. But if you're going to let me in on it, how about just spitting it out and let's get the hell on with it."

"Jack . . ." He put an almost genuinely hurt look on his face and shrugged at me, holding his palms up like he was an altar boy and I was accusing him of something venal. He was pretty loose, I thought, and almost enjoying parts of this. Of course, the two murders were out of his jurisdiction, and he was not on anybody's hot seat on this one. He was pretty well along for the ride. And nobody had whipped his ass either. He had a pretty high tolerance for pain when it was mine.

"Give it to me or shut the hell up," I said.

"Okay, here it is, as far as I've been able to put it together . . ." He leaned across the table toward me and tossed a look over his left shoulder at the closed door. "Jerry and Felicia were working an Operation Exodus deal . . ."

That was as far as he got before my ignorance reared its ugly head.

"Operation Exodus, Jack. It's been in the papers, for Christ's sake."

I made a note to start scanning the headlines in my neighbor's *Times Herald* in the future, instead of just Xeroxing his crosswords.

"So?" I answered, like who has time to read the papers.

"Customs not only catches people smuggling stuff into the country, they also catch people sneaking stuff out."

"You're kidding," I said. I really did not know that.

"No, I'm not kidding. That's why they call it 'Exodus,' get it?"

I nodded at him and he went on.

"High-tech stuff mostly, computer chips and whatnot."

"Two killings and a brace of feds kidnapped over computer parts?" I asked. It seemed extreme.

So Eddie explained it to me, or tried to. Did I know what a DRAM was, had I ever heard of them, he wanted to know. Yeah, I told him, it was like a shot of booze, a dram. No, no, he told me.

"Jack, do you know anything about chips at all?"

"It's hard to eat dip without them."

"Computer chips, Jack."

"What won't they think of next," I said.

So off we went from there. RAMs, ROMs, I don't know what all, and me sitting there thinking I wished he had brought the coffeepot in the little interrogation room with him, because I could have used another shot of caffeine so I could act interested. Back to DRAMs again. It turned out a DRAM was a particular kind of computer chip, one that can store 256,000 bits of information. Big numbers do not mean much to me, because I have always been busy with nickel-and-dime stuff. Like when I hear the federal budget deficit is a trillion dollars, what the hell does that mean? Who can picture a trillion of anything? Eight bits make a byte, Eddie told me, careful to spell it out so I would not lose track of things. From there he went off on another kind of chip, a computer chip he said could store one million bits of data. That one they called a SRAM. DRAMs were very important to the military as well as other people, because, Eddie explained to me, since they were tiny, you could do fantastic things with them. You could make weapons smart. Who knew, maybe you could make airplanes that could fly themselves, or anything. SRAMs were the latest thing in the business, and it was big news that some American and Japanese companies were supposed to be going in together and make the things. Naturally, the Chinese, Arabs, and others would kill to get their hands on these things. Thing was, there was a new kind of chip almost nobody knew about yet, even bigger and better than the SRAMs, which because of some kind of breakthrough, could almost double the capacity of the chip. Eddie could tell this was all over my head, but he assured me it was mind-boggling, breathtaking. It was a hell of a big deal.

The thing was, Doctor Teckmann was supposed to be the brains behind this new super-duper-chip thing. He went back a long way with the government and TI and who knew what else, and somehow he had come up with the angle that what they called "revolutionized" the chip racket. Only word leaked out one way or another, and one day this guy Galipolus, Borodin's ex-partner, turned up. He made a pass at Teckmann, showed him some serious money and promised there was a hell of a lot more where that came from. Friends of his were very interested in the doctor's work, and they would make Teckmann rich beyond his wildest dreams if only he would supply him with the secret of the superchips. A sample, maybe his notes, whatever it would take for them to catch up on the thing, so they would not get left at the starting gate. This new chip was that big a deal, Eddie assured me.

"So then what happened?" I asked.

"Teckmann did what a good citizen is supposed to do. He dropped a dime, called the feds, and told them what was up."

"He was making this chip on his own?"

"Nah, Jack, don't be silly. It takes an incredible amount of hardware to make chips. Teckmann had done some theoretical work on the thing, and he got with some people who had the plant to do the work. They were making a prototype."

"Does it work?" I asked.

"What do you mean?"

"I mean, does the goddamn thing work, whatever it's supposed to do? They've tested it?"

"Yeah, I guess so. I don't know all the details. Why?"

"Just wondering." I knew how devious you would have to be to think the way I was thinking, that you would have to be more than a little paranoid. But that did not bother me. Like they say, it ain't paranoia if the bastards are really out there.

"Anyway," Eddie continued. "One thing and another, it wound up here in Customs. Thompson put Adams and Sykes on it, to work a sting on Galipolus and his friends."

Eddie looked at me with one eyebrow cocked and a glint in his eye, but I did not say anything.

"They worked it out where Teckmann would put Felicia Adams in it and he would introduce her to Galipolus as his girlfriend."

"Sure," I said, shaking my head and fumbling for a cigarette. "They made such a pat couple."

"That was the idea," Eddie explained patiently. "Here was this old geeky computer guy running around with this hot little number, so that sets up his story why he's willing to sell his secrets, see? You gotta figure she's only going to stick around with him if he's spending money on her, and he doesn't have that kind of money, right?"

"How'd Sykes get into it?"

"That was Thompson's idea. Sykes is an old hand, just

transferred in from Silicon Valley out in California. Knows this high-tech stuff cold. See, Felicia is still a little green, I don't think she had worked any of these deals before."

Why did that make me feel the way it did, I wondered.

"So they told Galipolus that he was . . . who?"

"Her boyfriend. They let themselves be seen by Galipolus one night after a meet, and when Galipolus asked, it was like he'd caught them cheating on the old guy. I like that part of it. See, what they were showing Galipolus was this: Teckmann was turning around his country for money on account of the girl. Only she's turning Teckmann around for her boyfriend. I like that, because it makes Galipolus think he's dealing with a whole gang of cheaters, see? It's something he can relate to, he can believe that kind of stuff. I like it, don't you?"

"He would be comfortable with people like that, I guess," I said. I wondered what had gone wrong somewhere up the line between Galipolus and Borodin, who had turned whom around there.

"You're damn right. Also, it makes Galipolus think he's in on a secret, that he knows something Teckmann doesn't know, and he likes that, too, I'd be willing to bet."

"So what went wrong?" I asked.

"You."

"Oh yeah."

"Borodin and Galipolus are in the same racket, used to be partners. Maybe you already knew that. So, Borodin gets a line on his old pal somehow, gets wind of this big deal he's working on, and decides to cut himself in. Only he doesn't do anything that would screw things up. He scouts around a little first. Felicia caught his eye. He must have had somebody tailing Galipolus . . ."

"Anton, the butler," I offered. I had already told the feds about him and about Sasha.

"Right. And Borodin was smart enough to key on the girl."

"And he hired me to tail her and get pictures."

"Yeah. You couldn't have known, Jack. It's not your fault."

"Okay, if you say so. How did Thompson get wind of it, that I was involved?"

"His people had a tap on Galipolus's phone, at his house. They intercepted a call. Somebody, they think it was Borodin, called Galipolus and told him the girl was a fed."

"Did they say how they knew?"

"Yeah, said a private eye had shot some pictures of her."

"What, screwing in the pool? From that they figured out she was Customs?"

"Nah, man. Meeting with Thompson, that afternoon at the Wine Press. Somebody on the other side made Thompson. I don't know him that well myself, but apparently our friend Thompson was a pretty big player back East and made a name for himself. Anyway, somebody made him and put two and two together."

This feeling that I had been trying not to get came on me strong at that, ran up my back and around my neck, and licked down into my chest and tickled my heart. Because I had not taken any pictures of Thompson at the Wine Press. Not inside or outside or anywhere else, just the girl and Pink Shirt playing footsies in the car. This deal was beginning to smell a certain way, a particularly nasty way that I knew a hell of a lot better than I would have liked.

"I see" was all I said to Eddie. I did not say anything more, because I knew there was nobody I could trust. Eddie was all right, I was as sure of that as I could be of anybody, but I was also satisfied that the little room where we were having this conversation was wired for sound, and that others were probably listening. And who knew who would be listening later, when the tapes were played? There was nothing I could say to Eddie that I wanted any of the others to hear too, so I did not say anything.

CHAPTER
TWENTY-TWO

By THE TIME Eddie finished telling me the stories his fed friends had asked him to tell me and Thompson and his boys had said they were through with me for the time being but that I should not leave town, and Eddie had given me a lift back to my office building, it was late and I was hungry.

On the ride from downtown to my office parking lot, I had told Eddie he needed to watch his ass on this one. By saying only that, I had hoped that I could put him on his guard without getting him any more involved than he already was. Of course, you cannot handle Eddie like that. He pressed me for details. He laughed when I insisted that we find a better place to talk, but he humored me and pulled off the freeway and into a parking lot. He even went along with me when I wanted him to get out of the car, because I could not be sure somebody had not put one of those nifty voice-activated rigs in his squad car, his take-home Diplomat. After all, it had been sitting in the parking lot downtown for a long time.

Eddie quit grinning when I told him what I knew. What I knew was that I had not burned the two undercover agents. When Borodin made that phone call to Galipolus and knew about Thompson, he was not talking about anything I had told him or any pictures I had shown him, because I had not taken any photos of Thompson, and I had not bothered to mention the black man in the Brooks Brothers wardrobe. It was Pink Shirt I had thought was important, because he was the one screwing "Mrs. Borodin." All of which meant something I did not have to explain to Eddie. It meant there was a joker in the deck somewhere. Somebody else had tipped Borodin. Why Borodin called Galipolus at home when he knew the feds were working on him and his line might be tapped, that was anybody's guess. Another layer of deceit, another side bet on this little crapshoot. Two murders already, and who knew what was next?

"That was Teckmann in the house, wasn't it?" Eddie asked.

"His toupee, anyway," I answered.

"They got teeth. Part of a bridge. We should know something in the morning," he said. Then he looked at me as if I were not there for a couple of minutes, and I could tell he was doing some deep thinking. Finally, he told me that I was well out of it and I should stay out of it.

"We'll see. It's not your deal, Eddie," I said.

"Whatever. Why don't you take me back to my place now. You guys never even offered to feed me, and I'm starving."

"Stay clear, Jack. That's my advice to you."

"Whatever you say."

So that was how I came to be standing in the parking lot in front of my office building shortly after six that evening, wondering what it was about me that seemed to attract this kind of trouble. I did not come up with an answer, and since I had not spotted anything that looked like surveillance outside, I went in.

There was no one lurking in the lobby, I was glad to see, and I took the elevator up because my legs were still too gimpy for climbing stairs. So I was surprised when the door opened and I found I had company waiting.

Joe and Speed had made themselves comfortable around Della's desk and were playing what looked like a hotly contested game of hearts. They looked up when I stepped off the elevator, and I had a picture for a second of those looks on their faces if it had been someone else instead of me, someone with mischief on his mind and a gun in his hand. There had not been much about guns in this deal so far, except for Borodin asking me about mine. But I did not think a little gunplay was out of the question, and I did not care for the idea of Joe and Speed getting in the way of anything like that.

"Hey, man." Speed grinned up at me from the cards in his hand. "Where you been?"

"You're not moving too smooth there, Bro," Joe chimed in.

"What are you two doing here?" I asked.

"Waiting for you to show or call or . . . something." You could see all the way through Speed, the guy could not hide a thing. He was hurt by my tone of voice, I imagined. Or maybe it was the look on my face.

"Are you all right?" Joe asked.

"I'll live."

"What happened to you?" Speed wanted to know. "You didn't show last night, and . . ."

"Yeah, I guess I owe you guys a dinner," I said, making a little face to show them I felt bad about standing them up.

"Never mind that," Joe cut in before I could make up anything witty to say, the way hard-boiled private eyes are supposed to do when they're bunged up and a day late for something. "You get beat up or something?"

"Does it show that bad?"

"If you know what to look for. They didn't mark you up much."

Joe had been around the track a time or two himself, and he did not miss much.

"Only where it wouldn't show," I told him.

"Who was it?"

"I'm still working on that."

Joe slid off of Della's chair so I could sit down and went to drag himself up one of the straight-back jobs that lined the wall outside Mrs. Farragut's office.

"Why didn't you call us?" Speed asked.

"I should have, Speed. Sorry, but I've had a pretty busy day."

"Della was worried about you too," he added.

"Yeah?"

"Sure. We called her trying to get a line on you, and she said she hadn't seen you or heard from you all day. She was plenty upset when she left."

"How long ago was that?" I wondered aloud.

"Half an hour ago, maybe. What's the deal?"

"Yeah," Joe chimed in, settling into his new chair. "Is it part of the deal we were working on?"

"Probably." I pulled a cigarette out of the pack in my pocket and scrunched down in Della's chair, trying to get my back fixed so it would not hurt so much. I was trying to remember if there was any scotch left in the bottle in my desk drawer. If there was, it would not be enough to go around, and I did not feel like running out for some more. "This thing is all screwed up, guys. I'm afraid I've gotten us into something real nasty."

"So?" Speed demanded, thinking I might not tell him the rest of it, just because I had stopped to take a breath and light my cigarette.

So I told them how I had spent my day, at least as much of it as I thought they needed to know so I could be sure they understood that we had stumbled into something serious. I did not want them to be tempted to do anything cute when I told them to butt out.

"And that's it," I said when I had finished.

"Jesus, Jack," Joe whistled softly. "You got a knack for it, don't you?"

"I guess. Does that square me with you for not calling, Speed?"

"What the hell are friends for, Jack?" he answered me with his own question.

"Not for getting them mixed up in this kind of trouble. What I want you guys to do is to drift out of here and amuse yourselves for a couple of days. When this thing is over, I'll give you a call and make good on that dinner I owe you."

"You sure you don't need somebody watching your back?" Joe asked. His voice had about the right tone in it. He would stay in it if I wanted him to, if I needed him, or if I thought one more would make any difference, but he was by no means eager for it. His feelings would not be hurt if I waved him off. He was a young guy, in his mid-twenties probably, although I had never gone to the trouble of checking, with a straight dark face and a smile full of teeth that were white and straight. He rode motorcycles and had about the right outlook for this business. I knew he could handle himself in some pretty rough company, but he was not looking for trouble by any means either. He had told me about his family on a night or two when there was nothing else to do because we were lurking in the shadows somewhere waiting for somebody to screw up. His dad was very old, but still worked hard on their ranch somewhere down in south Texas close to the border. Joe was the youngest of a platoon of kids, and his people were very straight-laced and honorable. His mother worried about him because he lived in the big city and because when he had tried to explain to her what he did for a living, following people, she had gotten the idea that he was some kind of a spy, a secret agent like on TV.

"I'm sure," I told him, with a nod and a smile. He was a good man, and there was no point in wasting him on a deal like this.

"What about me?" Speed piped up. Unlike Joe, Speed wanted in, even though he did not know what the hell the deal really was. The little I had told him should have been enough to put him on a dead run for the nearest exit. That was how Speed was, and I attributed it to the fact that he read too much.

"No," I said, shaking my head with my eyes clamped down to show him I was not in the mood to argue about it.

"Okay," he said, muttered, actually, like a kid who was not going to get to go to the game after all. "Fine."

"Stick by your phone though, if you don't mind," I added. "If it breaks that way, I'll call you."

"I hope so."

174

I looked at Joe in a way to show him I would like for him to get Speed out of there before anything else happened and it was too late to keep him out of harm's way. Joe saw what I meant and got to his feet.

"Let's go, Speed-o," he said. "Man's got a lot on his mind."

"Yeah." Speed was not happy with me. He figured he owed me, and I was not letting him pay back.

Also he was probably worried about me, and silly enough to think I would have a better chance of it with him along. That was most certainly not the case, which is nothing against Speed. It was just that different people had things they could do.

Joe got Speed out of his chair and into the elevator in only another five minutes or so. At last the elevator door closed, and I was left alone. There was no answer at Della's apartment.

I dug the scotch bottle out of my desk drawer to find it was too near empty to suit me. But I did not feel like hiking out to get more, so I consoled myself with the notion that I needed a clear head anyway.

No matter how many I cadged from Della at our office parties or pilfered from Mrs. Farragut's supply cabinet while her back was turned, I never seemed to have any clean paper cups when it came time to drink scotch around my place. The particular cups I could not find on this occasion were white ones done up with red painted-on ribbons and holly wreaths, and bells if my memory served. They were from the office Christmas party. It occurred to me that I was looking for them in August, but that was not particularly relevant.

After wasting more time than the damn cups were worth, I gave up the search and lugged my bottle into the lobby of the suite of offices. I would have to make do with one of the white plastic cups in the dispenser beside the coffee maker, the ones Mrs. Farragut kept there for new customers. For old customers, she had real cups. But that did not work either, because apparently Mrs. Farragut was hip to the fact that I, or someone, had been borrowing supplies. The plastic cup dispenser was empty, and all the coffee cups, the real cups, were gone, probably locked out of sight in the supply cabinet to which only Mrs. Farragut had a key. I did not have a personal coffee cup of my own, because Della had appropriated it as a home for one of the desperate-looking plants she had come back from lunch with the other day. She had airily promised to buy me another, but then there had been the business with her boyfriend, and that is the way it goes.

So that is why I was sitting in my squeaky swivel chair with my feet up on my desk and my shoes off, drinking cheap scotch out of the bottle, when I heard the distinctive click of high heels on the tile floor in front of the elevators.

CHAPTER
TWENTY-THREE

IT IS NOT as if my circle of lady friends was all that limited, and of course if this had been the beginning instead of the tail end of a deal, it might have been a mysterious and troubled blonde coming to hire me to find her lost husband or ransom a jade necklace or something along those lines. But it was not the beginning of anything. So I assumed it was Della, dropping by to check on me. I even imagined I recognized the particular cadence and resonance of her high heels tapping on the floor outside my office. I was glad she had come, glad we would have a chance to talk. To show you how glad I was it was Della, I was even thinking about how I could bring myself to tell her I would apologize to her boyfriend if that would make her happy, when my office door clicked oddly and swung slowly in toward me.

It was not Della.

It was a gun, a blue-black stubby little fucker with a hole in the tip of its snout that looked big enough to shove my whole head into. In which case, I imagined that if I yelled it would have made an echo. It looked that big.

It was the gun that had made the odd click when my door

swung open, the gun bumping against the outside of the door. I made a note to try to snap on the sound quicker next time. Call me an optimist, I was thinking there might be a next time.

The gun was in a hand that looked pinkish and a little on the small side. I noticed that the finger that lay upon the trigger terminated in the pearl luster of a manicured nail. The arm was just an arm as I worked my way up slowly from the muzzle of the gun. Somewhere in the back of my head I thought whoever it was would not shoot me until I had looked into her eyes. So whether it meant anything or not, I stopped when I got to her mouth. It was pink too, a shade of rose, actually, and pouty in a way that seemed familiar. She had long hair and it was not done up, and of course I knew who it was, and I was relieved. Not enough to move or say anything cute, but relieved just the same.

"Mister Kyle," said the rosy mouth.

"Miss . . ."

"Adams."

"Thank you. Miss Felicia Adams."

I knew her as Sylvia Borodin, and that was why I had so much trouble with her real name. Beyond family and a handful of friends, I don't have much room for people in my head, and apparently not enough for more than one name apiece.

"You're alone?" she asked, with me still looking at her mouth because I thought it might matter.

"Not anymore. Come in."

She stepped across my threshold and managed to circle her right elbow around and push the door to behind her without letting the ugly snout of her gun travel more than an inch, not by any means far enough that if she had pulled the trigger it would have missed me. From my seat, it looked like she was holding it just about on the second button of my shirt. Center mass. Good girl, just like they taught you at the academy.

"Drinking alone, that's a bad sign," she said.

"Care to join me?"

"It's supposed to mean you're an alcoholic or something, isn't it?" she persisted, leaning against my door with her steady gun.

"Not in my case," I assured her.

"Why not?"

"Because I'm just a drunk, don't go to any meetings. I was grandfathered in, honorary membership."

"I see."

"Listen, Felicia . . ." I began, then halted when she moved. She was only turning the knob that locked my office door and not bracing to shoot. "May I call you Felicia?"

"If I can call you T.J."

"T.J.?" I asked, forgetting for the moment about the other thing, the gun and the purpose of her visit.

"Turnaround Jack. That's your name, isn't it?"

"I don't . . ."

"Your real name, I mean," she added quickly, with a twist to her voice that was supposed to tie in with my not being able to remember her real name or something.

"Not really."

"Isn't it?"

"No. Just Jack, thank you."

"Oh. Perhaps I was misinformed. I thought your real name was Turnaround Jack, T.J. to your friends, because you specialize in fucking over your friends, or is it getting fucked over by your friends?"

"You want to take a little care with the language," I scolded her.

"You're kidding."

It was not that I was prudish. But one of my pet theories and peeves is that people do not appreciate language. They have no idea how important it is. Any word may arise naturally from a person's nature and the circumstances, and carries the seed of poetry in doing so. It was unnatural, the way she said it. It put me in mind of how I thought it ought to be used and made me remember another time and another woman. Fresh into the cool adobe rooms from our day out on the boat on the shimmering blue, a tepid shower together. We had grappled over an unmade bed and drunk Mexican beer and made love and sat crosslegged and naked on the bed and drunk more Mexican beer and peeled and eaten shrimp and made more love. She had

179

used that word and it had been perfectly natural and nothing else would have done in its place. I snapped myself back into the unnatural present, which consisted pretty much of Felicia and her gun and too little scotch to go around. I resolved not to think anymore, certainly not at least until Felicia had done something reassuring with that gun.

"No, I'm not," I answered. From the look of her she had not missed me while I had been in my reverie. I thought again what a mysterious thing the mind is. "I don't object to profanity. Heartfelt profanity is one of my favorite things."

"Shut the fuck up," she barked. "You're drunk."

"Do you really think so?" I asked, and I meant it. I had not thought there was enough scotch for it.

"Put your hands where I can see them," she ordered.

The whole thing was bullshit, and as I raised my hands and put them on the top of my head, I considered telling her so. In fact, I did tell her so.

"This is all bullshit," I said.

"What do you mean?"

"Your heart's not in it, and, frankly, I resent the whole thing."

"What thing?" she asked.

"The . . . I'll tell you what . . . Felicia. Put your gun somewhere safe and I'll tell you."

"Fuck you."

"Well, either shoot me or put the son of a bitch up or else get the hell out."

You would have thought someone had talked to her that way somewhere along the line in whatever training school she had been through, but apparently they had not. She honestly did not know what to do. I was not sure what she ought to do either. Before she came barging in, I had been ruminating about the whole Borodin deal and very upset that there did not seem to be any way I was going to be able to deal myself in for the payoff. The feds had the case, it was big league, obviously not my style, and that was that. Eddie Cochran had made that pretty clear. I was to count my blessings, and abrasions, and sit on my thumbs until the story either broke in the newspapers or else did not break at all, in which case in a few months or whenever he thought it had all cooled down enough to breach security, he would let me know how it had worked out. I did not like that a bit and had been racking my brain looking for a way back in. I had scores to settle and daffy old Mrs. Teckmann had not deserved to have a telephone blow up in her ear.

Now, ta-da-a-a-a, enter the mysterious and ever bewildering Sylvia Borodin, aka Felicia Adams. There was still the off chance that I was about to be shot for having committed real or imagined wrongs.

"Come on, come on, come on!" I screamed at her. "Drop your drawers or get off the goddamn stage!"

As drunk and muddled as this may have sounded, I was pleased that she cocked her pistol and raised it to eye level, her arm straight as a board, her left eye squinted shut, her right eye looking down the stubby barrel through the square black gap of the rear sight and along the shallow grooves atop the barrel, aligning the bulged ramp that was the front sight with the second button on my shirt. She was calling my bluff. Only I was not bluffing.

"There ya go!" I heckled her. "That's the ticket."

Nothing happened. She squinted, she aligned, she breathed, then held her breath, then breathed again, then breathed halfway out and held it . . .

"You're talking maybe seven, eight feet, bitch!" I yelled at her, perfectly aware that now that she had cocked the hammer on her Smith & Wesson Model 19 .357 magnum with the 2½-inch barrel it would only take about four pounds of pressure to touch the damn thing off. "You don't have to compute windage! Just pull the fucking trigger!"

"Oh shut up," she spat, as in one motion she limbered her right arm to let the revolver tumble out of sight into the shoulder bag I had not noticed before. She sank into one of the two cheap chairs against the wall of my office.

CHAPTER
TWENTY-FOUR

AFTER WE SAT not talking for a couple of minutes, she asked if I would mind if she had a drink. I demurred, pointing out that I did not have any glasses. She said that she did not mind drinking out of the bottle, so I had to level with her and tell her that there just was not enough scotch to go around. To which she reacted pretty well, I thought. She got a twinkle in her eye and said something about it was going to be a long night. The hell you say, I said, or something to that effect. Too long to face sober, she said.

While I was pondering that, she stood quicker than I could have, which, the gun having been taken out of the picture and no longer monopolizing my attention, led me to consider her condition. It looked better than my condition felt. She was wearing something simple but, now that I noticed, incredibly sexy. Which, I realized after I had looked her up and down twice, had more to do with the way she was put together than with the outfit. It was what on a lot of people would have been a skirt and blouse. P-f-f-t. See 'em every day, all the time, right? Women wear them to the office, no big deal. But this kid was unlimited. By which I mean you could have put her in farmer's overalls and she still would look this particular way. She looked like she was moving around inside her clothes when all she was really doing was just standing there. There was something about her. She was a throwback, in a nice way. Nowadays—and I know this is tricky because what's in and what's out, it all changes all the time—we still have sex symbols, but they all look pretty streamlined to me. This kid, she was more the Marilyn Monroe type, only with dark hair. I mean, she had curves, like Rhonda Fleming had. She had that thing with the teeny waist you could put your hands around and hips that swelled, the kind of body that in the old days men were supposed to have leveled cities for, cities with walls around them and old churches. That was the kind of body she had.

She was saying something about stepping around to the corner package store and picking up a quart of something to while the night away. She was talking as if all that business with the butt-ugly revolver had never happened. Okay, I am a flexible person. I have learned to adjust, or whatever. Good idea, says I. You do that. Know where the nearest liquor store is, do you? I ask. She does. Won't I go with her, she asks. Thank you, no, I answer. Thing is, I've got my shoes off, and once I sink that low, I don't like to go out again. Besides, I am in no condition to be up and about. You see, says I, you may not believe such things happen in this day and time, but I was only this morning worked over by a couple of pros, and I have the distinct impression that one of their primary goals was to see to it that I did not get out of this chair and go anywhere.

When I said that, or whatever it really was that I actually said, was the first time that Felicia Adams did or said anything that I believed.

"Really?" she said, one eyebrow rising and her eyes narrowing. "The . . . uh, stun gun . . . ?"

How did she do that, I asked myself. With just her eyebrows and that about the . . . "uh, stun gun" . . . she let me know what she meant, that she had gotten only the stun gun. She was curious to know what else I had gotten, and why, too.

"It wasn't so much the cattle prod," I began. "It was when

they put down the implements and kicked the shit out of me."

"Oh?" was all she said.

But from that I parsed out a few things. First, her curiosity had been real about what had been done to me, which meant at least that she had not been in on that. Second, it had not been done to her, and this led me to surmise that she had gotten the better of the bargain, for reasons yet unknown.

Felicia seemed to be very worried that I would not be there when she got back. To put her mind at ease, I pointed out a few salient truths. She was going for scotch. I was too stove-up to go anywhere. I would be out of scotch soon. She would be back soon.

Finally, there was nothing left for it but that she go. And she did. She took the stairs, I noted, and she had not bothered to ask about getting back inside my building, even though it was supposed to be locked at night. Good for her, was all I thought. At least she could get through a door if she had to.

When I was sure she had gone, I called Eddie Cochran at home. There was no answer. I called his office, and a surly masculine voice told me Lieutenant Cochran was not in. When I asked when Lieutenant Cochran would be back, the surly voice put me on hold. In no more than seven or eight minutes he came back on the line, and did not mask his surprise that I had lingered so long. He said that Lieutenant Cochran was out of town and it was not known exactly when he would be back. I thanked him twice as many times as he deserved, which was once, and after a few minutes dialed Dallas Homicide again. This time I got lucky and a woman answered. Although I did not recognize her voice, I assumed, based upon the slightly interested tone of her voice, that she was not a policewoman but was actually that most valuable of City Hall denizens, a clerk-slash-typist.

"I'm trying to get hold of Lieutenant Cochran," I told her in as earnest a voice as I could muster. "I'm a friend of his, I used to be a Dallas officer, and it's really important."

"Jack Kyle, is that you?"

I did not know who she was, but I played it out the best I

could. The upshot of it was that Eddie was out of town for real, as far as I could tell. Some kind of school. Came up without much notice.

That part of it fit, once I had given up trying to get in touch with Eddie and sat back to think about it. He was somebody, something, more than showed on the surface. And people elsewhere did not want him on the scene when whatever was in the works came off. Great. Where did that leave me? Oddly enough, it left me in a pretty good spot, relatively speaking. At least it was the kind of a spot that I was getting used to. Okay, somebody had seen to it that Eddie was out of the picture. That left me and whatshername, Felicia, if she actually ever came back with the promised bottle of hooch. What were we supposed to do about the whole thing, and who had sent her to me? Whatever their game was, whoever they were, I had reasons enough to play out the hand.

CHAPTER TWENTY-FIVE

LO AND BEHOLD, she did come back. And she brought scotch. It was enough to make you believe in . . . something, anyway. Thirst and loneliness, maybe.

We poured some into two of the clear plastic glasses she brought back with her, the kind with the store logo on the sides. She left my office to prowl around inside the small refrigerator Mrs. Farragut kept out of sight beyond her locked supply cabinet, and came back with three or four cubes of ice in her drink. Then Felicia Adams made herself comfortable in one of the chairs by the door of my office, although I was pretty sure I had remembered to offer her a more comfortable one that I would not have minded stealing from one of my neighbors' offices. She wiggled her feet out of her shoes and tucked her legs up underneath her and looked as if she were set for a long wait.

"What are you doing here?" I asked.

"Drinking."

"No shit," I retorted. It was getting late and I did not feel up to a lot of cat-and-mouse bullshit. "Why?"

"Actually"—she took a pretty healthy slug of the stuff in her plastic glass—"I came here to kill you."

"I don't believe you."

"Why not?"

"Because you didn't."

"I might yet," she said, not smiling, and I noticed that her right hand dangled from the arm of her chair, not far from the open bag on the floor beside her.

"Do this any way you want to," I told her. "Because I'll admit I don't have anything better to do. Which doesn't say much for me, I know, but there it is. If you hadn't showed up, I can't say I'd be doing anything any more worthwhile than this anyway, except that I'd be out of booze by now. So take your time, do it any way you like. But I'll give you a tip. Level with me. It'll save us both a lot of time, and your badass act is really too lame to pass."

"Is it?"

"It's out of character, and you can't act for shit. Besides, the premise won't stand up."

"I beg your pardon?"

"What the hell are you supposed to be, a rogue cop? Rogue G-man, G-person, whatever the hell you are. You're a nice kid, clean enough record to get by the background check, too young to have gone far wrong, and you're on the job, for Christ's sake. Besides, I haven't done anything you'd want to kill me for. It doesn't make sense."

"You have a short memory, T.J."

"Don't call me that. And what have I forgotten?"

"You burned us, me and Jerry. This whole fucked-up deal is your fault. And Jerry . . . whatever's happened to Jerry, that's your fault too."

Her use of the word sounded more natural that time, and when she brought Jerry into it, suddenly she was a lot more convincing.

"Didn't anybody tell you? That wasn't my fault."

"The hell it wasn't."

"Ask Thompson. Even he knows by now." I was sure Eddie had touched base with him. "There's a leak somewhere. I didn't take any pictures of Thompson when you and Jerry met with him at the Wine Press, and he wasn't in any of my reports."

"I don't believe you."

"You don't have to. Ask Thompson."

"That would be . . . awkward," she said as she freshened her drink.

"I'd been told you were Borodin's wife, Sylvia," I explained, wondering as I did what she had meant about it's being awkward to ask Thompson. "My job was to see if you were having an affair. Pink Shirt . . . Jerry was my concern, not Thompson. And you were having an affair. What was that all about?"

"What do you mean?" she asked, with an odd look in her eye.

"In the pool. You and Jerry. That wasn't part of the drill when I . . ."

"You're a Peeping Tom, T.J. A sneaky, slimy . . ."

"Have another drink."

She did, and so did I. She drank deeply from her glass, and I could tell that most of her ice had melted, but she did not mind enough to go get any more. She had a lot on her mind, and I thought part of what was going on was that she was trying to decide about me, about where I fit into all of it. I could not be sure which way she would go, or what would happen next.

"Tell me about Jerry," I said.

That got her started. I tried to remember a time when a woman's eyes would have lit up like that talking about me, but I did not honestly think of one. Even my ex-wife, back at the very first, had never shown that kind of feeling for me. This kid was not worried about reasons, reason was not any part of it for her. Reason all went the other way, but as she drank and talked to me about Jerry, I wondered if she might not be in the wrong line of work.

Jerry Sykes was practically a legend in the Service, she told me, and I remembered that the gorilla, Welch, had used almost the same words. Jerry had been at it a long time, he was almost as old as I was. She did not put it that way to hurt my feelings, it just more or less slipped out. Only she compounded the insult by hastening to assure me that she meant no offense, that she liked older men, as long as they had taken care of themselves, as long as they still had a little fire, a little fun in their eyes, like Jerry. She did not say that I did not have fun or fire or anything else very exciting in my eyes, but she did not have to. I lit a cigarette and when I did she made such a face, full of tolerant disgust that bordered on pity, that I did not bother to offer her one.

Jerry was the hero of a dozen tales of derring-do in the Service, she told me. She had heard stories about him at training school, some of the amazing things he had done. He was cited as an example by the instructors of what an undercover agent should be. So I could imagine, she assured me, how she must have felt when she actually met him in person.

I could not imagine, of course, because I have not had any heroes for a hell of a long time. But she was into it by then, paying less attention to me and more to her drink and her story.

By the time I mashed my cigarette butt out in the cluttered ashtray on my desk, Felicia had gotten to the part that interested me. I had not paid such attention to the courtship stuff, or the first time Jerry stayed the night at her place, or walks in the rain, or any of the rest of whatever romantic bullshit she had gone through. It was when she mentioned Doctor Teckmann that I started listening again.

Teckmann had called somebody, the FBI, probably, to report that he had been approached by a man, a foreigner, about selling secrets. That was Galipolus. Teckmann was referred to Customs because the secrets Galipolus wanted were that kind of secrets, a distinction I did not exactly grasp. She tried to explain it to me, the business about this or that kind of computer chip, as Eddie Cochran had done, but it only put me in mind of Eddie, and I wondered as I often did what his real story was. Odd that a homicide lieutenant should know so much about computer chips and Operation Exodus. Odd, too, that he was so suddenly away at some school, things having gotten to the point they had.

At any rate, it had been decided, by Agent Thompson or

Jerry Sykes or somebody, that they would work a sting on Galipolus. And Felicia would have the opportunity of a lifetime,
a chance to work with her hero, with whom of course, she was
hopelessly in love. They coached Teckmann to play along with
Galipolus, and Jerry and Felicia would insinuate themselves into
the deal to handle the Cypriot, or whatever he was, while
Teckmann alibied out of direct contact on the grounds of nerves
or whatever. And it worked out just that way. Things were
going fine, until the night before, when all hell broke loose.
She had awakened to find Jerry gone from his place beside her
in bed and two characters in ski masks looming over her. From
there, it was about the same with her as it had been with me a
couple of hours earlier, except that once she was incapacitated
from the electrical shocks they had not gotten her down on the
floor and stomped her as they had done me. I wondered why.
All they had done was slap a handkerchief over her mouth and
nose until finally she had to breathe, and then she did not
remember anything more until the SWAT team had barged in
on her at Borodin's house later that morning.

"You weren't interrogated?" I asked.

She started, and turned to look at me as if she had forgotten I was there. It may sound weird, but I happen to think it's
true that in a way something has not actually happened to you
until you tell it to someone. It is putting it into words to make
somebody else understand it that makes it real, because choos-
ing the words, leaving this or that out and keeping this or that
in, is what hardens the thing into memory. And that is what
we remember, I believe, that first telling of the thing, more
than the thing itself. I thought that was why she looked at me
then in that wild and peculiar way. And if I was right, that did
not say much for any debriefing Thompson had done, because
whatever else he may have accomplished with her, he had not
drawn out of her this first telling of it.

"No," she said, and she made herself a fresh drink. This
time she looked into the plastic glass as if she could not figure
out what was wrong with it, then finally she stood and padded
barefoot out my door to get more ice.

"When did you last see Jerry?" I asked when she returned.

"Just before they jumped me. I was in the bedroom. He'd gone into the kitchen—"

"At the condo?"

"Yes."

"You didn't see him when the two in the ski masks jumped you, or later, at Borodin's house?"

"No."

"Have you heard from him since?"

"That's a strange thing to ask."

"I'm a strange man. Have you?"

"No."

"That 'no' didn't sound like the other ones. What's the deal?"

"Do you take the morning papers?"

"What does that have to do . . ."

But of course, before I finished the question I knew what that had to do with it. They had made up some kind of a code between them, something in the personals, a want ad. That was one thing she was doing now, waiting for the morning papers to come. I was not sure, but there was an outside chance that if she did not find what she hoped to find in the papers, if she decided that meant Jerry was dead, she might be serious about killing me. It did not make a hell of a lot of sense, but she was in love, and that makes a difference.

"Why don't you just go ahead and tell me the part that everybody's been leaving out?" I asked, trying to sound encouraging, not critical.

"I'm not—"

"Wait. Before you deny that anything's out of whack or lie about it, just . . . I don't know, give me the benefit of the doubt. You haven't been debriefed, at least not very thoroughly. You're hoping to hear from Jerry by some personal code the two of you have worked out for yourselves. You're here with me, for Christ's sake, instead of being down at the office, or the command post or ops center, or whatever you guys call it on a deal like this . . ."

"You're not as dumb as you look, T.J."

"Don't call me that. And nobody's as dumb as I look. I know what it is, I just don't know why."

"Oh?"

"Yeah. You're off the case. You're suspended or whatever. Thompson sent you home, didn't he?"

"More or less."

"Why? You don't look that roughed up to me, that's not it."

"No. I'm okay. A little sore."

"I could tell you about sore, lady. So, what's going on?"

"You're going pretty good, why don't you figure it out?"

If we had been anywhere else, I would have told her to screw herself and gone home. But I was already home, and it was her booze.

"Something's not right. It was supposed to look like I stumbled into the picture and screwed up your operation. Only we know I didn't, because the tap picked up Borodin telling Galipolus about your meeting with Thompson, whom they both knew from back East, and Borodin didn't get that from me. Which means there's a leak. Did they get an ID on the stiff at the house out in the county?"

"Teckmann."

"Positive?"

"Yeah. They made a dental."

"Yeah, Eddie said they found some bridgework. Still no sign of Jerry, though?"

"No."

"But you think he may be running an ad in the paper this morning. Jesus, that's it."

"What?"

"Jerry's gone over."

CHAPTER
TWENTY-SIX

"That's it, isn't it?" I insisted.

"No."

"It's gotta be. He has to be alive and free to take out an ad, and if he's alive and free, why hasn't he shown himself? That has to be it."

"He's not dirty."

But she said it all wrong. Not angry or sure, if either of which she had been, I would have expected her to come across my desk at me like a hellion. The way she said it was like she was not sure at all, like she only wanted what she said to be true.

"Thompson thinks he is," I said. It was a place to start.

"Yeah."

"Why?"

"There was a deal in California. Jerry was working in—"

"Silicon Valley," I interjected. "Yeah, I heard."

"It went wrong. Things go wrong sometimes, it wasn't his fault. That's why they reassigned him here."

"I see."

This was turning out to be my kind of deal all right, the

kind I wanted no part of, only they seemed to follow me around. Turnaround specialist, that was me, all right. Felicia had drifted off somewhere with Jerry, and I did not bother to bring her back to me, because I wanted to see if I could keep it all straight. I rooted around in my desk drawer until I came up with a pencil with a point. Out of the corner of my eye, I saw that Felicia had not paid me any attention, and I felt pretty sure she had no plans for me as far as the gun in her bag was concerned. Settling that in my mind was good news, except that it left me wondering what she did have in mind for me.

I turned over an unopened envelope that I was sure had an overdue bill inside and jotted a couple of notes on the back. As far as I knew, this thing started back some time ago with Borodin and Galipolus as partners. One of them sold out the other one and they went their separate ways. Now Borodin had dealt himself in on Galipolus's Dallas deal, in an underhanded way; by calling his old friend on a phone he had to suspect was tapped and tipping him off that Felicia and Jerry were feds, Borodin really put the heat on Galipolus. Another double cross, plus the one he pulled on me, and of course the one Jerry and Felicia were working on Galipolus, which was okay because they were the law. Now, it looked like Jerry might be turning everybody around, and Felicia's certainty that he was not was not much consolation. It was a ball of snakes.

"If they don't trust him, why did they put him on this case?" I asked, thinking she had had enough time to reminisce. There was a rhythm to these things, and we were starting to get somewhere.

"They trusted me."

"Oh."

"He was our most experienced undercover operative," she added, but I looked at her in a way to say that we both knew that did not make any sense. If he was dirty, what difference did it make about the experience?

"Is it a big deal, this case?" I asked.

"Not really, not compared to some."

"But I thought this new chip, this whatsit, was revolutionary and earth-shattering, stuff like that. It was going to fix it where airplanes would fly themselves, and Lord knows what all."

"Maybe, but what we're dealing with here is a prototype, one chip that will have to be tested, reverse-engineered . . ."

"Meaning if you didn't have the plans you'd have to look at the thing and work backward to figure out how it was made, right?"

"Yes. Materials are a problem too, so it's not like we're talking about handing over the whole process."

"But it ain't chopped liver? I mean, a couple of people have died—"

"A hundred thousand, tops," she said.

"That's it?"

"Maybe. We asked a quarter of a million. They were supposed to make a counteroffer. Jerry thought a hundred thousand, no more."

"He'd go over for that?"

"Of course not."

Don't get me wrong, a hundred grand is a hell of a lot of money. To me, it was like the national debt. Borodin's cash was the first I had handled since I had got out of the hospital, except for a couple of nickel-and-dime tail jobs I had picked up on the side from friends of mine who had more work than they could handle with their full-time crews. And I had done some risky things when I was working for the city back in the late sixties, making almost five hundred dollars a month. A hundred thousand dollars was not pocket change, but it did not figure. I was not up on what G-men were paid, but I knew it was decent if not extravagant. And Jerry Sykes was an old hand by all accounts, not that far from retirement. To him a hundred grand was three or four years' worth of pension. For that he would go over? Not likely. Of course, if he had been working for the other side in California, this might be part of a continuing arrangement. Or maybe the other side was blackmailing him. I did not think that Jerry had sold out in California, for a couple of reasons. One of them was that if he had, if the government had any kind of a case at all on him, they would have done something about it. If they could not prove anything, at the very least they would have buried him at a desk somewhere. God only knew they had enough of them. I did not think they would have put him in undercover on a deal like this if they were hinky about him, no matter how much they trusted this kid Felicia. Of course, she was the other reason I did not think Jerry was dirty. She believed in him, and I wanted to believe in her. That reason did not carry much weight with me, but there it was. There was another reason, but it was part of that thing about this whole case that I could not prove, the part that involved my knowing who had killed the man in the house and the daffy broad in Richardson, the one who liked to play with telephones and plastic explosives.

"The buyers—you've met with them?" I began.

"No, and that's not unusual. Galipolus is fronting for them. He has a contact with one of their people."

"Here?"

"Why not here?"

"I don't know, you just don't think about that big-league stuff going down in Texas, I guess. Istanbul, Beirut, you know, I can see that, or California."

"You may not think about it, but we don't think about much else in my outfit. You've no idea of the concentration of defense contractors and high-tech companies we have here in the Dallas–Fort Worth area. We're probably number three after Washington and the Silicon Valley."

"It's too weird," I protested, pouring myself another drink and losing conviction as I thought about it. "I'm a private eye in Dallas, Texas. I should be getting involved in . . ."

"In what?"

"I don't know, more usual stuff, a little ordinary crime, maybe."

It occurred to me that I was not sure what ordinary crime was anymore, because there had been so much new crap in town, more and more high-stakes gangsterism over the past few years. We had the drug gangs now, the Mexican Mafia and the bikers, the Jamaican posses and the Colombians, and the Cuban Marielitos, not to mention the old-timers, the guys with friends in Las Vegas and New Orleans, who met in restaurants and played golf and sponsored Little League baseball teams and catered to the tastes of the citizens and only now and then had somebody killed. There was the weird shit too, I had been hearing, a satanic cult in one of the suburbs, street gangs of high school kids who wanted to be like the big boys in L.A. The whole scene was getting out of focus, and I had to admit I did not know exactly what I meant by ordinary crime anymore. Who were all these people, and what the hell were they doing in my town?

She told me about some of the cases she had worked on, stuff I supposed was no longer secret or else she either did not care or for some reason had decided on her own that I was a good security risk. Or maybe she was just getting as drunk as I was. There was one with these two foreign guys. One of them conned the other into thinking he was some kind of a secret agent, and then the two of them hooked up with a guy from their home country's consulate, who was not exactly a diplomat, but pretty close, and they got into some big-time schemes to sell secrets for a lot of money. Only the whole thing was a scam, and it turned out there were not any secrets, and it was all a big washout and burned who knew how many hours of the agents' time for nothing, except that they had made a contact with somebody who worked for one of the midcities defense contractors, and if these guys had been for real, there was no telling how much damage they could have done. She said that kind of stuff happened all the time.

Before she could confuse me with any more details, I decided to cut to the bottom line, while I was still nearly sober enough to think clearly.

"So why are you here, really?" I asked her.

"Not to kill you, you were right about that."

"Good. So why?"

"To ask you to help me."

"Why?"

"Because you're the only one who can."

"I don't get it. You've got a whole—"

"No, I don't. Thompson benched me, I'm on my own."

"Because of your boyfriend."

"Yes. Thompson said I was thinking with my . . . Anyway, let's just say he doesn't think I'm being objective about it."

"And you're not."

"Probably not. But I know I'm right. Jerry's on the level, and he's in some kind of trouble. He'll need me to get out of it, and I need you to back me up."

"You don't know anything about me."

"Eddie Cochran vouched for you."

"That son-of-a-bitch."

"So, what do you say, T.J.?"

"Don't call me that. What's in it for me?"

"What would it take? I have a little money saved up, a couple of thousand. My car's paid for."

"What kind of car?"

"Better than that heap you're driving. Is it a deal?"

"You might have just asked me, as a friend of a friend."

"Eddie said you were good in a fight. He didn't say you were stupid."

"At least you didn't bother with the high-minded stuff, appeal to my patriotism."

"No, I understand you fell for that once already." She smiled.

"Vietnam, you mean? Yeah, it worked on me that time, all right."

The telephone rang.

"Are you expecting a call?" I asked.

She shook her head no.

I lifted the receiver and heard the last of the taped message on my answering machine, and then Della's voice.

"Jack, are you there?" she asked.

"Hi, kid," I said into the phone.

"Jack, did I wake you?" Della said, sounding tired and sad.

"No, I was just . . . shooting the breeze with a friend of mine. Where are you?"

198

"At home. Are you all right?"

"Yeah, fine."

"We were worried about you. Speed and Joe came by, they said—"

"Nothing to worry about, kid, I just got tied up with some business. What are you doing up this late?"

I tried to focus my eyes well enough to make out the hands of my watch, and decided it was within a few minutes of three in the morning, give or take. Agent Adams and I had been drinking and talking longer than I realized, and both of us were a little drunker than I would have thought.

"You're not alone, are you?" Della asked.

"I told you, I'm . . . shooting the breeze with a friend of mine. That's all."

"I just wanted to make sure you were all right, Jack. So . . ."

"What about you?" I asked, not wanting her to hang up. "Are you okay?"

"Yeah, Jack. Don't worry about me."

"What about the boyfriend."

"We can talk about him tomorrow. Good night, Jack."

Click and buzz, and that was that.

I did not call Della back to find out what it was that made her sound so tired or sad or whatever it was, or to insist that we talk about her boyfriend. I was interested, but I had other things on my mind.

"Okay, Jack. I'm all ears," said Agent Adams.

"Before you popped in, I was sitting here trying to figure some cockamamy way to deal myself back in on this thing. You show up, bang. I'm thinking I may get another crack at it. I'm listening. I really am. I'm ready. What do you do? You offer me your fed credit union balance and a used car. I don't want your money or your car. I've got business with these people for my own reasons."

"I see," she said.

"I doubt it. The thing is, I don't have a hell of a lot. In the realm of material possessions. What I do have is more along the line of what they call intangibles. Peace of mind . . . no, that I don't have. Let's see . . . honor. No, not so much of that anymore either. Uh, what it is . . . Jesus, this is depressing."

"Reputation?" she offered, trying to help.

"Not really. You can hear all kinds of things about me if you ask the wrong people."

"I heard your word is good."

"Yeah, that's true. I have my word. That's my bond. You can bank on my word. Thanks."

"You're welcome."

"And . . . I don't know, kind of a professional pride, I guess you'd say. Yeah, I do still take pride in doing my job, you know, doing it right."

"I haven't seen the videos, Jack, but from what I hear, you did a good job on me."

"I did, except that you weren't Sylvia Borodin, were you? See, that's what I'm in this for, I'm going to set that little deal right. That's it."

"So you're in?" she asked.

"Yeah."

"I didn't have to go to all this . . ."

"Nah, all you had to do was ask. That's what I'm telling you."

"Well, for Christ's sake."

"See, that's what I mean. If you were smarter about people, you wouldn't have to work so hard."

She laughed a little then, and I was glad that she did, because for all my advice to her about being a better judge of people, I was not so sure that I was so good at it myself when it came to women. I am notorious in some circles for being wrong about women. But she laughed, first only softly and in a tired, resigned way, and then a little more thoroughly, until she looked about halfway relaxed, as if she had been holding herself together for something and now she did not have to do whatever it was, and she could take it easy, take a little blow until the next crisis.

And then, as I stood watching her, the laughing crumbled

around the edges and I saw that she was crying, softly, her hands over her face. She hoped I would not realize she had succumbed to this softness that was a part of her loving Jerry Sykes, and also a part of her fear that whatever she had to offer would not be enough to save him.

CHAPTER
TWENTY-SEVEN

WE DID NOT wait at my office for the morning papers to come. Instead, I took Felicia to the Denny's where I go sometimes, at Preston and LBJ, for breakfast. The plastic twenty-four-hour utilitarianism of the place did not disappoint me, and I thought all that fluorescent lighting and a couple of pots of black coffee would not do my new partner any harm.

Our breakfasts came about the same time the man in the pick-up truck with the camper on the back pulled up in front and loaded *The Dallas Morning News* vending machine. I went out through the double set of glass doors and put a quarter into the machine and removed the third paper from the top. I don't know why I do that, it's just a habit not to take the top one.

Felicia dropped her fork on the plate with her uneaten short stack and eggs-over-easy and ripped through all the sections of the paper until she found the classified ads, then folded and refolded a particular section until she had the whole thing narrowed down to about an eighth of a page.

"Ah!" she said, only it was not much more than a noise that rose and caught in her throat.

"It's there?" I asked.

She nodded her head to tell me yes, it was there, she had her message from her lover. Her eyes went moist and I thought she would cry again, only loud and messy this time.

"Now what?" I asked.

She was not in a mood to talk, but I coaxed her to explain it to me and to eat her breakfast. I ate mine, also a short stack of pancakes and eggs-over-easy with bacon and plenty of hot coffee. She finally went to work on her food, but only because she wanted to think things through before she told me what was going to happen next.

"Tell me about Doctor Teckmann," I said with my mouth half full of pancakes.

"What? Why?"

"Humor me. I'm making conversation."

"He was a cute old guy. A nerd, I guess."

"Did he hit on you?"

"That was our cover, I was supposed to be his chip on the side."

"Yeah, but did he hit on you, for real?"

"Come on . . . no, he didn't. Not really."

"Not really?"

"You know, he kidded around some. Not really."

"Oh. Did he ever mention his wife, or his daughter?"

"Not that I recall. Why?"

"Conversation. I'm curious, that's all. Waiting for you to decide how much you want to tell me about what's in that paper."

"Read it yourself." She smiled, offering it to me.

"Very funny," I rejoined. "Like it ain't in some kind of code."

"He's in trouble, all right. I'm to meet him this morning at a place we know. He says come alone."

"That's it?"

"Yes."

"Where's the place?"

"Jack, are you sure you want in on this? It's not too late to take a pass."

"Are you sure you want me along? Sounds like you're having second thoughts."

"Yeah."

I had not expected her to admit it. Thing was, what did she need me for if Jerry was in good enough shape to take out an ad in the paper?

"There's something else, isn't there?"

"Maybe. Are you in or not?"

"I'm in. What kind of trouble is he in?"

"The third kind."

"Okay, I'm listening."

"We have three trouble signs, one through three. According to this, he's in the third kind of trouble, the worst."

"Give me a hint. Does that mean he's hurt, or being held against his will, or what?"

"Or both."

"Then how would he get the ad in the paper?"

"He's good, Jack. If somebody's got him, he could convince them to let him do it, you'll have to trust me on that."

"Okay," I said, thinking to myself that she should know, because Jerry had convinced her to do God only knew what.

"I mean it, you don't have to go through with this."

"What are you, schizophrenic? A little while ago you were offering me . . ." I paused when the waitress brought a fresh pot of coffee and picked up the empty. "Offering me practically everything you have, now you're trying to talk me out. What gives?"

"I don't want you to get hurt on account of me, I don't want you on my conscience," she said.

"Then don't fuck up. Now, what's the deal?"

She explained it to me, and I did not like it any more than I had expected to. The place they knew was an abandoned horse farm, one the feds had seized, not far from where we sat. In fact, the quickest way to get there was to take Preston Road north, out past the turnoff that would have taken us back to the house where the telephone bomb had done its work. She made it sound like maybe a half hour's drive. I checked my watch and saw that it was a quarter past five, only another hour or so until good daylight. I did not feel any particular way about the location. It was the job she had in mind for me that I did not like. She said that she had a rifle in the trunk of the car that she wanted me to use.

"It's a good one," she said.

"Get serious."

"I am serious. I checked you out, T.J. You were a sniper in the war."

"You don't know the first goddamn thing about it, do you? You think I just pick up a rifle out of the trunk of your frigging car and go throw myself down in the bush somewhere and shoot a cigarette out of somebody's mouth at a couple of hundred yards? Jesus Christ."

"It's Jerry's rifle. It shoots great."

"For Jerry. I'd have to sight it in. And there's no time for that."

"Are you sure?"

"Yeah."

We were both sobering up, and I liked the way she was handling it.

"Well then," she announced, pushing her plate to one side and reaching for the fresh pot of coffee. "That changes things, doesn't it?"

"How so?" I asked.

"If you can't use the rifle, then I'm not sure I see how you are going to be of any use to me."

"I'll go in with you, cover you. It makes more sense that way, anyhow. You can't work with a rifleman on a deal like this without radios, and a hell of a lot of teamwork, anyway. It makes a lot more sense if I just go in with you."

"The other way, you could get clear if anything went wrong. I don't want you getting into anything you can't get out of on my account."

"Why, you don't want to owe me a favor?" I said, trying to make light of it. Actually, she was making sense, and I would have felt about the same way about it if I had been in her place, except that I would not have gone to a stranger at all. Not even if Eddie Cochran had vouched for him. "How well do you know Eddie Cochran?"

"Not well."

"You said he vouched for me. You seem to put a lot of stock in that."

"He's a friend of a friend."

"Thompson?"

"Okay, Thompson."

The hell you say, I thought. Okay, don't tell me. My friend Eddie was full of surprises.

"So what's your plan?" I asked. It was getting to be that time.

"I'm going to go to the place Jerry named in the message. And . . . play it by ear."

"Hell of a plan."

"I'm open for suggestions, T.J."

"No, it's your call. You have some kind of a backup gun I can borrow?"

"Are you authorized?"

"Sure." From me, I'm authorized, I thought. From the Texas penal code, not really; from the police, it depended on if I knew them and what I was doing at the time. She should have known that PIs don't get to carry guns in Texas, but maybe she had come from some place where they had gun permits and like that.

"I've got my service issue in the car."

"What is it?"

"Model Thirteen, bull barrel. You'll love it."

"Yeah, fine."

As a matter of fact, it could have been worse. The 13 was an ugly little son of a bitch, but I had plinked around with one once, and it handled pretty good. Of course, that meant we were going in packing two revolvers, and I started totaling up the opposition. It depended on who was doing whom. Borodin had the two henchmen, henchpersons, Sasha and Anton; that made three at least, if it was Borodin's show. As far as I knew,

Galipolus was on his own. If the two Cypriots had joined forces, that added up to four. And, of course, I was a hell of a lot less sure of Jerry Sykes than the girl was. As a matter of fact, if I had figured it out right, Jerry was not going to be much help at all.

"You ready?" she asked, sounding perky, but I knew that was mostly the adrenaline kicking in.

"There is one other thing."

"What?"

"Who has the McGuffin?"

"The what?"

"The chip, the gizmo, what all this bullshit is about."

"Jerry does, or he did. I don't know now."

"I see."

"Once we get Jerry, then we can worry about the chip."

"You don't think maybe they already have it and they've left the country?"

"Maybe. I don't think so."

"Why not?"

"Jerry . . ."

She did not finish, and I figured there were a couple of reasons for that. For one thing, she thought enough of Jerry that she did not think Borodin or Galipolus or whoever could have gotten their hands on the whatsit without doing something really terrible to old Jerry. And she did not want to think about that. For another, there was the suspicion that Jerry was not straight, and however wild she was about him, she was not immune to that. Which, if it were true, might mean Jerry was somewhere counting his money. In which case, what was the point of the coded message telling her he was in trouble and to come to the ranch? She had a lot on her mind too.

"It's time," she said finally, checking her watch without really looking at it. "Are you in or out?"

"I'm in. Got time for head call?"

"Sure."

We had taken a booth on the side of the restaurant near the rest rooms because that was where they stuck smokers, so it was not much of a hike to the men's room. When I came out, I half expected her to be gone without me, but there she was, standing at the register, waiting for her change. I put a couple of ones on the table for a tip and noticed how she had left things. The newspaper was lying beside her plate, folded to the personals, and she had dropped her napkin inside her coffee cup. After I dropped the two ones on the table, I picked up her napkin and wiped my hands with it, noticing as I did that she had not left any lipstick on it, because we had been drinking all night and she had not bothered to freshen up. Then I tossed the napkin back onto the table and joined her at the register.

"I got the table," I told her.

"And I got the tab," she answered, with a smile that was only a little tight at the edges, as she took some silver and three ones in change from the waitress at the register.

"Then we're about ready to go," I said.

"After you."

I started toward the front door, and heard her snap her fingers behind me.

"What is it?" I asked, not bothering to turn around.

"Forgot my keys. Just a sec."

I studied the front pages of the other papers in their machines outside the front door while she hustled up the aisle between the row of booths along the big picture window and the long counter that made up the smoking section. She stopped at our table and I saw her lift a set of keys and shake it at me to show that she had found them before she started back toward the doors where I was waiting. I smiled and made a dopey face, cranking the index finger of my right hand in a tight circle alongside my temple to show her I thought she was goofy for forgetting her keys. Without making a big thing of it, I also bumped up onto the balls of my feet so I could see over the bottom edge of the window, which ran even with the booth seat backs, and noticed that her napkin was back in her coffee cup, the way she had left it the first time.

We smiled at each other and if I was not imagining things, we both quivered with a hint of a chill, although it was a regular August Dallas early morning and there was nothing cool in the air. It was us, we were getting a buzz because of what we were about to do, and I thought to myself as I waited for her to reach across the front seat of her car and unlock my door for me to get in, I thought: yeah, this is your kind of a deal all right, Jack old boy. Even this kid is turning you around.

CHAPTER
TWENTY-EIGHT

WE LEFT HER car somewhere off the road on a rutted trail that looked as if someone had driven up that way before a time or two, if not recently, and hiked in from there. She had to have been there before to find this horse place she was taking me to, and probably she had gotten there by the route we were taking, because it was still dark except for the high ground where the rising sun cast what there was to see in deep relief and made everything a nest of goblins. If you had only been there in good daylight, none of your landmarks would have been recognizable in this early light. I felt as if I were sneaking up on Bald Mountain, like in the Disney short, and catching all the rocks and bushes off guard as they were skittering around trying to get back into their daytime shapes. I tried not to make any noise stumbling along a faint and winding trail behind Agent Adams, thinking of my kid, my little boy.

I had taken Little Jack to see *Sorcerer's Apprentice* and some other Disney stuff a long time ago. He had not cared for it, it had scared him. I thought this version was pretty spooky, too, and wished for all I was worth that I had not conjured up my memories of the boy. If it had not been for Little Jack, I would not give a shit if I died. And that is about the right frame of mind to be in on a deal like this.

Agent Felicia had changed on the way from Denny's to the place where we had parked and begun our hike. She had a set of "grubbies" in a bag in the backseat of her car, and she had asked me if I would mind holding the steering wheel while she slipped into something more appropriate. I had done that, but I cannot say that I did a very good job of driving.

"See?" she whispered, leaning close to me and pointing at shadows to our front.

I squatted beside her and made an effort. In poor light, there is a whole volume of lore you need, tricks to help you see what is really there and not to see what only seems to be. Most of it I had learned, but did not remember, and this was not the first time that I had thought of myself, with a certain sardonic surprise mingled with exultation, as an old man. Exultation because there is something to be said for surviving long enough to become old in a life like mine. Alternately blinking and bugging my eyes, and making faces I was glad she could not see in the early morning grayness in the process, I finally got the general idea. My legs hurt like hell and began cramping for the hundredth time, so I shifted out of a squat and went prone. It helped a little.

We were on the last of a series of low rises that finally petered out and made a slope from about the spot where we lay in the cover of weeds and some other indigenous shit that I must have been allergic to, by the way my nose was beginning to itch and run. The slope from there ran at not too severe a grade down to a swale or glen, or whatever you call a depression between a couple of hills, that ran from directly in front of us off to our left. It was about the size of a football field. From the edge of this low and bumpy field there rose a low hill to our right, its top almost level, as far as I could see. If I had kept my bearings, the road was farther off to our right, the road down which we had driven to the point where my intrepid guide had chosen to leave her car. From there I supposed there ought to be a drive or lane that ran from the road to whatever those buildings were that I had finally been able to make out on the level top of the low hill to our right.

"That's it?" I murmured.

"S-s-h," she answered, which I had suspected she would, out of spite and her sense of her superior field craft.

Having been shushed, probably on the grounds that, as every kid knows who has ever seen a movie with this kind of crap in it, sound travels great in the early quiet morning out of doors, I signaled to my associate that I was curious why the hell we had stopped, and was this the place, by raising my hands, palms toward her, to my ears and arching my eyebrows as high as they would go.

She nodded, as solemn as a Hollywood Indian, and stabbed her index finger toward the buildings on the flat top of the low rise to our right front.

I, in turn, spun both hands on their wrists and then slung them toward the place, like the clown who introduces vaudeville acts, as if to say, "Let's get on with the show." She waved at me like a patient mom with a bratty kid and then moved off to her right. I followed.

It probably was not more than half an hour later that we both fetched up in a clump of trees and brush in a fence line that seemed to mark the border around whatever it was the buildings represented. It was daylight now, and I could see without any tricks what we were up against.

From our hiding place in the fencerow, which at that point traced the edge of the little tabletop that looked as if someone with machinery had whacked off the top of the little hill, we could see in the expanding light a bit of overgrown pasture and then what looked like a stable, in better shape than I would have expected from its being stuck out so far off by itself and not being in use. Felicia had told me about the place on the drive out, for no particular reason except that talking seemed to be her way of handling the nerves. Some of her Customs colleagues had raided a dope operation there, and the government had wound up seizing it, along with a fleet of cars, a couple of airplanes, and a helicopter. The aircraft were all stored over at the Addison airport, and she did not know what had been done with the horses the smuggler had built the stable for. She had joked that the horses had better accommodations than the man the smuggler had watching the place. From what she had told me, I figured that the little shack where the keeper had lived was the shabby frame job I could just make out beyond the stables. I knew there was more to it, the beginnings of a big house the smuggler had intended to live in, but I could not see it from where we were. I could see a gravel drive that led out of the brush farther off to our right and on to the level part of the hill in front of us. That was the way in if you came in a car, from one of the country roads that crisscrossed this part of the county between the highways. Of course, I was not sure which county, whether it was Dallas or Collin, but that was not important now. That would matter only when it came time to call somebody and tell them what had happened.

Felicia was quivering hard enough that I could feel her beside me. I could hear her breathing, but I was not worried about her. Probably, she was just pumped for what was going to happen next. If it was any more than that, worrying about it would not help. I knew she expected more out of the morning's exercise than I did, because she was sure that Jerry Sykes was in there somewhere, in the stable probably, or the shack beyond. She was going to rescue him. For my part, I had it figured quite a bit differently, and from the way I saw it, there was not going to be that much to cheer about when it was over, whichever way it went. To me, it was just something that needed doing, and I was the man for the job, for a couple of reasons.

After we had lain in the cover of the fencerow long enough to hear the noises somebody would have made if he or she had been up and about, Felicia turned to me and made a bunch of hand signals. Probably something she learned in Customs school, but of course I had not attended it. A couple of the signs I remembered from the service, the rest of it could have been anything. But by the time she had finished, I thought I understood pretty well what she had in mind. She would go in and I would cover her from the fencerow, or possibly follow her at a safe interval, one of those. What I thought would have made more sense would have been some kind of a leap-frog action, where she moved to cover, then I moved while she covered me, and like that. That way, one of us would be covering whenever the other one moved, and we would keep each other in sight all the time. But she had her plan, and it was more her deal than mine, so I just nodded and off she went.

She moved pretty well, once she got clear of the tangle of barbed wire that had accumulated alongside the rotted fence post behind which she had been hiding. Working very quietly, she picked herself free of it and she did not look back at me to see if I was laughing at her or anything before she moved forward. I was glad to see that she did not go too far before she dropped into the concealment of the weeds. When she rose into view again, it was from a different place, probably ten or fifteen feet beyond the point where she had dropped. That was good. The thinking is you should only advance about five meters at a time, then drop. That way, if the enemy spots you, you should not be exposed long enough for him to get a bead on you. Once you are down, you should crawl for a while, so when you show yourself again you won't be in the same place he last saw you. Then you drop after five meters, before he can get on you. Each time you move in a little bit different direction and distance before you show yourself again. It is not foolproof by any means, but it showed somebody had given some thought to the girl's preparation for this kind of thing.

There was not much for me to do except keep my eyes moving so I might spot somebody before they spotted her. Whether I would be able to do very much about it or not depended on how far away they were. The little Smith & Wesson she had loaned me was a .357 magnum, but she only had .38 ammo for it. That will work, but it does not have the same range, or the same authority either. With the three-inch barrel and my being pretty badly out of practice, I was not optimistic about doing any fancy shooting at much distance. If my eye was still any good, the nearest wall of the stable was about fifty yards away, everything else about the place was farther. I could probably hit the stable from where I was, but I doubted I could have hit one of the shutters that hung to either side of the three windows on the wall that faced me, windows where the smuggler's horses were supposed to hang their heads out and amuse themselves however horses do.

Time was not important enough for me to check my watch, but it took long enough for the careful girl to reach the stable that by the time I saw her turn toward me from the corner of it and wave her hand in a small circle that meant it was my turn, the sun was properly up and had gotten a start at making an August day of it.

Up from the cover of the brush and weeds I went, careful not to snag my clothes on any barbed wire. Unlike my friend Felicia, I was not dressed for wilderness war games. Due to my limited wardrobe and not having been told where we were going, I was wearing my only pair of shoes, the cordovan loafers, my gray pants and what had been a white shirt before I had spent well over an hour trekking through weeds, brambles, and underbrush. The shoes were done for, and there was enough prickly clinging crap inside them to fill a salad bowl. For these reasons, the discomfort that came of not being suitably dressed, and because I had a hell of a lot less to lose, I was not nearly as careful as the girl had been. Besides, I was ready to get this thing over and go get a drink. Or just get it over, depending on how it worked out. I didn't think my legs would hold up to a lot of combat maneuvering anyway.

This was about the point in these things that you find yourself wondering why you are here again, stepping off into another one of these things that is bound to end badly. As I jogged toward the stable, bent over in half-crouch and trying to keep my zigging and zagging irregular enough that anyone looking down a gun barrel at me would not detect a pattern that would make it easy for him, I ran it over in the part of my mind that does not involve itself in anything as practical as staying alive. While I prided myself on being a professional, by which I meant that I did not do anything I was not paid to do, it was pretty clear that I had not dealt myself in on this part of the deal on behalf of a client. Borodin had been the only one paying me, and he was on the other side. Mrs. Teckmann was part of it, but not all, by any means. Felicia? Since it had not been me who burned her after all, what did I owe her? Nothing really, but I had to admit I liked a couple of things about her. She could handle her booze and did not mind doing whatever she had to do to get her man out of whatever kind of a hole she thought he was in.

But I was in no mood to kid myself about noble motives. I was there because of my pride. Borodin had roped me into this thing, and I thought I knew what the real deal was. And I did not think the Adams kid was up to it, or Agent Thompson and his troops either, for that matter. That was it, I had the affrontery to think it was up to me to get to the bottom of it. And there was the thing about the two characters who waylaid me in my own office building. It is not good business to let an ass-kicking go unanswered. Sets a bad precedent. Next thing you know, people stop taking you seriously.

From the scowl she turned toward me as I trudged into place beside her, I could see that Agent Adams had not been impressed with my technique in crossing the more or less open ground. That was all right. I had made it.

CHAPTER
TWENTY-NINE

IF THERE WERE any sentries posted, it would be Sasha or Anton, it stood to reason. Maybe both of them. I did not think they would be armed with stun guns this time. From our places alongside the stable wall, we had a pretty clear view of the gravel drive that led away toward the road. That would be the way anyone else would come. While Felicia worked her way along the wall to each of the horse windows in turn and looked inside the stable, I kept my eyes on the drive so if anybody did come we would see them before they saw us.

She was doing it about the way you see it on some of the current TV cop shows, what they call the "peekaboo" technique. Which just means she would squat down low beneath or beside a window, then pop up for a quick look inside, then down again before anybody in there could shoot her. Looked great, but I was not sure how much she could see looking in such short bursts.

It did not matter, because we heard them before we saw them. I recognized Borodin's voice, his accent particularly. The other man's voice I had not heard before, but his accent was similar. I could not make out what they were saying. The voices were coming from inside the stable.

Felicia looked at me to make sure I had heard them, and I nodded that I had, then made a questioning face to ask silently if she had seen them. She shrugged to say she had not, she did not know where they were inside.

It would have been more to my liking if we had waited until we had some idea where the two thugs were, Sasha and Anton, but Felicia was not in the mood to wait. I knew she had her lover on her mind, and I could not blame her for that. Still, I knew we should have waited.

She made a couple of her mysterious signals at me, then moved out and slunk around the corner of the stable wall toward the center of the cleared area that was to have been a ranch if the anonymous smuggler had stayed clear of the law long enough. After a quick two-count, during which I did not hear anything, like shooting, I followed.

Around the corner quick and low, my borrowed revolver ready in front of me, and I settled into a crouch against the stable's front wall. There was nothing in front of the stable except a yard. The house across the way was caved in on itself from neglect and did not look as if anyone had been inside it for a long time. The yard had gone to seed, and weeds stood knee-high between the three cars parked there. I remembered two of them from the Borodin house, and I was pretty sure the third one was the one Galipolus had been driving the night I followed him home from the strip club on Industrial where he had met Felicia and Teckmann. The gang's all here, I said to myself. Almost.

By the time I had scanned the cars well enough from my position at the wall to think that there probably was not anybody in, under, or behind one of them, Felicia had made her way, duck walking, down the front stable wall to the door.

When she turned to motion to me, I had already begun making my way toward her. There was no point in trying to argue with her, we couldn't risk actually talking, and she and I had learned different hand signals. Like a generation gap.

Besides, I had some idea how she felt about Jerry Sykes, and I knew she was going in now, whether I went with her or not.

I moved up alongside her and she hopped across in front of the closed door to squat on the other side of it from me. She was looking at the door and beyond me, over my shoulder. I was doing the same for her. The knob was on my side, and she motioned with her free hand that she wanted me to try the knob, to see if it was locked. I nodded and reached toward it, but she started in at me again with the hand signals then, pointing to herself and then to me, making x's in the air and so on, until I pretty well understood what she had in mind. She wanted me to push the door open, then she would go in low and to our left. I was to follow, high and to the right. That sounded like a plan, and I was tired enough of screwing around in the early morning heat that I pretty well just wanted to get on with the thing.

The knob turned noiselessly in my hand when I tried it. She saw that and nodded. I cranked the knob clockwise until I was sure the bolt was clear of the channel, and then I shoved hard against the door and it swung all the way in with a clattering bang against the wall. Felicia was in like a shot, and as soon as she had cleared the threshold I went in too, angling to my right and throwing my back against the door to make sure that if anybody was hiding behind it they would not be in any position to do anything about it.

There was a lot of noise when I went in, with the door banging hard against the wall and Felicia caroming off an earthen jar that was half her size. It teetered and reeled backward from her like a drunken sailor, and then over it went and shattered on what I was surprised to see was a real tiled floor, a couple of hundred shards skittering and spinning away. Felicia had lost her balance in the surprise of hitting the big pot and gone to her knees with an earthy expletive. It was to her credit that in all the unexpected noise and excitement she did not do any shooting, from reflex.

"U.S. Customs Service!" she announced from the floor, as

if everyone in the place didn't know who she was already. She even flashed her ID at them.

Aside from the busted big pot and the banging door, Borodin and Galipolus were making a hell of a racket as well. Some of the broken bits from the jar made it across the room to go sliding beneath the table where the two men were eating their breakfast, and Galipolus in particular let out a yelp because one of the fragments had hit him in the shin or on the ankle, and with the surprise and all the noise, he thought he had been shot.

"I'm shot!" he yelled.

"My God!" Borodin said, spitting scrambled eggs on the tablecloth and the floor, because as he said that, he was turning toward the door, toward Felicia and me, his mouth agape. He probably believed Galipolus about having been shot, and the look on his face said he thought he would be next. "Mister Kyle! My God!"

The big jar must have been intended for some kind of a palm tree or banana plant or something, because there was a lot of dirt from it on the floor too, and what looked like the remains of something yellow and fibrous. Whatever it had been, it had not been tended any better than the overgrown yard outside.

First, after swinging my eyes and my gun right to left and then back to check the room, I double-checked behind the door but there was nothing there. Then I pushed the door closed and snapped the lock on, so nobody would surprise us.

"My God!" Borodin said again, his mouth still open and showing us his breakfast. His eyes were the size of hard-boiled eggs.

Galipolus had his hands in the air and did not look as if he had had much practice at it, the way he held them straight up. Maybe, he hoped he could reach one of the roof beams overhead and pull himself up out of sight somewhere.

There was a wall on our left that ran from the front wall to an open door near the rear wall, and the stalls with the windows were beyond that. That was why we could hear the men's voices from outside but Felicia had not been able to see them when she did her peekabooing. It did not look like the room we were in was as long as the stable building itself was wide, and I figured there was a walkway behind the rear room of the wall. To our right, there were three doors in a wall, two of them open.

Galipolus began to moan, softly at first, then louder. When he started talking in some foreign language, I told him to be quiet and he did.

"Where's Jerry?" Felicia demanded of them, still on her knees amid the wreckage of the big jar.

"Huh?" Borodin grunted.

"Where is he, goddamnit?" she insisted, and the sound she made when she thumbed back the hammer of her snub-nosed magnum was louder in its way than all the racket with the jar.

"He's . . . he's not with you?" Borodin asked.

Felicia scrambled to her feet and from the look of her she was about to do something rash, so I made it a point to keep my voice soft and flat.

"Take a breath, kid," I said to her. "Let's take it in order."

She did not say anything, but then again she did not shoot anybody either. It always makes me nervous when somebody cocks a handgun. It takes so little to set one of the damned things off single-action like that.

"Mister Kyle, I assure you . . ." Borodin began, then had to stop and either swallow or spit out the rest of his food. He swallowed.

"Save it," I interjected. "I'll start with the easy ones. Where are the butler and the water nymph?"

"But—"

"Anton and Sasha, goddamnit. Where are they?"

Borodin cut his eyes around to his left toward the wall with three doors in it as far as he could without moving his head. Neither of the two men was doing any moving.

"Call him," I said.

"Anton. Anton, come out."

Nothing. I listened hard in the silence of the room, but

all I could hear was everybody breathing. I jerked my gun at Borodin with a shrug of my wrist to tell him to try again.

"Anton, please. Please come out. It's all right."

I had pivoted a bit to my right from my place near the door so that I was facing the middle door. The borrowed revolver was braced in a two-hand grip, what they call an isosceles, chest-high. Locked in like that with my elbows snug in on my ribs, the gun pointed wherever I looked, because I turned my body as I turned my eyes, and I kept it low so it would not interfere with my vision. If something ugly popped through any of the three doors, I felt pretty sure I could hit it. Of course, I was out of practice.

Anton appeared in the last of the three doors, silently, and without seeming to have stepped into the doorway at all. As if he had been there all along, he was just there. He looked at me only, never at Felicia, and there was nothing in his eyes that said he was worried about me. I made a note of that.

"Step out where I can see you better," I told him.

He did not move, and the expression of his face did not change.

"Please, Anton," Borodin said.

From the corner of my eye, I saw that Galipolus had not moved and his lips were still working, but I could not hear him, and that was all I cared about. Also, I noticed that Borodin's color had improved, and his breathing was nearer normal. Maybe that was because my gun was aimed at Anton now.

Anton was too cool to be on the spot like he was, and I did not forget to worry about the other two doors. As long as Felicia covered the one door on her side, this thing should not go too wrong, whatever the little butler had in mind. That was what Felicia would be doing, I told myself. She handled herself pretty well, and she would know that was how we needed to do it. I had Anton and the right side of the room, she had the left. But then, I am not a good judge of women.

"Jerry!"

Felicia screamed her lover's name, and that told me that we were not exactly working together anymore. She had waited about as long as she could for him, and now she was going to make a mistake. It was not what I wanted to do, but I turned my head toward her, keeping my eyes on the butler but straining to pick Felicia up in my peripheral vision. She was moving toward Anton, putting herself between me and the one door in the left wall as she went forward.

"Stop!" I ordered.

She froze in midstride, but I could see that her face was turned toward me.

"He's in here," Anton said nonchalantly, a little dejected, as if the jig was up and there was no point in denying it. He took a short step to his left and pointed with his right thumb over his shoulder toward whatever lay through the doorway behind him.

"Jerry!"

"Felicia . . ." I started to tell her to hold her ground.

"He can hear you," Anton purred, smiling almost apologetically. "He just can't answer."

"Felicia, don't!" I snapped. But she was moving, I saw that out of the corner of my eye. As quickly as I could, I looked and saw that she had taken a couple of steps, moving toward the door where Anton stood watching her, the smile gone now. She would cross between me and the two men at the breakfast table. "Don't."

Then it all went to hell.

As I snapped my head back toward Anton, in the microsecond it took for the change in his expression to register, I also sensed a new stirring on my left, and I thought but could not be sure that there was the soft pad of a bare foot on the red tiles.

"Look out!" I yelled to tell Felicia that Sasha was in it now, but it was too late. The startled gasp and the brittle crack of a bone off to my left told me it had already happened.

Anton grinned and I shot him.

CHAPTER THIRTY

My gun was up and when I touched it off I had the picture of Anton's teeth just above the blue-black snout of the three-inch bull barrel. That was because he had dipped his head down as he went into a crouch to draw the gun he had tucked in his waist in the small of his back, and that put his head where his chest had been when I started my trigger pull. He was damned quick, you had to give the little bastard that. He already had the piece out and coming up toward me when my slug slapped into his face.

The roar of my gun filled the tile and brick enclosure of the room, followed half a beat later by Anton's bark, which sent a round skittering along the floor and into the wall behind me. There was smoke and the stench of cordite, along with the shell burst of gore that popped like a balloon atop the little man's scrawny neck. He jerked half toward me before what was left of his head careened back at a crazy angle from his shoulders and he collapsed, still turning, and his feet slid out from under him in the blood before he fell.

If he had not grinned first, if he had only made his move, I do not think I would have beat him. But that was old business. Before he crumpled into a pile and then toppled over backward, I spun as quickly as I could, pivoting on my feet to turn my body and the gun all together as I brought my eyes around to my left toward the girl.

Sasha had her. Sasha must have come out of the door on the left as Felicia moved toward Anton, leaving that door uncovered. Now Sasha was behind Felicia, holding the agent's broken right wrist in her left in front of Felicia. In Sasha's right hand was a pistol. It was nestled snugly into Felicia's right ear.

Sasha was standing behind Felicia and had her left arm run around Felicia's waist, holding Felicia's right wrist in a hold that would have hurt like hell even if it were not broken. Sasha's head was alongside Felicia's so that I could only see Sasha's right eye and a patch of her forehead no bigger than a cue ball.

It was not the kind of a shot I wanted to take, not with a borrowed gun anyway. Felicia was screaming, because Sasha was working on her broken wrist.

"Drop the gun or I'll kill her," Sasha said.

"Yeah, just like on TV," I answered, holding the fat-barreled revolver with two hands, trying to keep Sasha's right eye centered behind the front sight.

"Mister Kyle," Borodin said, rising from his chair at the breakfast table. "Please, no more shooting. Look what you've done to poor Anton."

Galipolus was on the floor, underneath the table, and it occurred to me how odd he looked. Here was this handsome, distinguished-looking guy, barrel-chested, with his neatly brushed black hair graying at the temples—he looked like some kind of hero—but he was on his hands and knees under the table like a frightened child.

"Hold it!" I snapped at Borodin, who had taken a step toward Anton. "Leave him alone."

"Maybe there's something I can do for him," Borodin offered, and I could not help noticing a tremor in his voice.

"What, a head transplant? Sit down."

I was keeping my eye and my gun on Sasha. She was the

threat. All this with Borodin and Galipolus was with peripheral vision. I wanted them at the table, where I could watch them. If they had guns or any intention of using them, they would have dealt themselves in already. I did not want Borodin anywhere near Anton's dropped pistol, wherever it had wound up on the floor.

Anton was not officially dead yet. He was making a lot of noise, blood gurgling up out of his throat and this and that oozing out of him, and his muscles and nerves were shorting out, making his body kick around quite a bit, like the dead frog you fooled around with in high school biology lab. But he was not my problem anymore.

"Surely you don't think I'm bluffing," Sasha said, jamming the muzzle of her pistol a little deeper into Felicia's ear. Felicia jumped and made some noise, but I could not tell if it was the gun or her wrist that caused it. "I'm not, you know."

Sasha did not have the hammer cocked on the little automatic, a Beretta .380 or one of the knockoffs made to look like a Beretta. That did not mean she was not serious, because the gun was double-action; all she had to do was pull the trigger and it would shoot. But that way it would take anywhere from ten to maybe fifteen pounds of pressure on the trigger. With the hammer cocked, maybe only a couple of pounds would touch it off. I made up my mind that if she put her thumb on the hammer to cock it I would shoot her. Of course, if she took the gun out of Felicia's ear and turned it toward me I would shoot her too. I hoped that would not mean hitting Felicia, but you can only do so much, and I was not about to give up my gun or try to dodge any bullets if I could help it.

I may have heard it a second before the rest of them, but by the scuffling of their feet on the tiles and the way Galipolus cut short his babbling, I knew they heard it too. Borodin turned his head to one side to hear better and looked up.

"It's over now," I said. "Put down the gun."

"Don't make me laugh," Sasha said.

As she said that, she moved her head a bit for emphasis, raising her chin toward me with an instinctive little movement. Her eyelid, the one I could see, fluttered ever so slightly. It was almost what I wanted. You cannot shoot a gun and talk at the same time. And when you blink you are blind for half a second or so. That is why the pros say that in a situation like this if you blink you'll die in the dark. That was what I wanted, for Sasha to talk and blink at the same time. She had almost done it for me, but not quite. Of course, it would help if Felicia would do a little more than whimper from the pain. It would help if she would make a move, give me a bit more of a target.

It was coming our way, fast. Like a stuttering great bird with wings beating incredibly fast, the wingbeats coming louder and louder.

"Tell her, Borodin."

"I don't—"

"She's wearing a wire, stupid!" I screamed. I was losing my patience. "Look for yourself, Sasha. That's the cavalry coming to the rescue."

I did not mind talking a little, in short bursts like that. Sasha would have to swing her gun around to get off a shot at me. From the look on what I could see of her face, she was entertaining the thought. That was okay too.

"Goddamn Jerry Sykes," Borodin muttered softly. "This whole thing was a trap."

Sasha let go of Felicia's wrist with her left hand long enough to check her for a transmitter, and she found it. She yanked it out of a pocket in Felicia's olive drab shirt and threw it on the floor. The fluttering roar of the helicopter's engine was close now, and loud as hell. The downdraft from its rotors slammed against the locked door like a storm.

You never know with one like Sasha. She might have been about to throw down her gun in disgust and call it quits, or she might have meant to try to dust us both and make a run for it through the bush, hoping to get out before the agents could surround the place. But, whatever she had in mind, I saw the barrel of her pistol move away from Felicia's head. Felicia slumped down a bit, and I could see most of Sasha's face for an instant. My finger tightened on the trigger, but before I could get the shot off, something funny happened.

Felicia, now that Sasha had let go of her busted wrist,

looked as if she would crumple to the floor. But she did not. Instead, she spun back toward Sasha, coming up from somewhere around her knees with her right elbow like a hammer.

What I saw looked funny. One second, I was looking through my sights, such as they were on the stubby little revolver, at Sasha's right eye, which widened into a whole face as Felicia dropped and Sasha's pistol moved. Then, quicker than you could imagine, there was the green blur of Felicia's sleeve and Sasha's face disappeared. By the time the sick little flat thud of impact registered, I heard the louder sound of Sasha hitting the floor, along with the clattering of her pistol as it flew out of her hand. If Felicia's punch had not been enough to knock her out, whacking her head on the tile floor had done it. She lay still on the red floor and her broken nose bled onto her top lip and the blood ran down one side of her face.

Felicia went after the Beretta and scooped it up in her left hand so quickly, and turned toward the two men at the table with such a furious look on her face, that I thought she would shoot them.

The booming voice of Agent Thompson on a powerfully amplified speaker swamped the place before Felicia could say anything. Borodin looked like he did not mind that the law was on the scene. Galipolus was making noises like he just wanted it all to be over.

"What have you done with Jerry, you son of a bitch?" Felicia demanded, moving toward Borodin with Sasha's pistol held out stiffly in front of her in her good hand. She reached up with her thumb and cocked the hammer on the little gun, and the significance of that was not lost on Borodin.

"I haven't done anything with him, I assure you," Borodin said. "This is all his doing. I don't know where he is."

"Liar!" Felicia hissed at him.

"You'd better do better than that," I advised him.

More from Agent Thompson's amplified and godlike voice. He was saying the usual stuff like in the movies, the place is surrounded, come out with your hands up, stuff like that. Sasha had dropped Felicia's transmitter in all the excitement, and I did not think the feds outside were able to hear what was going on inside anymore. They knew they had one of their agents in here with a gang of bad guys, and another agent still missing, and I did not think they would wait very long before they did something dramatic.

"I swear to you, Mister Kyle . . ." Borodin began, but he did not finish whatever he was going to tell me because Felicia was closing in on him with Sasha's gun, and he understood the significance of that too. She could almost shoot him with that gun and get away with it, if I was in the mood to back up whatever story she made up. He must have known that I was in that kind of mood indeed. "Okay, okay. Don't shoot me, will you, lady? Try not to shoot me, and I'll tell you everything. All right? How's that?"

"Depends on the quality of your story," I said.

So he talked.

"I got word that my former associate, Mister Galipolus here, was onto something promising here. Something high-tech, with military applications. So I came down and checked into it. As these things go, it turned out that he had stumbled into something with terrific potential—"

"Doctor Teckmann's superchip," I interjected.

"Yes. But of course, Galipolus here has no imagination. So he had arranged to get a prototype from Teckmann and sell it to some foreign clients."

"You had a better idea," I prompted.

"Of course. The Arabs, let's be honest here, they don't pay that well, and what would they do with such a chip? They'd have to get someone to build the damn things, even if they could reverse-engineer it. Do you know what they offered him for the chip?"

"I heard it was a hundred thousand dollars."

"Exactly. Can you imagine?"

"So who did you arrange to sell it to?"

"The Japanese, of course. Who else?"

Made sense to me. They were tops at copying high-tech ideas from other people, and they had the sophistication to mass-produce the things. Then, of course, they would sell them to the Arabs or whomever. Anything for a buck.

"When and where?"

"That's the catch." Borodin shook his head ruefully. "It was to have been today, here. Our buyers were to fly in today, then hop out here by chopper to make the deal, back to DFW and catch the flight out. That's why I thought . . . when I heard the helicopter coming just now . . . well, you can imagine."

"Yeah. Where's the chip?"

"Jerry has it."

Felicia made an ugly noise deep in her throat, and I put a hand on her arm to remind her not to do anything foolish at this stage of the game.

Agent Thompson was sounding pissed off by this time and was down to making threats against all the occupants of the house. I figured we had less than a minute before feds in Darth Vader outfits started materializing. They would probably toss in stun grenades first, I knew, or artillery simulators.

"Where?" I asked.

"I don't know. It was his idea to use this place, said it would be safe to make the switch, the chip for cash. He has it."

"So he was in on it all along?"

"No. He dealt himself in when he got wind of the Japanese angle, the million dollars."

"Million dollars?" I asked.

"Didn't I mention that? That's the price the Japanese agreed to. Ten times what this . . ."

Without finishing his sentence, Borodin finished his thought by kicking the cringing Galipolus like a dog. I told him to stop that, that we did not have much time before Felicia's friends outside assumed the worst and came boiling in.

"Then just open the door and let them in, for God's sake," the Cypriot said, exasperated. "We surrender, already."

"Not just yet you don't. And remember, it's not too late for you to end up like Anton over there."

"I really wish you hadn't done that—"

"Never mind. How did Jerry tell you all this, that he was dealing himself in, that you would use this place, and all that?"

"He sent word by Teckmann. I haven't seen Jerry since—"

"Since your friends Sasha and Anton grabbed me at the condo, right?" Felicia demanded.

"Right," Borodin answered, looking more and more worried as the seconds ticked off.

Thompson had stopped talking on his speaker, which probably meant they were getting ready to come in. The next time he spoke, it would probably be just a distraction for the assault. I did not waste the little time we had to ask why Sasha and Anton had done their little job on me. I could figure that out to my own satisfaction.

"Why did you kill the Teckmanns?" Felicia wanted to know.

"Mister Kyle . . ." he pleaded.

"Answer her," I said.

"She won't like it," Borodin warned.

"Tell her."

"She won't believe me."

"The truth," I cautioned.

"I didn't do that. It had to be Jerry," Borodin said, that last part so faint you could hardly make it out.

"You dirty . . ." Felicia snarled and may have been about to shoot the poor man for saying that about Jerry, but I grabbed her arm and turned her away from him.

"That's it," I told her. "That's all we're going to get here. Call off your pals out there. We've got things to do."

From the way she looked at me, I could see that she did not understand, that she thought I might be saying that I had bought the thing about Jerry being in on the deal, that I believed Borodin when he said Jerry had killed poor Doctor Teckmann and his dotty wife. But I made it clear from the way I handled her and the look on my face that I was serious and that she would just have to play along with me if she wanted to get to the bottom of things. She looked back toward Borodin like she would have preferred to take care of him right then and there, but she must have thought that I knew what I was doing, because she did as I said.

I rounded up all the loose guns, the one Anton had dropped when I shot him and the magnum Felicia had lost when Sasha broke her wrist. Felicia located her discarded transmitter and spoke into it. Lucky for us, it was still working, and from outside, from somewhere very near the front door, Agent Thompson announced on his loudspeaker that he had received her message. So we unlocked the front door and walked out into the sunlight to meet our rescuers. Of course, we made Galipolus and Borodin walk in front of us, just on the off chance that somebody had not gotten the word and might shoot the first thing that moved. But nobody did, and in no time Borodin and Galipolus were handcuffed and somebody was reading the Miranda warning to them from a wallet-sized card.

"Are you all right?" Thompson asked Felicia.

"I'm fine."

"Her right wrist is broken," I said.

"Let's get that tended to," Thompson said, turning to signal one of his men to bring a first aid kit.

"There's no time," I told him.

"What do you mean?" he asked.

Before I could answer, the noise of cars rumbling up the drive from the road drew my attention away, and I saw two carloads of reinforcements arrive.

"We're in a hurry," I said.

"To do what?" Thompson wanted to know.

"To get into your helicopter and fly like hell to the airport."

Thompson looked at Felicia to see if she knew what I was talking about. She didn't, but she shook her head with assurance as if she did, and Thompson looked back at me.

"We're in a hurry," I said.

He did not answer, just turned away and broke into a fast trot toward the clearing where the old smuggler had let his horses run free and where now a government helicopter stood waiting. I followed him, and when I saw that Felicia was coming too, I did not bother to try to talk her out of it.

CHAPTER
THIRTY-ONE

"How DID YOU know I was wired?" Felicia asked me, once we were airborne and on our way to Dallas–Fort Worth International. The helicopter was one of the big Hueys from the war, the model made to haul troops, and we were clinging to seats in the open waist of the ship. The engines and rotors made so much noise we had to yell at each other to make ourselves heard.

"At Denny's," I screamed back at her. "After breakfast, you put your napkin back into your cup. I figured that was a signal, in case you weren't transmitting."

She lifted her head as if to say "o-o-h," or something like that, then nodded at me several times, touching the side of her head with the index finger of her good hand to say that I was a pretty smart cookie, or words to that effect. She did not smile though. She had not smiled since we had failed to find Jerry Sykes at the smuggler's ranch.

Thompson had been on the radio with somebody and turned back to me and leaned close to tell me what he had found out.

"Delta to Tokyo's already gone," he yelled.

"It's not nonstop, is it?" I yelled back.

"Short layover in Portland."

"Oregon?"

"Yeah."

"Call ahead. Have your people there hold it up."

"Who are they looking for, man? That damn chip can be hard as hell to find. You think we're gonna search every passenger, all that luggage?"

"You're looking for a Japanese that flew into DFW earlier today. Odds are, from the West Coast, L.A. or maybe San Francisco. There won't be many people on that plane in Portland with that kind of an itinerary."

"How do we know they didn't just drop that goddamn thing in the mail?" Thompson asked.

"Would you?"

"It's worth a shot."

He turned back to his radio and his crew and did a lot of talking. They would be rigging radiophone patches and lighting up buttons all over the country, I figured. I turned back to Felicia and pointed at her busted wing.

"How's the wrist?" I asked, mouthing the words to make myself understood. I pointed at the wrist.

She gave me a thumbs-up with her left hand. The right wrist must have been hurting her like hell. She had it resting on her knee, and I could see from where I sat that the damn thing was already swollen to twice its size. She needed to be seen to, but I knew she would have none of it until this thing was done, and there was not much I could do for her. I gave her a pat on the shoulder for encouragement and she leaned close to tell me something.

"I'm sorry," she said.

"What for?"

"Fucking up back there, letting Sasha blindside me. For one thing."

"Don't worry about it. It worked out all right."

"And for dragging you into this."

"Don't be silly. I wanted in. Or else I wouldn't have come along."

Thompson rejoined us then and said he had set things up in Portland, assuming that everybody out there got the word and there were no screwups, which was always a chance.

"Now what?" he asked.

"Haul ass on to the airport. We've got business there."

"Any place in particular?"

"Yeah, the international terminal, as close as you can get. And see if there are any flights with Jerry Sykes on the passenger list."

"You don't think he'd use his real name, do you, Kyle?" Thompson asked.

"Did he have a passport in any other names?"

"Not that I know of."

"Then it couldn't hurt to check."

The copilot interrupted to say that we were only a couple of minutes out from the airport, and that he was getting some flak from the FAA people in the tower about going where he wanted to go. Thompson said he would handle it and went forward.

It wouldn't be long now.

CHAPTER THIRTY-TWO

THOMPSON TOOK CARE of the flight controllers and whoever else was raising hell in the tower, and our pilot brought us in low over the terminal buildings, low enough that I found myself looking up at people who were standing in the windows of their rooms at one of the airport hotels. Then he swung the big chopper around in a tight slewing turn and set us down about fifty feet from a door being held open by a couple of guys in uniform. Thompson and Felicia jumped down and I followed close behind them.

These were Customs people from the international terminal, the ones who check luggage and things like that, and they seemed to know who Thompson was. Felicia looked more or less official in her OD outfit, but I could tell they did not know what to make of me. I must have looked like hell in my screwed-up shirt and slacks with the gone-to-hell loafers and needing a shave. Or I guess it could have been the revolver butt sticking out of the waistband of my pants. Thompson waved a hand at me to let them know I was official too, more or less, and they let me in.

We were hustling down a corridor and one of the Customs

types was briefing Thompson on what they had come up with. By the time that was done, we had reached an intersection and stopped there, with three corridors leading away in different directions.

"Sykes showed up on this one," Thompson said, showing Felicia and me a computer printout with clusters of names arranged beneath boldfaced flight names that included their numbers and destinations. "Flight Four-Eleven to London. Jack, you take that one."

"Why?" Felicia practically screamed before she caught herself. "Why Jack?"

"Because it's the least likely," I assured her.

"That's right," Thompson agreed, eyeing me with an odd expression. "Felicia, you come with me. There's a flight leaving in about five minutes for Stuttgart. That's more like it, if he's been playing the other side."

She did not think that made any sense, you could tell by looking at her. Not only did she not believe yet that Jerry had gone wrong, the deal with Borodin and the superchip made it pretty clear that if he was playing games, it was money, not anything political. But whatever she thought about it, she wanted to find him, so off she went with Thompson.

Nobody made it a point to say so, but one of the Customs agents had been assigned to go with me, and he led the way, showing me to the boarding gate for the London flight.

We made it with a couple of minutes to spare, and it did not take long to find out that Jerry Sykes was a no-show. There were not any other names on the passenger list that looked promising either, but the airline people did not seem to mind if my Customs friend went aboard the plane for a look, just to make sure. They almost certainly did mind my getting anywhere near their aircraft, in my disheveled and obviously armed condition, so I stuffed the piece under my shirt where it would not be so offensive and straightened myself up the best I could. And, since Customs vouched for me, the ticket taker, or ground attendant, or whatever you call him, did not make too much fuss.

It did not matter. A quick stroll up and down the aisles, with lavatory checks to make sure, turned up a blank. When we stepped off the boarding ramp into the terminal again, my Customs pal asked me what I had in mind for my next number.

"What do you have going to Mexico?" I asked.

He checked and found a flight due to leave in ten minutes. I told him that was my next trick, and off we went at a gallop. It was a pretty good jog to that gate, and when we got there we found that Thompson and Felicia had beaten us to it.

"Well?" I asked as I came panting up behind my Customs escort, who I noticed was not even breathing hard.

"Nothing," Thompson answered. "Nothing on the Stuttgart flight, so we came here because this is the next one out."

"Jack, are you sure he's here?"

"No. But, if Borodin wasn't lying, the Japanese guy flew in today to meet somebody."

"Yeah," she said. "At the ranch."

"No, that was bullshit. That's what Borodin and his gang were supposed to think. That kept them out of the way. Us too. So the meet was here. The Japanese swaps his briefcase full of cash for the gizmo, catches his plane for Portland and points west, and our boy steps down the hall and boards his plane for wherever it is he wants to lie low and spend a million bucks. It's gotta be."

"Or maybe he took a cab and now he's on a Greyhound, or driving a rented car he booked on some bogus ID he's been saving for just such an occasion," Thompson offered.

"I don't think so. Get the people off the plane," I said.

"Do what?" Thompson asked.

"Humor me."

"I told you, we went all through that airplane, and he's not on it," Thompson insisted.

"Trust me," I said.

The public address system announced final boarding for flight 1139 for Mexico City.

I motioned for Thompson to step away with me a few feet

and whispered my idea into his ear. He looked at me as if I had kissed him instead, he was so shocked at what I told him. But I could see in his eyes that he knew I might be right.

"What is it?" Felicia wanted to know.

"Okay," Thompson said. "Okay, we'll see about that."

He turned away from us and walked briskly toward the entrance of the boarding ramp. I could see that he was explaining things to the airline people there, who were confused but apparently impressed. One of the ladies turned and hurried down the ramp toward the plane. On the apron outside, I could see the aircraft crew in their cabin and the ground crew, making ready to push the big plane away from the terminal. Then everything stopped, and the captain looked up from his controls, looked into the terminal toward me. I wondered what he thought was going on, and imagined he was worried about his schedule.

Through the entrance ramp door, I heard the muffled but melodious voice of one of the attendants explaining to her passengers that something had come up, it was nothing to worry about, but that they would be deplaning briefly, and would they please remain in the gate area just inside the terminal because they would be reboarding in a moment. It was not long after that before people started coming out of the ramp, looking around to see if they could figure out what was going on. All there was there for them to see was Agent Thompson, a handful of his uniformed Customs people, Felicia in her GI Joe outfit, and me. I did not think that put their minds at ease.

Most of them looked like tourists, which is what I guess most of the people are who fly from Dallas to Mexico City in August. I was not sure, but I thought you probably had to go through Mexico City to get to Cancun and most of the other places tourists go. I had been to Mexico a number of times, loved to go down there fishing, but I did not often fly.

Tourists look pretty much the same everywhere, and this bunch was no exception. They were outfitted in the usual Bermuda shorts and golf shirts, the women in every kind of sundress and god-awful pantsuit you could imagine. There were probably two cameras for every three couples, and a smattering of kids who already were chafing from their confinement aboard the airplane, which had been all of fifteen minutes.

Thompson turned to look at me every couple of seconds as the tourists and here and there somebody who looked like he might actually have business in Mexico shuffled off the plane and out the ramp door into the gate lobby to see what came next. He was not seeing anything that looked like it might prove me right, and I imagined there probably was somebody he would have to explain things to somewhere down the line, somebody he would have to convince that this had been a good idea. It was probably a pretty big deal to unload an airplane and make it real late taking off. That was the problem with being part of a big operation like the government. The upside was you could do a lot of neat things, like grab a helicopter and tell the FAA to kiss your ass and go skimming around in restricted airspace, and stuff like that. But the catch was, you had to find what the hell ever it was that you were looking for in the first place. And in that department we were not winning any ribbons so far.

Agent Thompson had not liked me from the first. Lately, he had been rethinking that, what with the business at the ranch and with the thing about the Japanese guy on the plane to Portland. He must have figured I had been of some use. Now, he was revising his opinion again. I could see that in the way the veins in his neck had started to rise.

"Well?" He turned to me and lifted his hands at his side.

"Is this everybody?" I asked.

Thompson turned to one of the flight attendants who had accompanied the passengers off the plane to ask if this was everybody, but before he could ask her anything, another attendant came up. She was not running or doing anything that would alarm the passengers, but she was walking very fast, and I thought by the way she was nibbling her lip that I might have been right after all.

Before I could find out what the lip-nibbling flight attendant had to report, I heard the jingling of equipment behind me and turned to see a sergeant and a couple of officers from the airport police coming our way. They were not exactly running, but they were not wasting any time. The sergeant went directly to Agent Thompson, and the two officers pulled up short. I noticed that they happened to stop so that they were in really good position to cover me, so that if they had to do any shooting in my direction they would not have to worry about cross fire. Out of curiosity, I looked over my shoulder and saw that from where they were standing there would not be any passengers in the line of fire either, or even anything of value, only a blank wall. These guys were good.

The sergeant spoke with Agent Thompson as if he knew him, or at least knew who he was, and waved one hand in my direction as he seemed to be explaining something to Thompson. He was explaining something about me, I could tell. I was glad to see Thompson smile, even though it was not much of a smile, and raise his hand, palm up, toward the sergeant. He rocked his big hand back and forth a couple of times as if he might be erasing a blackboard and shook his head.

"They got a call on you, Jack," Thompson informed me. "Man with a gun. Thought you might merit a little attention."

"Glad you vouched for me," I told him, smiling and nodding at the two officers.

"I had to think about it," the agent assured me.

"Excuse me, Agent Thompson?" The flight attendant who seemed to be in charge stepped forward, motioning for the one who was nibbling her lips to come too.

"Yes, ma'am?"

"We have one passenger who refuses to deplane."

"Oh?"

"Yes, sir. Tell him, Kelly."

Kelly was the lip nibbler. She made her report: "The gentleman in Twenty-nine-A refused to deplane. He said, he said . . . 'I guess this is as far as I go.' Words to that effect. And he would not come off the plane with the rest of the passengers."

Felicia stepped forward, and the look on her face was such

a poignant mix of confusion and hope it would break your heart if you knew what I knew.

"White male, mid-forties, slender and blond?" she asked the attendant.

"I beg your pardon?"

"She's with me," Thompson said.

"Oh. No, that's not what he looks like at all. He—"

"Excuse me, ma'am," I cut in. "Did he say anything else?"

"Yes," the poor lady answered without being told who I was, apparently having decided that we were all in this together, one way or another. "He wanted to know if . . . his exact words were, 'I wonder if, by any chance, there's a young lady out there by the name of Felicia Adams.' Those were his exact words."

Felicia would have bounded right up the ramp and onto the plane if I had not grabbed her.

"I see," I said, holding Felicia and trying to make it look as if it were easy. "And did you happen to notice if he had any carry-on luggage?"

"Why, yes he did. He had a largish tote bag. We weren't sure we'd be able to fit it into the overhead storage area, but he said that was all right, that he would hold it in his lap anyway."

"The money!" Thompson snapped. "Let's go."

"Yeah, only let's don't be in a hurry, all right?" I said, more for Felicia's benefit than for Agent Thompson's. I was ambivalent about seeing him with his brains down his back, but I would have hated to see anything more happen to Felicia. She was a tough one, but she had already been through a lot.

By the time we got as organized as such a motley gang could get and started down the ramp to the passenger section of the airplane, there were four of us: Felicia, Agent Thompson, and the airport police sergeant, a lean and sharp-eyed kid who said he was Sergeant Frieman, with a long *i*. I was the fourth, of course.

Thompson got there first, stepping into the first-class section ahead of me and Felicia and stopping short when he found himself facing the recalcitrant passenger, who had taken it upon himself to upgrade his seat from 29-A to first class.

"Well, I'll be goddamned," Thompson said.

Felicia looked around the edge of the door at the man but did not say anything.

So it was more or less up to me to think of something cute when I sidled past her into the compartment and looked at the man all the fuss was about.

"Doctor Teckmann, I presume?"

CHAPTER THIRTY-THREE

"WHO ARE YOU?" the man asked.

"Name's Kyle," I answered, not letting it show that I was disappointed he did not know me somehow. "Jack Kyle."

"Yes, but who are you?"

"Private investigator."

"Big deal."

"Yeah, that's what I say."

Doctor Teckmann looked different this time. For openers, of course, he was not wearing his toupee, which had after all been left in the little house in the country with the Dobermans in the yard, not far from the bombed and burned body of Customs Agent Jerry Sykes. He was missing some teeth too, for much the same reason. He had left his bridge with the body along with the rug so everybody would think it was him.

Besides all that, there was his wardrobe. There were no pens or pencils in the pocket of his flowered Hawaiian shirt, which was mostly an electric kind of blue color, with enormous white flower petals and here and there a dash of hot pink. There may have been rainbows on it too, but I could not be sure because he was slouched down in an aisle seat and I could not get a clear look at him. I could not help noticing his shoes, however. He was sitting with his legs crossed at the knees, which had to be wrinkling his white pants, because they were linen. He was accustomed to wearing polyester, of course, and not worrying about that. The right leg of his pants was hiked up because of the way he was sitting and showed his long white sheer socks with patterns on the sides, and his shoes were soft leather, so white he had to have put them on for the first time somewhere inside the airport, because he could not have walked even across a parking lot and left them so pristine.

"Felicia," he said. "Darling, good to see you again."

He had taken the liberty of foraging for himself a large bottle of champagne and raised a glass in his left hand to toast poor Felicia. He smiled at her as if he really expected her to be glad to see him, as if he did not understand what that meant, that if he was still alive, then it had to have been Jerry Sykes that we found dead. But in his defense, I could not help noticing that he was quite a bit drunker than he could have gotten on the bit of champagne that was gone from the bottle on the floor beside his seat. The good doctor had been doing some drinking before he ever boarded the Mexico City flight.

The noises that Felicia was making had no place in the normal repertoire of human sounds. They were the sounds of a horrible truth hitting home. Jerry Sykes was dead. Like a fool, I had hoped there would be a way to shield her from this. She cried at last, and that was the best I could hope for her now, and she sank against the bulkhead beside the door, in the corner made by the inner wall of the passenger cabin and the closet partition where travelers hung their garment bags. When I was sure she could stand, I left her there and went back to the edge of the partition to see what else Doctor Teckmann had in mind.

"Teckmann, you are under arrest for the murder of Customs Agent Jerry Sykes and for the unlawful sale of military goods to a foreign power."

"And for the murder of your wife," I added.

"Yes," Thompson said, with a look toward me and, beyond me, at Felicia. "That, too."

"Says you," Teckmann answered, sticking his tongue out at us.

"You shit-eating little . . ." Thompson muttered as he started toward the doctor.

"Hold on a second," I cautioned, my hand on Thompson's shoulder.

"What?" Thompson was out of patience with me, the more so because I had been right about this. "Wait a second for what?"

"I have a bomb," Doctor Teckmann announced.

"There," I said, nodding at Thompson. "See?"

"I have a bomb," Teckmann repeated in exaggeratedly solemn tones.

"This guy's twisted off," Thompson whispered to me, turning half around toward me and sweeping his left hand across his mouth so Teckmann would not hear. "Bugsy."

"I heard that," Teckmann yelled, slapping his foot down on the floor. "Not nice. Not nice!"

"Well, I tell you what, motherfucker, I'm just gonna have to see your goddamn bomb."

Thompson said that with a conviction and sincerity I admired.

Up shot Teckmann like a jack-in-the-box, into the aisle, his champagne glass tumbling unbroken to the aisle carpet, his hands outstretched toward us. In his right hand, he held a Zippo cigarette lighter, open and aflame. In his left, he held his carryon bag. It was not too wide or too long, but it was fat, as if stuffed with something, and I could see how the attendant had thought it might not fit in the overhead storage compartment.

"There! Seen enough?" Teckmann demanded.

"Hang on a second, Doctor Teckmann," I interjected. "I think maybe you've gotten a little mixed up here. That's the bag with your money in it, the million dollars the Japanese gentleman gave you for the superchip. If you drop your lighter in there, it will burn, but it won't explode. Maybe you forgot and checked your bomb with your luggage, huh?"

The way he laughed, Teckmann sounded like, I don't know . . . a little girl, or else maybe the late Truman Capote on a TV talk show. It was this high-pitched giggling sound that you would not associate with anything as sinister as a bomb. However, that eerie little laugh under these circumstances chilled me like you would not believe.

"He's bullshitting," Thompson said.

"No, he's not," I said.

"No, he's not," said Sergeant Frieman with the long *i*.

"How do you know?" Thompson demanded of the sergeant.

"Trust me," the sergeant answered evenly. "He's not bullshitting. I'll be right back."

Sergeant Frieman backed out of the aircraft compartment tugging his radio out of its carrier on his belt. I watched to see if he would actually use it, but he caught himself before he keyed the talk button and slipped the radio back into his belt. Then he turned and disappeared up the ramp corridor around the turn it made going into the well-lighted and somehow cheery-looking terminal. Things would start happening now, I knew.

The reason that Sergeant Frieman did not use his radio to notify his people of the possible bomb situation on flight 1139 is that until you know what kind of bomb and what kind of detonator you are screwing around with there is always the chance that a radio transmission may set off the bomb. I remember a bomb threat call I got one time downtown at one of the oil company corporate offices. One of my pals had a brand-new rookie he was training. I'll never forget, the kid found a briefcase with a long string hanging out the top of it, like a trip wire deal somebody had not had time to rig up. So what does he do? He's so proud of himself for finding the damn thing, he not only picks it up and takes it with him, he gets on his goddamn portable radio and calls our sergeant to report what he's done! I swear, if our sergeant had not been afraid it was a real bomb and he might touch it off, he would have shot that goddamn rookie on the spot, and none of us would have blamed him.

"Gee, Doctor Teckmann," I said, with that thought in mind. "I thought they checked for bombs when you came in here. Didn't they check you, or what?"

"Who are you?" Doctor Teckmann asked again.

CHAPTER
THIRTY-FOUR

"NAME'S JACK KYLE," I said. "Private investigator."

"Big deal."

"Yeah, that's what I say. So, didn't they check you, or what?"

"What do you think I am, stupid? Of course they checked me. They check everybody. You think I didn't think of that?"

"Oh, I see. You mean you figured out a way to beat 'em, right?"

"No, I relied on magic." Again the weird-assed Truman Capote laugh. "Of course I figured a way."

"No shit?"

Suddenly, he stopped giggling, which scared me even more.

"No shit," he said. "I really did, you know."

"Wow," I said.

"Yeah, wow, you dumb shit. I'd explain it to you, but you're so dumb you wouldn't even know what I was talking about."

"Come on, give me a chance."

"I don't mean the bomb, stupid. Anybody can understand that. I simply stuffed the lining of my bag with a substance that is inert but potentially volatile. Add fire and boom! Anybody could have come up with that. I was talking about the real stuff. You wouldn't even know what the heck I was talking about."

Then I quit worrying. Then I knew it would be all right. Probably.

"Excuse me," I said to the doctor. "Listen, Agent Thompson . . . what is your first name, anyway?"

"Gus."

"Gus Thompson? Really?"

"Yeah, what's the matter with it?"

"Nothing." There was a street in Mesquite, a Dallas suburb where I lived when I first moved to Dallas, named Gus Thomasson, but I did not see any point in bringing it up. "Listen, Gus, why don't you take Felicia up the ramp and put her in a little safer spot, okay?"

"While you do what?"

"Nothing. We'll schmooze, me and the doctor. Nothing."

"You'll schmooze?"

"Go on, get her out of here, will you?"

"Yeah, yeah. I'll be right back."

"Where's he going?" Teckmann demanded as soon as Thompson moved behind the screen made by the partition.

"Who cares? He's stupid," I said.

"Sit down," Teckmann ordered me. "Over there."

He pointed to a seat near the front of first class, on the opposite side of the aisle from his. I stepped lively and plopped into the seat, then sat forward to adjust the pillow and everything to make myself comfortable. Also, while my hands were out of Teckmann's line of sight behind the backs of the seats, I yanked the revolver out from under my shirt and stuck it in between the back of my seat and the armrest.

"Wait a minute, wait a minute!" Teckmann piped. "Stand up. Stand up, mister!"

I stood up.

He wanted me to show him I was not armed, which I did not mind doing, since I had ditched the magnum in the seat. So I pulled up my shirt and turned around and went through a

couple of other gyrations before he was finally comfortable with me. Then he told me to sit down again, and I did.

"What are you going to do with the bomb?" I asked.

"Highjack the plane, I guess," he answered, the queer little voice sounding pouty, disappointed. "Or else . . ."

Yeah, that was how I figured it too. It would be the "or else" thing more than likely, because I knew that Thompson and especially Sergeant Frieman and his friends were not likely to let him get off the ground. I knew that all the big calls had been made by now, more than likely, that things were happening outside, on the taxi apron and the runways, up in the control tower, in the terminals, all over this end of town, for that matter. As I understood it, the FBI's Special Weapons people handled this kind of thing too, along with the airport police, but I was never sure about the FBI. This was an international flight, and that probably made whatever Teckmann had in mind a federal offense, but I did not know what the particulars were. All of which was to say that I was not sure whether the snipers looking through their scopes at the windows of the plane would be feds or locals. Not that it made a hell of a lot of difference.

"Yeah," I said, to keep him from thinking about the "or else" too much too soon. "So I guess you've got the situation pretty well in hand then. I've got to hand it to you."

"Thank you," he said, brightening a bit. I had hoped he would perk up at a little flattery, because there were a couple of things I wanted to get out of him, and I knew he did not have much time left, whether he knew it or not.

"It was your plan all along, wasn't it, Doctor Teckmann?"

"Would you care for a drink?" He asked, suddenly in much brighter spirits. He hefted the champagne bottle and rose from his seat to find me a glass. "This stuff is really very nice."

"I'd love a drink, Doctor. But none of that bubbly stuff, if you don't mind. Do they have any scotch?"

"Oh, I'm sure they do," he said, and set down the champagne to adjust his carryon bag. He slipped the shoulder strap of the bag up over his left shoulder and held the cigarette lighter in his left hand, about six inches above the open bag. Then, with his right hand, he rummaged through the cabinet in the service bay between first class and tourist until he found it. He produced maybe half a dozen of the small airline bottles of scotch and held them up for me to see. "There you are. I told you!"

"Great. Any ice?"

This he also located, along with a couple of plastic glasses and even some swizzle sticks. He even asked if I would like some soda with it, but I said no. What I wanted was for him to have his hands full for a moment, so that he could not hold his lighter quite so ready to drop into the bag. That was what I wanted, but he was too cute for that. Instead of trying to juggle the scotch bottles and a bowl of ice, he simply put the stuff on one of the wheeled tables the attendants used to serve the passengers and pushed the thing up the aisle toward me.

"There you are," he said, smiling.

"All right, thanks."

That had not worked out at all. Not only had he not let down his guard, but now the cart stood in the aisle. That would make it even harder to rush the little man. Not that I had any such thing in mind, but someone might. You never can tell. I had no plan to rush him or anything else, except to ask him a few questions. If he got in too big a hurry to set off that bomb of his, I might try to knock him down with my loaner revolver, but that was about all I had as far as a plan, and that would be just to stop him from blowing me up with the plane. Once I found out what I wanted to know, I planned to excuse myself and then he was on his own. There were plenty of pros in the immediate area to take care of him, I was sure of that.

"So, tell me," I began again while I poured the contents of a couple of the tiny bottles over some ice in one of the plastic cups. "It was your plan all along, right?"

"What do you know about it?" he challenged me.

"Nothing, that's why I'm asking."

"You have no idea."

"Yeah, I know. That's why . . ."

"How old are you?"

"Forty, give or take. Why, Doc?"

"Because I'm sixty-fucking-three, that's why!"

"Oh."

To show you how weird these things can get, I was surprised that he used the "f" word like that. Mind you, I had him figured for the murder of his wife and Jerry Sykes, and for arranging it so that Borodin and Galipolus and company and Felicia (I didn't think he meant for me to get mixed up in it, probably didn't even know about me before I walked onto the airplane) would run into one another at the smuggler's ranch that Sykes used sometimes for a hideaway or a rendezvous, probably hoping that they would kill one another or otherwise occupy themselves until he had sold a priceless American invention to some ruthless foreigner who would at the very least use it to kick our country another rung down the ladder. I had him figured for all of that, and I had known he was the one behind it from the very first, when we found the body in the little house and Eddie told me what the Richardson officers had found at the Teckmann home. But it surprised me to hear the old man say "sixty-fucking-three." For one thing, it was the way he said it, with his face twisted and his eyes sparkling, as if he had not had much practice at it and the word was still new to him, and meant something terribly nasty.

"Do you have any idea how many years of my life I gave them?" he asked.

"Counting your time in the service, I'd say about forty," I said.

"What? How did you know about that?"

"I've been in your house, Doctor Teckmann. I met your wife."

"What?"

"And I saw your daughter's picture."

"Who are you?"

"I told you, I'm a private investigator. Name's Kyle."

"You're not a cop."

"No."

"The cops didn't figure it out, not the cops. Not any of Jerry's friends, I know that."

"Why not?" I asked.

"They didn't trust him. They thought it was him, didn't they?"

"I think so."

"They bought the whole thing, I bet. Didn't they?"

"Pretty much," I assured him. There was something he wanted to know, I could see that. And I figured as long as he wanted something too, he was not going to do anything dramatic with his trick bag. "They thought it was you that got blown up with the telephone bomb. That was a nice touch with the dental work."

"Yes, yes. That would have done the trick, for as long as I needed, anyway. They might have seen through it if they'd dug a little deeper, but I knew it would give me some time. Do you know, by the way, if the dentists are any good in Mexico City? Orthodontists, I mean?"

"Probably," I said. "If you can afford them. And you can, naturally."

"Yes. You're not rich, are you?"

"Hardly," I admitted.

"I never had been either," he confided. "Until now. I've been rich for"—he checked his watch—"just over half an hour now, and I have to admit, it hasn't been as much fun as I'd expected."

"Yeah well, this isn't the best part. That will come when you get to Mexico," I promised him.

"I imagine."

We looked at each other, and I could tell he had a lot on his mind, but I could not be sure if he knew I was lying to him about Mexico.

"Where did you have in mind to settle down there?" I asked.

"They say Quintana Roo is nice, down around Cancun and Cozumel."

"Yeah, it's beautiful," I told him, and I meant it.

"I understand you can't buy on the beachfront, but renting would be better anyway."

"Absolutely," I agreed. "Buying can be tricky at best."

"You knew, didn't you," he said, out of nowhere, just as I had begun to think that I had led him off into pipe dreams about his future.

"Knew what?" I asked, wondering how best to handle this. Maybe it was the way to get my answers.

"Don't be coy, Mister Kyle, Private Investigator. How did you know?"

"I'll tell you, if you'll tell me a couple of things."

"Okay."

"It was your wife. You were the only one with any reason to do that. She wasn't a threat to anybody. She didn't know anything. If she had ever known, she'd forgotten. When they told me that she'd caught a phone bomb too, I knew it was you. I didn't know why or how it all fit together, but I knew it was you who killed her. And that meant it wasn't you dead at the other end of the line. So it had to be Sykes."

"The toupee, the dental work? That didn't trick you, not even for a moment?"

"I'm afraid not. Thing was, torching him was a bit too much. Oh, I understand you had to do that. Even with his head blown off, there was enough difference in your sizes that you had to burn him if you wanted anybody to think it was you. But that was the only reason I could think of for somebody burning a bombed hulk like that. It had to be you."

"The fire might have been accidental, started by the bomb," Teckmann suggested.

"Maybe. That's probably the way the experts figured it. But I don't know that much about it, so I thought it all pointed to you."

"Very interesting. Do you have any particular method you use in these matters, Mister Kyle? Or is it simply intuition? I'm curious."

"I don't know that I have what you'd call a system," I said. "I guess I just assume the very worst and keeping pushing. I usually turn out to be right."

"Interesting."

"It was for the money, then?" I asked.

"Of course. For what the money could buy, I mean."

"And your wife?"

"You said you met her. Can you imagine her living without me? Without someone to take care of her?"

"Euthanasia," I said, with a wry smile.

"In a manner of speaking."

"You couldn't have taken her with you?"

"That would have defeated the whole purpose, surely you can see that."

"If I knew what your purpose was," I said.

"A second life, of course. For as long as it lasted."

"Could be a long time, with a million dollars."

"I would not have lasted as long as the money, I can assure you of that," the little man said.

Before I could ask him exactly what he meant by that, Felicia stepped back into the cabin of the airplane, with Thompson close behind her. I turned and saw that someone had put a splint on her broken wrist, and that she was no longer crying for Jerry Sykes. She looked recovered, collected, and almost calm. In other words, she looked deadly.

"Thompson, what are you doing letting her—"

"It's all right, Jack," she assured me, turning her head in my direction but keeping her eyes locked on Teckmann. "I have business here."

I looked up at Thompson and I must have had a look on my face that told him I thought he was out of his mind. There was no telling what she would do, and I was glad that the serving cart was blocking the aisle.

"Then take a seat and take care of it," I told her, trying to be gentle and firm at the same time. I did not want her making a hotheaded move on Teckmann. She had made it this far, and she would get over losing Jerry Sykes, whether she knew it or not. I did not want her to throw herself away on this crazy little man who was not going anywhere.

She settled gingerly into a seat across the aisle from me, her eyes still locked on Teckmann, and sat on the corner of the seat, her legs under her in a way that she could spring up like a cat if she decided to.

"Why did you kill Jerry?" she asked.

Thompson stood in the aisle between me and Felicia, his hands empty and resting lightly on his hips. He was ready to move too, I thought, and hoped that he meant to keep Felicia from getting hurt if that was what she had in mind.

"I had to," Teckmann said. "He was the odd man out, you might say."

"How do you mean?" I asked.

"He was the only honest one. Everybody else was betraying somebody. Jerry was just doing his job. They didn't trust him, but he was doing his job. Even she betrayed him."

"Felicia?" I asked.

"Ask her. You did, didn't you, dear?" Teckmann said it without any malice or satisfaction. "You were supposed to be his partner, but you were really spying on him, weren't you?"

I looked at Felicia, and she did not look like a cat about to spring anymore. She looked as if she might sag into the soft plush first-class seat and disappear.

"We had to cover the bases," Thompson explained. "Felicia was under orders to keep an eye on Jerry because we had reason to believe he might have become a security risk. That's all."

"It looked like more than that to me," I said, thinking of the two of them in the pool at the condo.

"I loved Jerry," Felicia said, her voice soft and sad. "We fell in love. I wanted to tell him how it had started, but I couldn't."

"He knew," Teckmann said. "He told me. But I don't think he cared. He loved you, too, dear."

What an odd little guy.

"Actually, that fellow Galipolus got it all started," Teckmann went on. "He made a pass at me for the chip. He'd learned somehow that I'd been brought out of retirement to work on it. You see, they'd found that I had been onto something before, when I worked for them. They hadn't thought it was so much then, because they didn't know how to do what I was trying to describe to them. But they came around. It didn't even occur to me to play ball with Galipolus. I mean, half of a hundred thousand dollars . . . but Borodin had bigger plans. He offered me a split of a million. Of course, I had the chip, and there was no reason I couldn't have all the money. But I didn't want anyone looking for me, so I had to have a body. Not Jerry's particularly. I liked Jerry. But he was too smart and too honest for his own good. It was his idea to "burn" you, dear, to get you out of harm's way. So, anyway, it had to be him. Everybody was too busy cheating and lying to get in my way."

After he had explained all that to us, the old man stopped and drank some more champagne. He looked at us, from me to Thompson to Felicia, with this little flutter of his eyelashes as if there was nothing left to say. And I could not think of anything more to ask. I looked at Felicia and so did Thompson. She sat with her head down, her shoulders slumped. She was crying softly.

"Does anyone know if they have caviar?" Teckmann asked. I looked at him and he was pouring himself another glass of champagne. "I've never had caviar."

"Let's get her out of here," Thompson said, and I saw him lift Felicia by her shoulders, gently, out of her seat and turn her toward the door that led out.

"Yeah," I said. "Let's."

"Lovely girl," Teckmann offered as Thompson led Felicia away. "My daughter would be about her age."

"Yeah, I know," I said. I retrieved my gun from the seat and slipped it back inside my shirt before I rose to leave.

"Where do you think it would be, if they had any?" the little man wanted to know. "Caviar, I mean."

CHAPTER THIRTY-FIVE

THE WHOLE GANG met at Red's Bar a few nights later to have some drinks before going somewhere nice to have that dinner I had promised what seemed like such a long time ago. Speed was there, and Joe. Della even showed. Joe brought a date, a lovely young computer operator at some place downtown where Joe got a lot of the information he needed from time to time for his surveillance jobs.

Leslie did not show, and Speed admitted that they were on the outs again. He did not want to talk about it, which meant of course that he would get drunk first and then talk about nothing else until we all went home and left him to drink himself to sleep or maybe kill himself trying to drive home.

Della was drinking scotch instead of her usual wine mixers or those dopey sweet cocktails with the cute names, which told me she was in a terrible funk. It turned out that she and her boyfriend, the big blond kid I had roughed up in the office a lifetime ago, had split up. I told her that was good news to me, but it turned out that she had not chucked him because he beat her. Quite the contrary, he had dumped her for somebody else, and Della was sick about it. She kept putting my quarters into

Red's jukebox and playing the saddest goddamn songs she could find, and there were a couple of wailers, the old stuff.

Eddie Cochran stopped in, as he often did after a day's work, and bought a round of drinks.

"I feel bad as hell, Jack," he told me. I believed him. "I didn't know they were going to rope you back into the deal, or I never would have left town."

"You're not my baby-sitter, Eddie," I told him. "Don't worry about it."

But he was worried about it, and he even promised to tell me what it was all about someday. I had been doing a little drinking myself by that time, and I wasn't sure what he meant by that. If he meant what the case was all about that I had just finished, with Borodin and Felicia and the late Jerry Sykes, I thought I knew what that son of a bitch had been about, and if I didn't, I damn sure didn't want to. That was not what he meant though. He meant that he would tell me why he had left town so suddenly to go to this particular school and why it was that he happened to have so many friends who turned out to be spooks of one kind or another. It was a hell of a deal, he assured me. Which brought us to the matter of Doctor Teckmann and his bomb and the airliner he had hoped to hijack to Quintana Roo and a second life before he ran out of time. He really did not have much time, it turned out, because a malignant tumor was growing inside his head. The bag deal had not been a real bomb, it turned out, and the old man had not had any luck trying to get one of the airport cops to shoot him and put him out of his misery. They had taken him alive and he had not even managed to burn up the million dollars in cash which was all that he had had inside the bag. His lighter had run low on fluid from his snapping it on and waving it around for the couple of hours that the negotiations had gone on about his threats to set off the bomb he did not have. So when they closed in on him and he tried to burn the money so at least nobody else could have it, the old Zippo fizzled out on him.

The usual pack of lawyers had dealt themselves in on the

thing and muddied the waters about what laws the Japanese guy had broken, if any, but the main thing was that Thompson's friends in Portland had gotten the gizmo back.

We were a pretty downbeat group, with one thing and another, and poor Eddie did not stay at our table long. I had invited Felicia but did not think she would come. She had been on leave since the day we had gone out to the smuggler's ranch and ended up at the airport, and when I had spoken to her on the phone she had sounded awfully low, saying she was thinking about quitting her job and doing something else, something different. She did not know what.

Joe put up with the rest of us as long as he could, and his date kept shooting him looks and making faces like she expected more of him than this wake; and it became obvious after a while that we would not be moving on to dinner later, that this was pretty well going to be our evening, crying in our drinks here at Red's. Finally, even Joe could not take any more of it and made his excuses. I did not blame him and told him so. Joe was the kind of guy who had a gift for enjoying himself. He took things as they came and found something to smile about in most of it. As good a friend as he was, he and I both knew there was nothing he could do for us in our current conditions, and there was no point in letting us ruin his plans for the evening. So he and his date left us to go out in search of a good time, and I thought that reflected pretty good judgment on their part.

Della was cursing men in general and this one big blond bastard in particular, telling me and Speed things about her personal life that neither of us had any business knowing, and Speed was just about drunk enough by then that he was getting ready to try to top her with his stories about women as a breed and this one semiretired whore in particular, when Felicia walked into the place.

She looked better than I would have expected, in a black sheath dress and a chic white sling for her busted wrist. She stood inside the door and looked the place over until she spotted us at our table in the back, then I watched the way she moved as she made her way over. So did almost everybody else in the place. She still had that about her.

I scraped my chair back from the table and rose unsteadily to my feet to introduce her to my party, which by now had dwindled to the two hapless lovers, Speed and Della. It was not much of a party. But before I could do that, Felicia spoke first.

"T.J.," she said to me, with a nod and a little smile that told me a lot about her condition, a lot that was good. It told me that she was on her way back.

"Hi, kid," I said to her. "Glad you could make it."

FOR THE BEST IN PAPERBACKS, LOOK FOR THE

In every corner of the world, on every subject under the sun, Penguin represents quality and variety—the very best in publishing today.

For complete information about books available from Penguin—including Pelicans, Puffins, Peregrines, and Penguin Classics—and how to order them, write to us at the appropriate address below. Please note that for copyright reasons the selection of books varies from country to country.

In the United Kingdom: For a complete list of books available from Penguin in the U.K., please write to *Dept E.P., Penguin Books Ltd, Harmondsworth, Middlesex, UB7 0DA.*

In the United States: For a complete list of books available from Penguin in the U.S., please write to *Dept BA, Penguin, Box 120, Bergenfield, New Jersey 07621-0120.*

In Canada: For a complete list of books available from Penguin in Canada, please write to *Penguin Books Canada Ltd, 10 Alcorn Avenue, Suite 300, Toronto, Ontario, Canada M4V 3B2.*

In Australia: For a complete list of books available from Penguin in Australia, please write to the *Marketing Department, Penguin Books Ltd, P.O. Box 257, Ringwood, Victoria 3134.*

In New Zealand: For a complete list of books available from Penguin in New Zealand, please write to the *Marketing Department, Penguin Books (NZ) Ltd, Private Bag, Takapuna, Auckland 9.*

In India: For a complete list of books available from Penguin, please write to *Penguin Overseas Ltd, 706 Eros Apartments, 56 Nehru Place, New Delhi, 110019.*

In Holland: For a complete list of books available from Penguin in Holland, please write to *Penguin Books Nederland B.V., Postbus 195, NL-1380AD Weesp, Netherlands.*

In Germany: For a complete list of books available from Penguin, please write to *Penguin Books Ltd, Friedrichstrasse 10-12, D-6000 Frankfurt Main 1, Federal Republic of Germany.*

In Spain: For a complete list of books available from Penguin in Spain, please write to *Longman, Penguin España, Calle San Nicolas 15, E-28013 Madrid, Spain.*

In Japan: For a complete list of books available from Penguin in Japan, please write to *Longman Penguin Japan Co Ltd, Yamaguchi Building, 2-12-9 Kanda Jimbocho, Chiyoda-Ku, Tokyo 101, Japan.*

FOR THE BEST IN MYSTERY, LOOK FOR THE

☐ A CRIMINAL COMEDY
Julian Symons

From Julian Symons, the master of crime fiction, this is "the best of his best" (*The New Yorker*). What starts as a nasty little scandal centering on two partners in a British travel agency escalates into smuggling and murder in Italy.
220 pages   *ISBN: 0-14-009621-3*

☐ GOOD AND DEAD
Jane Langton

Something sinister is emptying the pews at the Old West Church, and parishioner Homer Kelly knows it isn't a loss of faith. When he investigates, Homer discovers that the ways of a small New England town can be just as mysterious as the ways of God.   *256 pages*   *ISBN: 0-14-012687-2*

☐ THE SHORTEST WAY TO HADES
Sarah Caudwell

Five young barristers and a wealthy family with a five-million-pound estate find the stakes are raised when one member of the family meets a suspicious death.
208 pages   *ISBN: 0-14-012874-3*

☐ RUMPOLE OF THE BAILEY
John Mortimer

The hero of John Mortimer's mysteries is Horace Rumpole, barrister at law, sixty-eight next birthday, with an unsurpassed knowledge of blood and typewriters, a penchant for quoting poetry, and a habit of referring to his judge as "the old darling."   *208 pages*   *ISBN: 0-14-004670-4*

☐ THE PENGUIN COMPLETE FATHER BROWN
G.K. Chesterton

Here, in one volume, are forty-nine sensational cases investigated by the high priest of detective fiction, Father Brown, whose cherubic face and unworldly simplicity disguise an uncanny understanding of the criminal mind.
718 pages   ISBN: 0-14-009766-X

☐ BRIARPATCH
Ross Thomas

This Edgar Award-winning thriller is the story of Benjamin Dill, who returns to the Sunbelt city of his youth to attend his sister's funeral—and find her killer.
384 pages   ISBN: 0-14-010581-6

☐ APPLEBY AND THE OSPREYS
Michael Innes

When Lord Osprey is murdered in Clusters, his ancestral home, with an Oriental dagger, it falls to Sir John Appleby and Lord Osprey's faithful butler, Bagot, to pick out the clever killer from an assortment of the lord's eccentric house guests.
184 pages   ISBN: 0-14-011092-5

☐ GOLD BY GEMINI
Jonathan Gash

Lovejoy, the antiques dealer whom the *Chicago Sun-Times* calls "one of the most likable rogues in mystery history," searches for Roman gold coins and greedy bird-killers on the Isle of Man.
224 pages   ISBN: 0-451-82185-8

☐ REILLY: ACE OF SPIES
Robin Bruce Lockhart

This is the incredible true story of superspy Sidney Reilly, said to be the inspiration for James Bond. Robin Bruce Lockhart's book tells the thrilling story of the British Secret Service agent's shadowy Russian past and near-legendary exploits in espionage and in love.
192 pages   ISBN: 0-14-006895-3

☐ STRANGERS ON A TRAIN
Patricia Highsmith

Almost against his will, Guy Haines is trapped in a nightmare of shared guilt when he agrees to kill the father of the man who will kill Guy's wife. The basis for the unforgettable Hitchcock thriller.
256 pages   ISBN: 0-14-003796-9

☐ THE THIN WOMAN
Dorothy Cannell

An interior designer who is also a passionate eater, her rented companion who writes trashy novels, and a rich dead uncle with a conditional will are the principals in this delicious thriller.   242 pages   ISBN: 0-14-007947-5

☐ **THE BODY IN THE BILLIARD ROOM**
  H.R.F. Keating

The great detective and lovable bumbler Inspector Ghote is summoned from Bombay to the oh-so-English Ooty Club to discover why there is a dead man on the very billiard table where snooker was invented.
                          256 pages   *ISBN: 0-14-010171-3*

☐ **STEPS GOING DOWN**
  Joseph Hansen

Frail old Stewart Moody is found one morning strangled with the oxygen tube that was keeping him alive, in this powerful tale of obsessive love and the tawdry emptiness of evil.   *320 pages*   *ISBN: 0-14-008810-5*